5442845
P9-DDG-802

Seriously Shifted

Tor Books by Tina Connolly

Ironskin

Copperhead

Silverblind

Seriously Wicked

Seriously Shifted

Seriously Shifted

TINA CONNOLLY

A TOM DOHERTY ASSOCIATES BOOK
NEW YORK

This is a work of fiction. All of the characters, organizations, and events portrayed in this novel are either products of the author's imagination or are used fictitiously.

SERIOUSLY SHIFTED

A Tor Teen Book
Published by Tom Doherty Associates, LLC
175 Fifth Avenue
New York, NY 10010

www.tor-forge.com

The Library of Congress Cataloging-in-Publication Data is available upon request.

ISBN 978-0-7653-8375-4 (hardcover)
ISBN 978-1-4668-9322-1 (e-book)

First Edition: November 2016

Printed in the United States of America

10 9 8 7 6 5 4 3 2 1

This one is for Eric,
who is in favor of the witch's latest plan.

1

The Do-Badders Club

I was hanging up the snakeskins to dry when the first witch rang the doorbell.

"Coming," I called as I folded the skins on my shoulder and hurried to the door. It does not do to keep witches waiting. They get cranky.

A tall, pale blonde wearing a lot of perfume swept into the room. Ugh, Esmerelda. "I see Sarmine hasn't managed to get any good help," she said. "Are you the familiar?"

"You know perfectly well I'm her daughter," I said through gritted teeth. I'm not what you'd call happy about having a witch for a mother, but that didn't mean I was eager to be insulted, either.

"Mm," she said. "Here's my coat. It's pure unicorn; don't let that werewolf of yours sit on it."

"His name is Wulfie and he is *housetrained,*" I said.

"He's *three,*" she retorted. She stalked over to the coffee table in the living room of our ordinary old split-level, clutching her emerald-green purse tight. "And hurry up with the drinks. Vodka martini, no vermouth, one eye of newt."

I had no sooner dumped the coat—and the snakeskins—in the spare bedroom upstairs when the doorbell rang again. "Sarmine," I hollered down the hall. "Your witch friends are here."

My mother, Sarmine Scarabouche, the wicked witch of the neighborhood, etc., etc., appeared briefly from her bedroom. We both are tall and white but otherwise don't look particularly alike. For starters, my regular outfit is jeans and a vaguely amusing tee. Hers is a starched button-down and a pencil skirt of the most unflattering length possible. My hair is nutmeg that does whatever it feels like, and hers is a perfect silver bob. She was sorting through the herbs and powders she kept in the white leather fanny pack she always wore. "Camellia, how many times have I told you not to shout? I will be down after I replenish my packet of dried beetle wings."

"That can't wait till after they go?"

She rolled her eyes. "Would you trust any of them not to start throwing hexes?"

She had a good point. I didn't trust any of them one bit. Witches are nasty, paranoid, sarcastic creatures—and the list gets worse from there. Sarmine is maybe, *perhaps,* one of the ever-so-slightly better wicked witches, if such a thing can be said to exist. I mean, she frequently imposes horrible punishments on me like turning me into a windmill and making me power the house for the day, and there's that whole thing about how she wants to take over the world, but hey, nobody's perfect.

The doorbell was now screeching like a peacock in heat, and since our doorbell didn't normally do that (witches usually try to blend in), apparently the witch who was waiting was a tired-of-waiting witch. Wulfie had run up from the basement and was now howling at the door.

"Coming, coming," I shouted. I scooped Wulfie up, put him back in the basement, and hurried for the front door.

This time the November wind blew in a short, stout lady all in black, with brown skin, heavy black eyebrows, and frizzy, graying hair. I had met Esmerelda a few times at various witch functions Sarmine had dragged me to over the years. But this lady was new to me. She had a cane and she stabbed it at my feet as she walked in. I jumped backward.

"Took you long enough, girlie," she said. "In my day we jumped to when our elders asked us to do something."

"When was that?" I said politely. "Around the time of Christopher Columbus?"

She looked at me side-eyed, as if trying to figure out if I was being rude or not. "Around the time of you can get me a bourbon and soda and make it snappy," she said. "With two maraschino cherries and a newt eyeball." She tossed me her black wrap and headed for the couch, mumbling something about how back in her day, there were ashtrays everywhere and everyone kept cartons of cigarettes on hand for their guests. Now that she mentioned it, the wrap I was holding reeked. I put it on top of Esmerelda's coat.

Esmerelda inclined her head toward the stout lady while I wheeled out Sarmine's minibar. And yeah, yeah, fifteen-year-olds are not supposed to be serving drinks to their mother's friends, I'm sure, but in the grand scheme of all the things Sarmine had me do, making a martini ranked low on the leading-me-astray scale.

I poured the vodka out of the cocktail shaker for the blonde, plopped in the eye of newt with a shudder, and passed it over. It's not that I'm squeamish—it's just that the witches have this real callous disregard for human and animal life. One of the many things my mother and I disagree on. I started to look for the soda for the shorter lady when the door knocker banged three times and then the door blew open. The freezing November wind swept through the house, bringing in an eye-watering gust of crumbling leaves and chilling me to the bone.

Esmerelda and the stout lady froze, their wands at the ready. I froze with the soda siphon in my hand. Everyone froze at the apparition confronting us.

Her cheekbones were sharp. Her hair was purple. She appeared to be wearing a scarf made out of an entire snake. If this were a movie there would be a dramatic music cue right now that said that *Evil Had Arrived.*

Sarmine chose that moment to appear on the staircase. "Malkin," she said in a super-not-excited-to-see-you voice. It sounds a lot like her regular voice, actually, but if you've been around the witch as long as I have you can pick up on the minute changes in expression. "How nice of you to drop in."

"Bowling night was canceled," quipped Malkin.

Sarmine continued down the stairs. "I thought perhaps we'd never see you again."

"Your lucky day," said Malkin. I guessed she was Caucasian, with a surprisingly deep tan for November. Maybe she'd been at the beach. She strode casually to the living room, surveyed the other two witches—who were both staring at her with varying degrees of wariness and stink-eye—and me. Her eyes drilled through me. "This one belongs to you, doesn't it?"

Sarmine did not deign to answer the obvious.

Malkin did not move, but such was the power of her presence that it seemed as though she were an inch away, studying my brain or witch blood or whatever it was. A gust of cold wind from nowhere brought a musky, animal scent. "Bats," Malkin said at last, in a voice like imminent death. "The upside-down tree. Rivers, running." It sounded like I was a tarot card that she was reading. "Potential, unrealized."

Sarmine sniffed. "You're telling me."

"Excuse me," I managed. "I don't belong to anybody. I'm my own."

A bark of laughter. "Funny kid." Malkin's gaze let me go and she raked the rest of the room.

"Last I heard you were in Borneo," said the blonde.

"That was three years ago," said Malkin. "Sorry to disappoint you, Esmerelda."

The short witch chuckled. "She's just hoping you're not still ticked about that time in college that she hexed you with five hundred green warts right before a date."

"Please," said Malkin. "Swept under the rug." She leered. "Surely you're not afraid I've come back to get you?"

"Nonsense," the blonde said coldly.

"And you, Valda? Still worried about that time you betrayed me to Student Housing for my side business of infectious diseases customized to your professor? Gonna peel out before the festivities start?"

The short witch snorted. "You think I'd miss this? Not likely."

"Good," said Malkin. "Then I'll put my drink order in and stay a while. Whiskey, neat, one eyeball." She plopped down in Sarmine's rocking chair and propped her combat boots on the table. They appeared to be made out of a gray wrinkly leather with insets of ivory.

I set down the soda siphon and switched over to making Malkin's drink. There was silence for a minute while I poured the whiskey and all the witches stared each other down, trying to suss out everyone's real motivation, and waiting to see who would make a move first. It was like watching a poker game between tigers.

Esmerelda tried another angle. "Revenge business getting slow?"

Malkin shrugged. "Too good. Fact is, I've been so busy the last decade I haven't gotten a chance to see my dear old friends." She smiled broadly at the three other witches. Nobody smiled back.

"You mean, you decided to take a break from hunting the lindworm," said Valda. "Having had no luck."

"They're extinct, Malkin," said Esmerelda. "Give it up."

"That hunt has consumed your life," said Valda.

Sarmine said nothing, eying Malkin suspiciously. "She's never going to give that up," she said. "Not as long as the Witchlore claims the fangs of the lindworm can be used to . . . what is it, Malkin? Cause pestilence, plagues, famine? Et cetera, et cetera, no doubt."

Malkin smoothed down her snake scarf. "Oh, that old thing," she said.

"*That old thing?*" said Valda from the couch. "You once called me at two a.m. because you heard from a friend of a friend that they'd once met a French shopkeeper whose grandmother had heard a rumor of a single lindworm scale. You were positively squealing with excitement."

"Bosh," said Malkin. "I never squeal."

"Squealing," said Valda.

"At any rate," said Malkin, "it seemed like a good time to pop in and see my old friends."

"Sounds suspicious," said Esmerelda.

"As you get older, you miss those good old college days," said Malkin, trying to look wistful. "The old gang."

"The club," said Valda.

"So what is this, a reunion?" I said.

"You could say that," said Esmerelda. She finally sat down on the edge of a wooden chair, her back stiff and straight.

I looked around the room again, realizing that these women who looked thirty (Esmerelda), forty (Malkin), sixty (Sarmine), and eighty (Valda) were all actually the same age. It was hard to imagine them all having been in college together. Harder still to imagine the poor college.

"We meet once every two years," explained Valda, "come from whatever parts of the globe we're now in for a week-long vacation, catch up. . . ."

"And a reenactment of our favorite old game," said Malkin. "A little bet we have between us, to see who the most skilled witch is."

"Malkin, we haven't done that in years," put in Esmerelda.

"This year was Sarmine's turn to host," continued Valda. "But it's been at least a decade since Malkin bothered to show up. I didn't think we'd ever see her again."

"Lucky you," said Malkin. She began cleaning her nails with a darling little two-inch dagger, no doubt carved out of tiger teeth or baby rabbit bones. "Shall we get started?"

I handed Valda her drink. "If you don't mind my asking . . . what is the name of your club?"

Valda grinned. Esmerelda showed a tight-lipped smile.

Malkin rocked casually back in her chair, flipping her little dagger around. "The Do-Badders Club," she said.

"I suppose it would be too much to hope that the Do-Badders Club meets in order to bring peace and joy to the world?" I said.

"Yes," said Malkin. "It would."

Sarmine slapped her hand down on the coffee table. "And I

keep telling you, the Do-Badders Club has outlived its purpose. It was a lark when we were nineteen—"

"Hence the silly name," put in Esmerelda tartly.

"But there are real things to focus on now," said Sarmine. "The world is going to hell in a handbasket, women. The oceans are rising, the air is burning, the sixth extinction is upon us. . . ."

"I knew you'd be difficult," Malkin said. "You're all so soft without me."

"I'm not," Esmerelda said indignantly.

"Peer pressure," snorted Valda.

Sarmine rolled her eyes.

Malkin tucked the little dagger away and held up her hands. Her silver rings flashed in the lamplight. "All right, all right. Will this sweeten the pot? I've got something extra special to ante up for the bet." She pulled a small envelope from some hidden pocket and waved it at us.

"And what's in that?" said Esmerelda.

"Pony up one of your mermaid fins and you can find out."

"I only have one," protested Esmerelda. "They're terribly hard to source."

"Afraid you're losing your touch?"

"Well, I'm in," said Valda. "What is it you want from me?"

"Still have your Bigfoot claw?"

Valda sucked in breath. "Hard bargain, Malkin," she said. "Still, I'll play the game. Whatever's in that envelope better be worth it."

"It's something you all will like," promised Malkin. "Even fuddy-duddy Sarmine over there. It's related to a spell I've been putting the finishing touches on. Works along the principles of sympathetic resonance."

Sarmine looked more closely at Malkin. "Is this what you were working on in college?"

"Yes," said Malkin. "Interested now?"

"Perhaps," conceded Sarmine. "I'll offer up a vial of dragon tears to find out, anyway." She sat down on the couch next to Valda. "Straight gin, please, Camellia."

"Excellent," said Malkin, writing all the wagers down on the back of the envelope. "Now. It's my turn to pick the area of havoc for the game." She stretched out her leather-clad legs, casually considering. She appeared to be reasonably well-muscled all over—no doubt from her time spent hunting those things she was wearing—and I thought that she would be pretty darn foreboding even if it weren't obvious from the other witches' reactions that she was powerful, too. "I did have an idea on the broom ride over, but I wasn't all that fond of it. And now, I think I have a better idea."

Her eyes fell consideringly on me and I suddenly found that my fingers were trembling on the gin bottle. What was this witch going to propose?

"Don't drag it out, Malkin," Sarmine said crisply. "Where are we going to set the game?"

Malkin pointed at me, a finger like a gun going bang. "Her high school."

My knees started to go. "Now look," I said, as firmly as I could. "I just stopped a demon from eating a boy's soul, and I stopped a phoenix from exploding. And that was all in one week, so I think my school's earned a bit of a break." Resolutely I turned away and poured Sarmine her gin.

Malkin jumped up, and suddenly she was near me, actually was this time. The animal musk smell was stronger. "Soft," she said. "Untried. Full of dangerous ideas about ethics and morals."

"Correct," I said, plopping the requisite newt eyeball into Sarmine's gin. I took a deep breath. It turns out that it is hard to state your opinions to someone who not only thinks they are ridiculous, but who can turn you into a potato to boot. But I tried. "I believe that there is such a thing as a good witch, and that I can be one." I handed Sarmine her gin, pleased with the firmness of my voice.

Malkin laughed. "Oh, you've got a live one here, Sarmy," she said. To me: "And just how do you propose to do that?"

"Not plot to do bad things at my high school, *obviously*," I said. The first flush of temper shot through me. I didn't know what the Do-Badders Club did but I could make some educated guesses.

"Stop bothering the girl, Malkin," said Valda. "I'm delighted to revisit high school. Come tell us the rules for this year's game."

Malkin pulled a deck of cards from yet another hidden pocket and tossed them to me where I stood in the center of the room. "Cut the cards and shuffle them," she said. "While you're doing that, tell me what classes you have at school."

"Er," I said, because this obviously sounded like a trap. But witches usually work spells by combining powders and ingredients and then touching them with their wand, and so far she hadn't done either of those things. "Algebra II," I said. I thought about the day only a couple weeks ago when Jenah and I had first seen Devon in our class. And I had been failing, but Mr. Rourke and tutor Kelvin helped me get caught up. . . . I realized Malkin was looking intently at me.

"Good, good," she said. "What else?"

I rattled the rest off more quickly. "French, English, American history, AP biology, and gym," I said.

"Any extracurriculars?"

I snorted. I spent all my "free" time catering to the witch's crazy demands. When would I ever do clubs or sports or things? "They exist," I said, envisioning some of the lucky kids headed off to them after school. "Drama club, football, debate. You know." The cards smelled vaguely of cinnamon. "Did you put something on these?"

"Cut the cards."

I did, placing the deck on the table.

Malkin flicked her gaze around the room. "You may all draw a card," she said. "Do not show anyone else."

Esmerelda drew the first one. Her eyebrows rose, then she smiled. "Oh, this one looks perfect," she said.

Rage and fear flashed up to my eyes. "What are you doing?"

Before they could stop me, I grabbed a card myself and flipped it over. The wide, pale face of my math tutor was imprinted on it. On the top and the bottom, where the numbers and suit usually are, was his name: Kelvin. Below it ran a list of his classes and clubs: drama club, 4-H, calc I. . . .

"If you're quite through with the dramatics," said Valda. She took the next card and peered at it over her plastic glasses. A snort of laughter escaped her nose. "Well, this will be entertaining."

"Stop it!" I scooped up the cards, holding them tightly. "I don't know how you did that without a wand, but you can't."

Malkin flashed her palm at me. I saw now that a small wand was fitted under several rings on her second finger, like some sort of conjuring trick. The casing must be made out of fabric or something flexible that bent with her hand. "Plucked plenty of good images of students from your memory," she said. "You can't even shield properly."

"Tsk," said Esmerelda, presumably just to annoy me.

Sarmine rose to her feet. "Mind reading was outlawed by the Geneva—"

"The Geneva Coven, I know, I know," said Malkin. She leaned casually back in her chair. "So were a number of other things, weren't they, Sarmine?"

Her sentence clearly held some deeper meaning, a reminder of something in their past. Sarmine's mouth closed, an angry, thin line.

Malkin gestured to the other two witches. "Those will be your students," she said. She pulled out her phone to check the time. "Let's see, it's Sunday evening, eight forty-two p.m. . . . You have exactly five days to make their lives as miserable as possible."

"You can't do this," I said, standing. "You have no right. Sarmine, tell them they can't do this."

Sarmine sighed. "Put the cards back on the table, Camellia."

"But . . ."

"No *permanent* harm will come to the students, correct, Malkin?"

Malkin shrugged. "If that's how you want to play it."

"And you will only go after the student on your card?"

"Rules," groaned Malkin. Her manner was flippant, but her eyes were so cold I could not tell what she was thinking.

Sarmine rapped the table to turn my attention back to her. "Think of it as a character-building exercise, Camellia. We"—she gestured to the club—"have done this little game before. You will find your fellow students are in fact toughened up by this experience. They will learn and grow and be able to achieve greater things." She held my eyes. "Put the cards back on the table."

Reluctantly I reached out and set down the stack of cards. I had been through enough of Sarmine's punishments and "learning exercises" to know that she was a big fan of this method of character-building. I wasn't going to be able to stop their fun.

Malkin fanned the stack of cards across the table, running her ringed fingers over them. She pulled one from the middle of the pile. That didn't seem like proper card etiquette, but I was not going to be the one to tell her that. She studied the card, reading the name and stats. "*Lovely,*" she said. I couldn't tell if she was being sarcastic or not.

"Well, if we're going to do it *that* way," said Sarmine. She fanned the cards in the other direction and held her hand above them, considering. Then she picked one of her own. The other two witches rolled their eyes at the one-upmanship. Sarmine barely glanced at the card before sliding it into her fanny pack. Her poker face, as always, was excellent. Sarmine was the only one of the four who might conceivably know some of my friends and not-friends at high school. Potentially she could have drawn someone she knew—Jenah or Devon or even Sparkle. But I had no idea.

Four witches, four cards. Four students—possibly friends—about to have their lives destroyed by wicked witches for fun.

"Well, that was entertaining," said Esmerelda with a delicate yawn. "Who's up for another drink?"

"I'll take a prickly pear margarita," said Valda. "With a little umbrella."

I shook my head, steeling myself. I might not be able to stop their game. But a good witch would fight. I was going to go down trying.

I put my hand over the pile of cards.

"Oh, did you want to play?" said Malkin. "There's always room for a fifth."

"No," I said. "I'm going to stop you."

All the witches howled laughter at that. "Stop us!" said Esmerelda. "You're just a baby."

"A whelp."

"A pup."

"With dubious ideas about morality," put in Malkin.

"You don't even know who's been chosen," said Esmerelda.

"That prevents cheating," explained Valda.

"So how would you even find them?" said Esmerelda.

"What you're doing is not right and I'm going to stop you," I said stubbornly. I was getting angry and that was not safe. Any one of these witches could destroy me on a whim. Okay, my mother would probably stop me from getting *destroyed* destroyed. But she was big on me learning lessons, so I doubted she would stop anything less. She might even join in. "How were you going to decide who wins, anyway?"

"With this," said Malkin. From an inner coat pocket she pulled out a bubble wrap–swathed package that really shouldn't have fit in an inner coat pocket. She unrolled the bubble wrap to reveal four slender glass tubes that she then placed on the coffee table. They looked like repurposed thermometers—the kind that have water in them and little different-colored bubbles that float up and down with the different temperatures. These only had one bubble floating in the cylinder. Each cylinder had a witch's name written on the stand in curly gold letters. Esmerelda, Valda, Malkin, and Sarmine.

"Whoever's bubble gets closest to the bottom wins," explained Valda. She took her dark glasses off and cleaned them on her skirt. "I remember a time when it was neck and neck between Sarmine and Malkin, but then Malkin covered her victim in birdseed and sent seventy-two hungry pigeons after her. That was an exciting finish."

I looked more closely at the tubes. Horizontal lines marked off the levels of happiness. From the top down it read: 6-Ecstatic, 5-Pretty Darn Happy, 4-Content, 3-Vaguely Dissatisfied, 2-Really Not Great, and 1-Despair. Between 3 and 4 was a painted red line marking the midpoint.

"The bubbles aren't even," I said. "Valda's bubble is in four but everyone else's bubble is down in three."

Esmerelda shrugged gracefully. "The luck of the draw. It only matters where the bubble is at the end of the game."

"Oh, man," said Valda. "Once I had a five and he would not leave it no matter what. I threw locusts and plagues at him and he whistled down the street saying things like, 'Gee, it's great to be alive.' He was the worst."

"I'm still going to stop you," I said stubbornly. "I'm going to make all four bubbles finish above the red line."

"But you don't even know magic," scoffed Esmerelda. She glanced at Sarmine. "Or have things changed dramatically since the last time you dragged her out in public?"

I rounded on Sarmine. "Look, you," I said. "You're always saying I need to practice more spells. Well, now I'll practice them. You can help me learn the spells I need."

"How do you know she won't cheat?" pointed out Valda. "You're asking her to play both sides."

I looked at Sarmine. "Will you?"

She made a *considering* face.

"*Really?*" said Esmerelda. "*This* girl? No magic, no lust for mayhem . . ."

"Too many ethics," put in Valda.

"And you think you can waltz in here and join our game? You're not even a member of the club."

"A fair point," said Valda.

Malkin narrowed her eyes at me. "A test," she said. "The teensiest little initiation, just to see if she can join the club at all."

I swallowed. "I don't need to join the club," I pointed out in a sort of soft, squeaky voice. "I could just try to stop you."

Malkin was suddenly near me/not near me again, and that sense of power and musk overwhelmed me. "Sarmine, we have been too lax," she said. "We have allowed an outsider to overhear our meeting."

"This is true," said Valda.

"Confirmed," said Esmerelda. Their expressions were suddenly very dangerous.

"True," admitted Sarmine. "Are you going to impose the Ultimate Punishment on her?" I couldn't tell from her expression whether she would try to stop them or if she would help dole it out.

"The Ultimate Punishment," I croaked. "That's something nice, right, like a hot fudge sundae?"

"First we encase you in leeches," said Malkin. "Next, we—"

"I would absolutely love to join your club," I put in. "What do I need to do?"

"Everyone still have their newt eyeball?" said Malkin. "Esmerelda, demonstrate."

Esmerelda popped the eyeball into her mouth.

"Make sure you crunch on it," said Valda to me. "I don't advise swallowing."

Esmerelda got a funny expression on her face as she bit down. Then she parted her lips—and emitted a small stream of fire, straight into the remains of her vodka. The alcohol flamed up, burning blue. The witches applauded.

Sarmine crossed to the minibar and pulled out the jar of newt eyeballs. I noticed now that the handwritten label claimed them to be *Ye Finest Olde Newte Eyeballs, Steeped in Unicorn Hair Vodka, with Especiale Ingredients*. Witches like that fake ye oldey stuff. They think it makes them look classy.

"I'm not sure . . ." I demurred. I mean, fire-spouting eyeballs sounded scary enough. What if I accidentally swallowed it? Plus, there was the thought of crunching down on those newt eyeballs that probably some newt would have rather kept.

"Got a dud," said Valda through a cough. I looked over to see a cloud of smoke around her. She pursed her lips and blew a smoke ring.

Sarmine picked an eyeball out with the cocktail tongs and dropped it into my hand. It was slimy. "Bottoms up," she said, and then she and Malkin both crunched on theirs at the same time. Malkin burned a hole in our coffee table. Sarmine lit Malkin's pant leg on fire. "Oops," said Sarmine.

"My deepest apologies," countered Malkin as she snuffed her pants.

I looked at the eyeball in my palm. My choice at this moment was between the eyeball of something that was already dead, and the lives of four kids at school.

Deep breath, Cam.

I crunched and blew.

Fire shot out into the air and then burned itself up and vanished.

I laughed with relief, feeling my face. I was fine, I was fine. My lips were warm, and my mouth tasted disgusting, but I was fine. I almost jumped with glee.

Valda rose and clapped me on the back. "Well done," she said. "There's the makings of a wicked witch in you after all."

"A *good* witch," I said. "Not a wicked witch."

Valda snorted. "Don't know many good witches who snack on newt eyeballs."

A side glance at Malkin showed that she was laughing at me. There was a nasty feeling forming in the pit of my stomach. "But I had to," I protested. "In order to not be encased in leeches."

"Ethics," said Malkin, petting her snake scarf. "A slippery slope."

"Enough of this," said Esmerelda. "I have to get up early to drop the kid off at school. Can we make it official and go home?"

"Almost," said Malkin. "There's the little matter of what the baby witch will ante up."

"I don't have anything," I said.

"I know I've been jealous of Sarmine's little helper all night," she continued. "Shall we say one week's servitude to the winner?"

Valda shrugged. "Fine by me."

I could hardly think of anything worse than to be at one of these witches' beck and call for a week. But in a strange way it seemed fair. The other kids from school didn't have a say in being included in the witches' game. I was stuck, too. "As long as I win all your treasures," I said. "*When* I win."

"Of course," said Malkin, writing down my wager. "And *now* we can make it official." She spat on her hand and held it out.

Around me the other three witches did the same.

I looked at the wet palms dubiously.

"That's how you seal the deal, Camellia," Sarmine said crisply.

"So it's fair, and we're agreeing that we're mostly not cheating," put in Valda.

"Witch spit?" Reluctantly I spat on my hand and began shaking around the table. The process was . . . moist.

"Then it's settled," Malkin said at last. "Whoever's bubble is the lowest on Friday evening wins." She looked at me. "Or, if all the bubbles are above the red line, then Camellia wins, and she gets the prize." She tossed the prize envelope on the coffee table and it skidded to a stop next to the thermometers.

"Not that that's going to happen," said Esmerelda.

Malkin curled her lip. "No," she said. "It's not."

2

Who Esmerelda Had

Monday morning I came downstairs bright and early. I had all the witch's regular chores to do, of course, but before that I wanted to check on the glass bubbles. They were all floating at the same level they had been last night. I guess none of the witches were early risers.

So that was good, right?

After I let Wulfie out to do his business, I sunk down on the couch, staring through the thermometers into nothing. There was a lingering scent of burned coffee table in the air. A lingering taste of newt eyeballs in my mouth.

So much for my "good witch" ethics.

I mean, I wasn't a vegetarian or anything. The witch had served newt burgers a couple times and I had eaten them. But this wasn't food—these were party tricks. And I was against the idea of using animal parts for the personal gain of magic spells.

Yes, I had been doing it to try to save the kids from my high school. But did that make it right?

To be honest, what really bothered me was how quickly Malkin had been able to talk me into it. A good witch needed to be firmer than that.

I found a piece of paper and started a list. I had a feeling I was going to need it this week. I wrote:

Good Witch Ethics

1. Don't use animal parts in spells.

Okay, so it wasn't much, but it was a start.

The Kelvin card had fallen on the floor. I studied it more closely. It was slick plastic, rounded corners—a perfectly normal playing card. His entire class schedule was neatly printed on it, with locations and everything. The witches would have no trouble finding their prey. I sighed and set Kelvin on the table. At least I knew one of my friends was safe. I was still worried about Jenah and Devon, though. I mean, Devon had just survived a demon infestation, brought about by my mother. Our friendship/relationship/whatever-it-was-ship was dicey at best. If he got caught up in this, he'd never forgive me.

A small noise and I looked up to see Sarmine coming down the stairs. Sarmine never got out of bed before ten o'clock. *I* was the keeper of the five a.m. chores. It was a shock to find her up.

"Coffee," she muttered. Her hands waved vaguely around for it like a zombie seeking brains.

I raced to start her coffee brewing. "Worried I'm going to tamper with the thermometers somehow?" I said over my shoulder. I shoved the coffee mug directly under the dripper to catch the first cup of coffee.

She rubbed sleep out of her eyes. "That would be a shortcut."

"I don't follow."

Sarmine sat on the couch, smoothing her silver hair into place. She might be out of bed, but she was still in her starched white nightgown. "Cam," she said. "You are going to win this thing."

"I am. I mean, I am?"

"I am going to help you."

I could hardly believe it. It must be a trap. "Wouldn't you rather watch me stumble through this on my own and then laugh?"

Sarmine yawned. "Nonsense. We need to get one up on Malkin. If she thinks she can waltz in here after a decade and start this nonsense up again she has another think coming." I handed her the full coffee mug and she breathed in the scent before she spoke again. "Besides, in fourteen years I have never once heard you beg me to teach you magic. What kind of a mother would I be if I didn't seize that opportunity?"

"Well, great," I said. I sat down beside her and watched her try to get caffeine out of the steam. And then, tentatively, I said, "But aren't you, you know, kind of working against me with your own student you're supposed to make miserable? How do I know you won't cheat?"

The witch drew herself up. "I never cheat," she said loftily. "Unless circumstances require it." She looked thoughtful. "Besides, Malkin is up to something. I can tell. I wouldn't trust her farther than I could throw her off of a broomstick."

"You and me both."

"All that nonsense about telling Esmerelda and Valda what to ante up. I don't know what Bigfoot claws are used for but I can tell you that mermaid fins are used to contain magical creatures. The more powerful the animal, the stronger the spell needed to contain it."

"Suspicious," I agreed.

"Camellia," she said, with the air of someone bestowing eternal life and a million dollars, "I will cancel your morning chores this week in favor of early-morning spell-crafting sessions."

This was getting better and better.

"But. If I am going to help you—and work against my own self in doing so—I need a promise from you."

"Such as?"

"That you will promise to learn the spells I teach you," she said.

Ah. There was the trap. "If they're *nice* spells," I said, thinking of the list I had started.

Sarmine set down her coffee so she could gesture in frustration. "Camellia, do you imagine that I deliberately do things just to annoy you?"

That was exactly what I did imagine, but I knew better than to say it.

"I'm not going to be creating the spells I give you to learn," she said. "The spells are the spells. If you want to know how to cast a certain spell to help one of the victims, we'll have to find a copy or buy it from another witch. A *reputable* witch—not one of those crazies you find on WitchNet."

"So wait, you've never created spells on your own?"

I could feel the eye roll like a disturbance in the fabric of the universe. "Creating spells is one of the most dangerous and exhilarating tasks a skilled witch can undertake," Sarmine said. "It takes years of study and practice."

"So that would be a no?"

"In all the catalogue of spells I personally have created, Camellia, I highly doubt there is one for 'passing a pop quiz' or 'finding out if that boy who sits in the front row secretly likes me' or whatever else it is that goes on at your high school."

My turn to roll my eyes. "Actually I *learn* things at that school," I said. "Biology. Lab tests. You ever heard of a little something called the scientific method?"

"Well then," she said. "You'll be all set to come up with new solutions to anything that bothers you in these spells."

"I, uh. Well . . ."

"Now. First things first," Sarmine said. "Please recite for me the elements you need to cast a spell."

"Well. The spell itself," I said. "Time to study it." Witch spells were written like some horrible combination of word problems, logic puzzles, and bad puns. "The ingredients." The witch was always sending me around to fetch the unusual ingredients she needed, like leprechaun hairs or organic elk butter. "And a wand." I had my father's old one—one of the few things I had of his.

"Very good," said the witch. "Now, as long as you cooperate, I will provide you with certain ingredients from my own stores—subject to availability. And cost. Unless I think it's a better learning activity for you to track it down." I was beginning to get the idea that there would be a lot of fine print to this agreement. "You will of course need a fanny pack to carry your supplies . . ."

But there I drew the line. "Esmerelda had a purse," I said. "Can't I do something like that?"

Sarmine sniffed. "If you want to spend your precious free time sewing hidden pockets into your backpack, be my guest," she said. "In the meantime . . ." She handed me an orange leather fanny pack, well-marked with gray, green, and dark red splotches. It smelled of ginger, garlic, and compost.

"Thanks," I said dubiously. I could always stuff it in my backpack.

"Now, is there a particular spell you would care to learn?" she said.

I thought about this. The problem with trying to stop the witches was that they could do literally anything. Whereas I knew about three spells so far and none of them were going to necessarily be the right ones. Like, if a witch broke a kid's arm, I didn't know a healing spell. If a witch turned someone turquoise, I didn't know how to change them back. If a witch made someone float away, I didn't know how to de-levitate them. You get the idea.

"Malkin had an aura of . . . menace about her," I said. "Was that a spell? Or just natural charisma?"

"Both," said Sarmine, adding modestly, "all witches are naturally charismatic."

"Naturally."

"But Malkin also had a favorite spell that she loved to work in college to make everyone more afraid of her. I'm sure she's still doing it, or a more refined version."

"I didn't see her combine any ingredients or wave her wand," I said. "Although, she did have that disguised wand. . . ."

Sarmine sniffed. "Malkin is fond of sleight of hand," she said. "Like any common street magician."

Actually it seemed pretty convenient to be able to hide what you were up to, but I didn't say anything.

Sarmine crossed to the bookcase and brought back a limp

leather-bound volume. "Some of the spells I wrote down in college," she explained. "We were all building up our collections, and we would often trade spells." She set the journal down on the bar between us and began flipping through. A small smile appeared as spells struck memory. "See, that's definitely an Esmerelda spell. 'How to Make Someone Always Appear Ugly in Pictures.'" That did sound like Esmerelda. "And oh, look, there's one from Valda I'd forgotten about."

"'How to Drop a Piano on Someone's Head,'" I read. "Lovely."

"I wonder if Malkin's early sympathetic resonance spells are in here," Sarmine murmured as she flipped. "Oh, here's the one you want. Malkin used this daily. 'A Mystikal Spelle of Great Power.'"

"I think there's a Mystikal in my grade at school," I muttered.

"Creative spelling aside," said Sarmine, "this is a nice beginner's spell for looking more powerful, and it shouldn't give you any trouble. I'll leave you to it."

I glanced at the handwritten spell, which started, in typical witch fashion: "If the day of the week begins with S, find yourself some slugs." I looked back up at Sarmine. "I thought these were lessons."

"They are."

"But I have to work out the spell by myself?"

"While I drink coffee, yes."

I rolled my eyes and grabbed a piece of paper. I'd almost rather be hanging up the snakeskins.

☾

An hour later, my paper was a mass of scribbled blue ink and I was no closer to deciphering the spell. I sighed as I got a fresh sheet and began copying the spell again. Among other things, I was hung up on the line that read, "If the day of the week begins with Y. . . ." Was I supposed to be reading all the days backward? Yadnom. Yadseut. Wulfie was curled on the couch next to me, busy shredding a chew toy into tiny bits. I stroked his fur as I tried to make my brain do brainy things. "Can't you give me a hint?" I said.

"Whiny teenagers get turned into solar panels," the witch said.

I shut up. I shoved the book into my bag. Maybe I could find some time to work on it at school. In between finding the four victims of the witches, and trying to retain my tattered bits of a social life.

"Interesting," said Sarmine. "Esmerelda's bubble is rising."

"That's good news though, right?" I said. "Her victim is having a good day?"

"Perhaps," said Sarmine. "Esmerelda does enjoy building people up. . . ."

She trailed off and I filled in the rest. "And then tearing them down, I bet," I said. Classic mean-girl strategy from a middle-aged witch. "She might be at the school already." I stared at the thermometer, watching to see if it rose or fell.

"Well, hurry up," said Sarmine. "You won't find Esmerelda here."

"I don't suppose you'd drive me? This once?"

Sarmine's eyebrows shot through the roof.

"Right."

I caught the next city bus to school. It left fifteen minutes earlier than my regular one, but it definitely didn't get there any faster or smell any better. I reviewed what strategies the four witches might use. Sarmine, of course, dearly loved to teach people a lesson. But she had promised me not to make her victim miserable. I didn't know whether to trust her or not. Or, even if I *could* trust her, would she understand the difference between teaching someone a lesson and making their lives a living hell? For example, last March she dropped live eels down the chimney of the guy who was still running his Christmas lights display. (They were *electric* eels. It was supposed to make some sort of symbolic statement about wasting energy. I don't think he realized that.)

Still, whatever Sarmine got up to would probably not be as bad as Malkin. Malkin was the most frightening witch I had ever met. I shuddered to think what she would do to her victim. Probably only her promise of no *lasting* harm would stop her from turning her student into little tiny pieces and calling it a day.

Valda? Valda I didn't really know yet. I tabled her for later.

Esmerelda—yes, Esmerelda would probably try to humiliate her victim. She had looked pretty happy at her card last night, so maybe she thought she had an easy mark. A geeky boy she could seduce. A nerdy girl she could destroy.

I got off the bus and made a circuit around the school, scanning the grounds for any sign of either Esmerelda or of an incident about to go down. Not for the first time, I wished Sarmine would let me have a real phone like everyone else. I could text Jenah and Devon and see if anyone had tried to drop an anvil on their head.

The crowd was growing by the minute as kids parked or got dropped off. It was crisp but not freezing—jean jacket weather. A couple girls were clustered on the steps, and I studied them, but they were griping about being up this early, going to class, et cetera. I kept going around the building. A few boys were playing Hacky Sack. They also did not look like they were having an incident.

And then I saw a tall blonde in a pink suit with a green handbag disappearing into the side door.

Esmerelda.

I hurried after her. How had she gotten permission to actually go on campus? I had thought the witches would at least be stuck outside of school bounds. I went into the side door, trying to look casual and keeping a sharp lookout for a certain blond witch.

The pink business suit bobbed and weaved through the growing crowds. I followed her upstairs. Ducked behind a door as she reached her destination. The art room.

The first few art students trickled in. There were a couple in ordinary clothes. As we got closer to the bell it was more black and chains and goth and punk and tattoos and piercings and every other different kind of style. I heard one of them say as they entered the room, "Where's Mrs. N?" and then another: "Dude, the sub is *hot*."

Of course. What better way to get into the school than to pose as a sub? Just magic up some teaching credentials and a clean background check. Further, it seemed a reasonably good bet that her victim was an art student. Esmerelda must have learned that from the victim's playing card. I hoped she hadn't done anything to Mrs. N.

The bell ringing shocked me out of my fugue. Crap. Rourke was not going to be happy with me for being late to his class.

I hurried off to first period, trying to formulate a plan for the day. I could stake out the art room between classes. I could surreptitiously ask around if anyone was having a bad day. No, I was terrible at that sort of thing. My best friend, Jenah, was great at it, though, and she knew everyone.

It was weird asking Jenah for help with this. I mean, we helped each other with mundane things all the time. But I had only let her in on my big secret about my personal life a couple weeks ago, when all the crazy demon nonsense was going down. So it wasn't my first instinct to ask for assistance with a wicked-witch standoff, you know? But I had promised Jenah no more keeping secrets from her.

I firmed my resolve. I was never going to get through this week without Jenah running backup. She would have to be let in on it.

I mean, for starters, if Esmerelda was just showing up to school now, then Sarmine and I were wrong about her interacting with her student twenty minutes ago. Which meant that the victim had been happy for some completely unrelated reason, like getting to eat waffles for breakfast. I groaned. How on earth was I going to figure out which art student was her target?

Malkin had said she was plucking the images from my memory. Did that mean that everyone chosen was actually a friend of mine? I tried to reassure myself. I must have seen every kid in school—and it was a big school—walking around at some point. On the negative side, that would make it harder to figure out who the victims were, but on the positive side, hopefully I didn't have to see any of my close friends get their lives destroyed.

Not that it was right to destroy anybody's life. Of course, there were some obnoxious kids in school. If only I had gotten to pick. . . .

No, I reminded myself firmly as I hurried into algebra II and dropped into my seat, panting. No one's life should be destroyed by an overgrown witch club.

"Glad you could join us, Camellia," said Mr. Rourke dryly.

On the other hand, if the club had gone after teachers, I could think of one to give them. Frankly, the only nice thing about Rourke's class is no one laughs when he says rude things because they know he might call them out next. It's kind of a mutual bonding experience—everyone who's managed to survive Mr. Rourke's teaching.

Across the aisle, Devon smiled sympathetically at me. Which made me feel a little better. Devon is white, with floppy blond hair and a sweet face. He's the new boy in school, and we sort of had one date ten days ago, not that I was counting or anything. Date one was mixed up with a lot of annoying things like demons and exploding phoenixes so I wasn't really sure if there was going to be a date two or if he thought high school would be a little easier if he stayed away from me.

Okay, to be fair, he had been sick all last week after recovering from fighting a demon out of him.

Still. When you've only had one date, and you have no way to contact your crush because your phone only connects to the witch system, you spend time obsessing about that perennially stupid question of "Does he like me? Circle here Y/N." It was kind of amazing I had any brain cells left to stop wicked witches, when you came right down to it.

"Camellia," Rourke said with the air of someone who has said it five times, "Please come to the board and work through the first homework problem for me. Unless, of course, the answer is to be found on the side of Devon's head."

There *were* a few snickers at that as I took my homework and my red-faced self to the board. Traitors.

I made it through the rest of class with a minimum of angst. Algebra II was going a lot better now that math whiz Kelvin had caught me up to speed. Rourke's terrible word problems even made sense, which was good, because that meant I had a prayer of solving Sarmine's spells. I wished I dared pull out the Power spell to keep working through it, but I figured I was on thin ice today. I kept my head down and tried not to glance over at Devon for the rest of class.

When the bell finally rang I mustered my courage and turned oh-so-casually to his desk. "How are you feeling?" I said. Witty banter, that's me.

"Much better." He smiled at me and then I guess we ran out of conversation. He smelled like soap. I like that in a guy.

"So, I . . ."

"Look, would you . . ."

I stopped. "You first."

"Well, uh," he said. "So I have band practice after school."

"Okay?"

"And then the band's going to get pizza. Like five-ish. At Blue Moon. I thought maybe you'd like to come?"

"Yes," I said, lighting up. I would worry about what the witch would say when I got home. "I would love to."

Next period's students were filing in and Rourke was swooping down on us to say something sarcastic.

"I, uh, better go," he said. "See you then."

"See you then."

And then of course we both gathered our books and had to go out the same door, so it was like, awkward for a second. But I got another smile from him before he turned to go the other direction, so it was worth it.

"I have a date, I have a date," I sang-chanted to Jenah when I caught up with her at our locker. Jenah is Chinese-American and my best friend from way back. She is tiny and chic-punk and knows everyone in school.

She looked amused. "With Devon?"

"And his band. But whatevs."

"Hey, baby steps," she said. Today she was wearing solid white with a million neon bracelets. She retrieved a yogurt tub from the depths of the locker and pulled out even more bracelets, loading up each arm. "That boy may look like a boy-band boy, but he's really kind of shy."

"He is, isn't he?" I said. "I mean, he is." Hard to figure out sometimes if someone was shy or just not into you. Especially when they were cute.

"Worth it, though," she said.

I took a breath. "So . . . I'll see you at lunch?"

"Of course?"

"I have Important Things that I need your help with."

Jenah lit up. "Ooh! Is that secret code for Witchy Things?"

"Hush," I said. "Secret code should stay secret."

"Wouldn't miss it," she said.

☾

The next two hours passed reasonably without incident. I was caught up in English, so I snuck Sarmine's spell out during that class. I decided to ignore the *Y* business for now and went back to "If the day of the week begins with *M,* find yourself a monkey," because today was Monday, after all. Once I focused on that, the spell started coming together. Witches like to throw in nonsensical stuff to distract you, and it had worked.

I wrote down the final list while Mr. Kapoor rambled on about the geopolitical climate of *Macbeth*. A pinch of ginger, one dragon's tear, one of my own hairs, and, because it was Monday—yes, there it was. A teaspoonful of monkey brains.

I was livid. Sarmine had deliberately given me a spell to work that she knew I would not want to perform. *This* was helping me?

This was working on the same team? I crumpled up the paper and shoved it into my backpack. I was so angry I even pulled out my phone, ready to text her something I would likely regret, when I realized Mr. Kapoor's eyes were upon me.

I dropped my phone into my backpack and my backpack onto the floor.

"What do you think, Miss Hendrix?" Mr. Kapoor said patiently. "Are the witches really to blame for Macbeth's downfall? Or did he bring it all on himself?"

"Blame the witches," I said. "One hundred percent."

☾

By the end of class I had calmed down enough to not send a scathing text to someone who regularly threatened to turn me into a wind turbine. I mean, I hadn't worked through the entire spell yet. Maybe it was just Monday that was a problem. Maybe on Tuesdays you only needed happy thoughts and rainbows.

Maybe.

I shouldered my backpack and headed to the cafeteria. I would have sent several texts to Jenah to relieve my feelings, but as I mentioned before, I have this stupid phone which only connects to WitchNet and the witch phone system. So Sarmine and any other witches can text or call me anytime they want (yay), and I can access all of Witchipedia and all the witch websites. But I couldn't call my best friend on it, or stalk my crush on social media, or anything useful. Maybe if the witch stopped giving me so many chores I could get a real-person job and pay for a regular phone myself, but at the moment, I didn't have time or money or a reasonable mother, so that was totally not in the cards.

At any rate, while I stood there wishing my phone would turn into a useful communication device, a text from my mother popped up. It read:

E'S BUBBLE PLUMMETED.

Oh, no. I looked frantically around the cafeteria, searching for someone undergoing public humiliation. But nothing.

Across the caf I saw Jenah getting her tray from the lunch ladies. I waved at her. She waved back and hurried my way.

That's when a kid burst through the swinging doors on his bike. "Hey, Brandon," he yelled at one of the jocks. "The delivery truck smashed your car!"

The athletic kids got up en masse; an irritated teacher went for the kid on the bike. The kid weaved, dodged—and plowed right into Jenah. The tray of lasagna she was holding splattered her white shirt and jeans as she went down hard.

"Jenah!" I shouted, and ran over. Around me I could hear some kids saying "oh, no," and some kids laughing. Jerks. Poor Jenah must be humiliated. I helped her up, but she was laughing it off. All four feet ten of her jumped on the bench, dripping cheese and tomato sauce.

"Thank you, thank you," she said to the cafeteria. "For my next trick I will make the food here edible."

There was genuine laughter at that, and Jenah jumped back down. "Ugh," she said. "Help me wash this off in the restroom, will you?"

We weaved between the bicyclist and the teacher trying to catch him, and left the cafeteria. "Well, that sucked," I said.

"Bad luck," she said.

But was it bad luck? My mind immediately jumped to the bet. I looked again at the text on my phone. But that news had come *before* the attack on Jenah. Plus, how could the witches have predicted that Jenah would be standing there? I thought again that it would be hard to determine who the victims were. Bad luck happened to people all the time. At least we knew that Esmerelda had drawn an art student. That was a clue in the right direction.

"What am I going to do?" Jenah said. "I don't have any extra clothes except my gym clothes, and . . ."

"Yeah," I said. Jenah usually looked ten times cooler than the rest of us, but not at the moment. "If anybody could make plastic shorts a statement, it'd be you," I offered.

"This is never going to come out," she said, rubbing vainly at the tomato sauce. "I wish there were a spell for . . ."

We both looked at each other at the same time. I had magically dry-cleaned her a couple weeks ago when she had rescued me from a giant pumpkin. "Unicorn hair sanitizer," I said, snapping my fingers. "Of course. Let's go somewhere private."

We headed up to the second-floor bathroom, which is in the old wing but next to the teachers' lounge, and so, paradoxically, is the best one to hang out in for witchy stuff because there isn't a permanent crowd of burnouts there glaring at you. On the way up, I explained about the witches and their bet and how I was going to stop it. This is how you can tell Jenah is a good best friend—she didn't look skeptical that I could stop them, she just said, "Of course you are, and I'm going to help you. After you fix my jeans."

Once inside the restroom, I scanned the floor under the doors and didn't see any feet. "All clear," I said, digging in my backpack for the vial of sanitizer. I pulled out my gross orange fanny pack in the search.

"Ew," said Jenah. She poked it with a finger.

"I know, right?" I said. "The witch gave it to me. It's got some of the powders and stuff I'm gonna need in it."

"Labeled, I hope," said Jenah. She opened it to see. "And nope."

"Typical," I said. "So it's useless."

"Unless you can tell a toe of frog from a toe of dog."

I made a face. "That one I could probably do. But I'm not going to use either, so it doesn't matter." I kept digging. Books, water bottle, crumpled-up spell . . . "By the way, what day of the week begins with *Y*?"

"None of them?"

I passed the spell over to her with all my scribbly notes, and the solution I'd found so far. "See, today's Monday, so I have to use monkey brains. But I'm not going to do that."

"Obviously."

"So I want to see if this is a spell I can work on some other day of the week, or if Sarmine has reached a new and horrible low, even for her." Promising the world one moment and taking it away the next. And yes, she had suggested I could experiment to find some substitutes—but really, on the very first spell?

"It looks like *S* days would use slug guts," said Jenah.

"No."

"*W* is walrus tusks. Oh look, *Y* is only yak fur. You wouldn't mind that."

"If I could find a day that started with *Y*, sure," I said.

"Here we go. If the day starts with *T*, find some thyme. So you *can* work this spell—tomorrow."

"On Tuesdays and Thursdays I can be powerful," I mused. "It's better than nothing. I won't kill my mother just yet."

"Epic witch battle?" said Jenah. "I'd see that."

"Speaking of epic witches . . . Any good gossip today? Anything out of the ordinary?" I needed to triangulate on the witches' victims.

"One of the cheerleaders decided to make over one of the nerds and date him," she said. "And two jocks have a bet going about who can get the French exchange student to date them first."

"Business as usual, then."

"Oh, there's something funny going on in the art classes today," Jenah said. "Something to do with a hot young sub."

"Right," I said. "The sub is Esmerelda, she's really like sixty, and I'm pretty sure the card she drew is an art student. Aha!" I finally found the bottle in the depths of my backpack. "Spin around for me."

Jenah twirled as I spritzed her. The unicorn hair sanitizer took her from disgusting to sparkly clean, literally. Silver stars of cleanliness fizzed around her. Even the tomato-cheese smell vanished, replaced by a pleasantly antiseptic scent that had overtones of apple and mint. By the time she finished twirling, her outfit was so white it glowed.

That's when we heard the muffled shriek.

I whirled. No one was in here. I had looked under the doors.

"Uh-oh," said Jenah. "I should have checked for auras." She walked down to the last stall and said firmly, "Whoever it is, come out right now. I can tell you're in there."

The stall opened and two legs swung down from the seat. A vaguely familiar-looking girl walked out. She was curvy and rumpled, all in black, with a nose piercing. She had brown skin and tangled dark hair, and her eyes behind her glasses were red, like maybe she had been crying. I would have asked her about it, except I was currently more worried about the look on her face, which said she had seen everything through the crack in the stall and was now trying to decide if she was going nuts.

"What were you doing in there?" I said.

"Me? What were *you* doing out here?"

I shrugged, trying to be casually offensive so maybe she'd give up and leave. "Not spying on people, I suppose."

She put her hands on her hips. "I wasn't, not at first. I was drawing."

"In the bathroom?" said Jenah.

"I had to escape for a minute," the girl said. One hand pushed up her glasses to rub her reddened eyes. "And the art classroom has a session this period so I couldn't hang out there. Not that I'd want to, not with *her*."

Jenah and I looked at each other. This must be her. This must be the girl who Esmerelda was busy making miserable. Now that I thought about it, I realized why she looked familiar—our lockers were near each other. I must have had plenty of images of her in my head for Malkin to steal. "You're Henny Santiago-Smith, aren't you?" said Jenah. "Freshman? *Art crowd?*"

Henny nodded woefully.

I started to say, "What can I do to help?" but I was forestalled by Henny opening her mouth.

"Let's cut to the chase," she said, and her woeful look transformed into a calculating one that I didn't like at all. She pointed at me. "Are you a witch?"

"No," I said.

"Yes," Jenah said simultaneously.

"Jenah," I hissed. I mean, come on. *She* wasn't the witch. If anyone was going to be giving up my deeply held secrets it should be me. Besides, there was something about this girl that bothered me. I think it was the way she was looking me up and down like I was the solution to a very big problem.

"What are you in here for?" I said. I wanted to be sure that this was Esmerelda's victim. "Did something . . . happen to you in art today?"

Her eyes bugged out. "You really are a witch. How did you know?"

"Lucky guess."

Henny sighed. "Ugh, we have the worst sub today. And the weird thing is, it's like I'm the only one who can see how awful she is. I mean, our regular teacher is Mrs. N, and she's the best art teacher I've ever had. She's amazing, seriously."

"But today?"

"But today we got this sub called Emerald or something—"

"Esmerelda."

"And, oh my god, the boys love her."

"Of course," said Jenah. We both rolled our eyes at the thought.

"And everything the boys do is right. She seriously has not said one bad word to any of them. Plus, and I don't even really think this is appropriate, but she said we were going to do some life drawing so we were all like, yay, and then she herself stripped down to a pink bikini and sat up on the teacher's desk for us to draw her."

"Um," I said. "That is a little bit . . ."

"Right?" said Henny. "And then she said we'd do a critique of everyone's stuff, right in front of everyone else, you know? And, I mean, Mrs. N does that to get us prepared for how tough they are in art school, so you get used to being dissected in front of everyone. But she basically raved over everyone's work in the entire room until she got to me."

"And then she trashed it," I said.

Henny nodded. "In a real vicious way, too. Like, 'It must be hard for you to draw my abs since you don't have any.'"

"That woman is insane," said Jenah. "The school should yank her out of there."

"She's probably hoodwinked the administration," I said. "They call her in, she magically makes them forget what they were doing."

"I mean, if regular art school teachers are like that, then I'll—I'll drop out of art," Henny said.

"You should *not* do that," I said firmly. "This woman has a vendetta against you personally."

"She's probably jealous of you," put in Jenah.

"Me?" said Henny dubiously. She looked down at her faded black hoodie and paint-splattered black jeans. The hoodie had a twelve-sided die on it, and read ELVES RULE AND WIZARDS DROOL. "I'm not really a pink bikini sort of person, y'know? I mean . . ."

"Don't sell yourself short," said Jenah firmly. "You are super great just the way you are and Cam will be happy to magic up a spell to fix your problem with this teacher."

"I will?" I said. Frankly, Esmerelda was starting to sound as terrifying as Malkin. I poked my own softish abs and wondered how easily she would vivisect me.

"Well, some kind of spell then," said Jenah. She nudged me significantly. "To make her week? Go better?"

Henny was clutching her tablet tightly, her eyes bugging at us. "You really are witches."

"Look, you can't tell anyone," I said. "Or . . ." I didn't know if I should plead with her or threaten her. Sarmine would have straight away turned her into a newt, so I supposed I should do the opposite of that and said gently, "Please don't tell on me. It won't be good if I attract attention."

Henny nodded, and then tilted her head. "Would you do something for me if I won't tell? Quid pro quo? I mean, I'm not threatening you. I could make your lives pretty miserable but I'm not the sort of person who would do that. Even if it would be amazing for me."

Okay, this girl was kind of rubbing me the wrong way. "I *am* trying to make people's lives better," I admitted. "And maybe even specifically yours." I didn't think it was a good idea to tell her the details of Esmerelda's goal for the week. "But how do I know I can trust you? I've never even heard of you."

She crinkled her nose in a quick glare, like she understood that I didn't know who she was but at the same time wished that were not the case.

"Why did you say it would be amazing for you to destroy us?" Jenah said.

"Well, not destroy you *intentionally*," Henny said. "But I do an online comic. It's called *Henny's Pathetic Love Life*." She sighed. "It does *not* have a massive following. But *Henny Meets Two Witches Right Here in Her High School*? Now that, I think, might get some traction."

"Yeah," I said reluctantly, "it might."

"Oh, man," Jenah said. "High school crossed with crazy witch hijinks? I would read that."

"I know, right?" said Henny. "And I can already see how I would draw you two. You're such perfect sidekicks—one cute, short, punk girl with amazing hair, one tallish, sort of average girl who looks even more average by contrast . . ."

"Okay, let's get one thing straight," I said. "I am the witch. Jenah is not. If anyone is going to be a sidekick, it's her." I turned to Jenah. "No offense."

"None taken."

"And thing two: there's not going to be a comic. There are lots of dangerous witches out there. Let's just say I'm undercover."

Her eyes bugged again. "Okay, when you said that, you stopped looking average for a moment and looked all fierce. You really would be amazing to draw."

"*No.*"

Henny sighed. "All right, all right, Scout's honor."

"What is it you want us to do for you?" said Jenah. "If not try to destroy Esmerelda." She was studying Henny with her questioning, *I'm going to figure you out* look. It was good she was on the case because even though I wanted to like Henny, I was feeling a little grouchy about her, "Boy, it would be awesome for me if I could expose your deepest secret" statement.

"Well, there's this boy," said Henny.

"*Obviously,*" I said, "Or I presume the comic would be *Henny's Amazing Love Life that She's Totally Got All Figured Out.*"

Henny shot me a dirty look.

"Of course," said Jenah, soothingly and helpfully. "And what have you done to try to win him so far?"

"Nothing," said Henny glumly.

"I think I've solved the source of your comic's woes," I said brightly. "People like action. They want things to *happen.*"

"I can think of something that happened today," Henny said darkly.

"Cam, give it a rest," said Jenah. "I can tell by Henny's aura that she's a good person in need of our help. It has these lovely, smudgy, baby-blue bits. You *wanted* to help her."

It was true. I did. So why was I balking? I guess, because when it came right down to it, I had wanted to both somehow help her and not get found out that I was a witch. Having my cake and eating it, too. I shoved down my irritation. "Okay, Henny. You're in."

"Ooh, secret witch club."

"One spell. But I don't know if I can do the thing you want. I'll have to go home and research it, and see if it's A, possible, and B, possible by me. I'm just a beginning witch."

"I know," said Henny. She must have seen my look, for she hurriedly said, "I mean, I'm sure you're great. But you didn't understand the clue in the spell you guys were talking about, and it was even trying to lay it out for you."

"It—what?" I floundered. It wasn't fair that this random *human* was better at solving spells than me. "What clue?"

She gave us an expression that said she was certain she knew the answer but uncertain about the advisability of proving to us that we were morons.

"Go ahead," Jenah said gently. "She won't turn you into a newt. I promise."

Henny picked the spell off the bathroom floor and pointed to the day-beginning-with-*Y* business. "That's your clue," she said. "To start thinking outside the box. There isn't a day that begins with *Y*."

"Obviously."

"So what else could it be?" She looked at our confused faces and simplified. "What's another way to describe Sunday?"

"You mean yesterday?" I said, and then did a double take.

"Now you see," said Henny.

"And I can't do the spell yesterday, but I *could* do it today, and today starts with *T*. . . . So then it's *always* today, and I can always use the thyme! Henny, you're a genius."

She beamed.

"Go ahead, lay it on me," I said, feeling more generous toward her now. "I'll try to do whatever spell you want. Do you want a makeover or something?"

Henny looked hurt. "Of course not. Despite what that horrible witch said, I'm fine with the way I look. I just need *him* to see me for who I really am."

"Like, you're friends but he needs to see you as something more?"

"Oh, I've never talked to him," said Henny. "I worship him from afar. My three loyal readers know the ups and downs about how I've crushed on him all semester."

"Okay," I said. "I am not the premier expert on boys but I think the first rule of thumb is that you should talk to someone you like. Wouldn't you say so, Jenah?"

"Sure," said Jenah easily. She was studying Henny. "Do you think he knows who you are?"

Henny lit up. "Well," she said eagerly. "I always use the computer lab during lunch. Because sometimes I do hand-drawn comics and need the scanner, or sometimes it's nice to see my stuff on the big screen instead of my tablet. You know? Anyway, a couple weeks ago he started coming into the lab. Every. Day. During. Lunch. I mean, that's awfully suspicious, right?"

"Or he can't afford his own computer," I pointed out.

Henny shot me a dirty look. Our bond was already deteriorating. "He is not the sort of person who would *need* to use the computer lab," she said frostily. "He clearly has ulterior motives."

"Of course," soothed Jenah.

Henny's face went all blissed out and she said, "Last week he asked me what the Internet password was." She opened her eyes. "And he could have found that on the board, you know?"

Patiently Jenah said, "Who's your crush, Hen?"

She sighed, and her brown skin flushed right up under her glasses. "Leo."

"Mmm-hmm," said Jenah. "You're not going to make this easy on us, are you?"

The name sounded vaguely familiar. "Who's Leo?" I said.

They both looked at me like I had sprung fully formed from the toilets a moment before and had no knowledge of anything. "Football quarterback," they said in unison.

"Ah. And how do you expect me to get the football hero to fall for you?"

"Love potion," said Henny.

3

A Mystikal *Spelle* of Great Power

"So what, some kind of Look at Me spell?" I said.

"Love potion," Henny said firmly.

I had never particularly thought about love potions before. And yet, the second Henny said it, I immediately knew what I thought.

Not a good idea.

Being a good witch meant not doing things *to* people like Sarmine and Malkin and all the rest did. It meant *asking* people what they want. And there was no getting around it. Forcing a boy to fall in love with a girl was not going to be fair to the boy, no matter how great a match the girl thought it was and how much she wanted it.

Of course, Henny had us over a barrel. She could spread the word about us immediately.

Was this another case like the newt eyeball dilemma? I could only do good in one place by doing harm somewhere else?

I opened my mouth to say something weaselly like, "Let's think about it overnight," when a commotion drifted up to our ears from outside the bathroom window. We all ran to the tiny window to see a green cloud of smoke billowing up in the air, just off campus.

"Didn't that kid in the cafeteria say Brandon's car got hit by a delivery truck?" said Jenah.

"Would that cause clouds of green smoke?" I said.

"Let's go, let's go," said Henny.

The three of us clattered down the stairs and out the door. A largish group of kids in the same lunch period as us were clustered at the edge of the parking lot. It's technically a closed campus, so everyone was nose to the edge, so to speak.

The parking lot was jammed full, as usual. You have to be a senior to get to park there at all, and even so you're not guaranteed a spot. Juniors' and sophomores' cars crowd the streets around the high school. The school is at the top of a hill, so everyone and their brother drives (and I mean that literally; car culture around here means a car for each driver in the family, plus a spare).

At any rate, the green smoke was not on school property. It smelled terrible—a mix of burning plastic and something medicinal. I shoved closer to see a black, shiny, massive SUV—no delivery truck anywhere in sight. Green gas belched from the SUV's windows, its sunroof, its tailpipe thingy, and from the lug nuts on its tires. Also it was wheezing like an elephant slowly collapsing under the weight of eighteen other elephants.

The wheeze became a shriek. The smoke thickened. Then with one final gust, the tires popped off as the car shuddered and collapsed on itself. Then the fire truck finally arrived, sirens going.

Through the crowds ran a tall, tanned, white kid I recognized as a popular sophomore, one of those summer birthdays who had been held back long ago and thus could now drive before everyone else. Total obnoxious prepster sort. Caden, that was his name. He was wearing pristine sneakers and perfectly ripped jeans. "My car!" he shouted as he ran. "Who did this? You're gonna pay!"

One of the firemen held out an arm to keep him from getting too close. Caden began swearing and threatening lawsuits.

The bell rang for the end of "A" lunch and everyone but me straggled back. Caden was busy telling everyone how his father's dealership was going to replace his car *immediately,* and then sue whoever'd done it.

Me, I stayed staring at the dead SUV for another five minutes. I didn't see any familiar faces in the crowd. No pointy hats hiding behind the bushes. And yet . . . normal cars did not belch green smoke. Despite not having a license myself, I felt relatively certain of that. No, the witches were involved somehow.

Which meant I had identified another victim.

On the bus ride home from school, I sat and worked on a list of what I knew:

WITCHES	**VICTIMS**	**HOW TO MAKE THEM HAPPY**
Esmerelda	Henny	Love potion (Is this ethical?)
Valda		
Malkin		
Sarmine		
(not S or E)	Caden??	Fix his car?

I knew Esmerelda had Henny. I mean, as sure as I could know without seeing the card. But if I started second-guessing myself I was never going to get anywhere. I didn't know who had drawn Caden, but Sarmine had promised that she would help me, and Caden certainly had not been helped by his car explosion, so I could cross her off of his list. He must have Valda or Malkin.

Oh, fantastic. This was worse than working through spells. I should draw one of those logic puzzle grids and check off the boxes. *Which Witch Has the Dudebro?*

My phone cackled in my pocket and I drew it out to see the witch's list of afternoon chores popping up one by one. Too much to hope that Sarmine would have cut out *all* my obligations. No, I would still have to dust the salamander skeletons while saving the world.

Not to mention trying to carry on a romance. Given that it was almost impossible to sneak out of the house when your mother was a wicked witch, this was going to be my first "real" date, even though it wasn't entirely real since it apparently involved the rest of Devon's band and did not involve the words "alone somewhere under a full moon." Still, you take what you can get.

Once I got home, I let Wulfie out to do his business, then cycled through a bunch of piddly witch tasks like salamander dusting and roasting some pixie wing/pumpkin seed mixture. I also quick-crammed a half PB&J since I hadn't gotten lunch. Finally I had to go to the RV garage and stir some new bubbling mixture the witch had going in a cauldron. It smelled like rotten bananas.

The RV garage used to be home to our dragon, and seeing her old quarters made me remember today's spell. A pinch of ginger, a pinch of thyme—thank you, Henny—one of my hairs, and one dragon's tear. Dragon's eyes naturally water—very slowly—and Sarmine and I had collected her tears for as long as she had been with us. Dragons are one of the elementals, and their magic is particularly powerful. It had been good business for Sarmine.

I walked over to an old spice rack that held a number of vials of dragon's tears. Sarmine had said she would supply me with some of the ingredients, right? So I took one, though my heart sped up as I did so, and I glanced over my shoulder for the witch. Old habits die hard.

I sighed as I put the vial in my pocket. I'd rather have Moonfire back than any number of her tears, no matter how powerful. It had only been ten days since she left, but I missed her. I was sure she was happier now that she had found some sister dragons. Still, I hoped someday she'd come back and see us. You know, if you set the robin free it should come back to visit you and all that. My eyes were getting misty, and several of my own tears plopped down into the banana mixture. I hurriedly backed out of the stinky, humid garage and shut the door. At least if I was going to cry I could do it where it smelled nice.

But instead I wiped my face as I realized the witch was working in the back garden. The witch doesn't like tears. Looking sad and lonely while asking for a favor might work on other parents, but not Sarmine Scarabouche.

I had been running through various scenarios in my head all day for asking Sarmine if I could go on a date with Devon tonight. I mean, the strategy that seemed most likely to work was to lie to her and say that I was hot on the trail of Esmerelda or Valda and I needed to see what they were up to.

But I didn't want to start out my career as an ethical witch by lying to people. Sarmine had promised to be straightforward and try to help me with the bet. And I would like to start us off on a good footing. And also, I thought it only fair to tell her what I was going to do, because I felt that it was totally okay for a tenth grader to get to leave the house once in a while and go have pizza, right? *Right?* So I was going to be honest.

And if she said no . . . well. Maybe I'd make a run for it.

I took a breath. In a rush I said, "I've walked Wulfie and stirred the cauldron and dusted the salamanders and roasted the seeds and pruned the deadly nightshade and now I'd like to go meet Devon and his band for dinner at Blue Moon Pizza."

Sarmine rocked back on her heels and considered my request while holding the remains of a squash vine. Being a witch requires a lot of random ingredients, and what better way to make sure that they are organic and pure than growing them yourself? Also, we eat a lot of vegetables.

"That is a reasonable request," she said at last.

"So I can go?"

She nodded. "But a witch always uses her time wisely," she said. "I happen to be in need of some inferior Parmesan for a spell. Please pick me up two packets while you are there."

"Okay," I said. That also seemed like a reasonable request. This was great. Here we were, two reasonable people. I turned to go.

And then I turned back. "Whoops," I said. "Can I also borrow some money? To chip in for the pizza?" I didn't know if Devon planned on paying for me, but I certainly didn't want to look like I thought he was supposed to.

The witch raised her eyebrows at this.

"I do a lot of chores around here," I pointed out. "And I do not get an allowance."

"I train you in the ancient arts of True Witchery," the witch countered. "For which I receive no compensation."

"If I do not have a ten to chip in for pizza," I said, "I will have to throw myself on the mercy of a *boy*."

The witch relented. "Very well," she said, and she drew off her gardening gloves and pulled a ten from her leather fanny pack. "You agree that this does not constitute as setting a precedent?"

"Right, right, just because you did it once doesn't mean I get money ever again," I said, rolling my eyes so hard I practically sprained them. "Thanks, Mom."

She actually squeezed my hand, not in a death grip way but an affectionate way, before putting her gloves back on and turning back to her squash.

I took my ten and hightailed it back inside the house, practically dancing for joy. This was big. This was huge. I was going somewhere to do something other than track down elf toenails for the witch. A thousand band members tagging along could not dampen my bliss.

I showered the rotten banana stink off me and dug through the clean laundry hamper for my favorite jeans. I had a pretty nice blue sweater that didn't have any pixie juice stains or anything so I put that on. That was about as fancy as it got. No matter how Jenah encouraged me, I just couldn't get motivated to change my style for more than a day or two. Maybe Henny and I weren't so dissimilar after all.

The pizza place was near the school, so I grabbed my jacket and backpack, and hurried out to catch the bus. I thought, not for the first time, that it would be nice to have a bike again. About a year ago, the dragon had sat on my bike and it had gone to that great bike graveyard in the sky. When I had asked for a new one, the witch had merely looked at me and inquired if I thought she was made out of bikes, and why didn't I take the nice public transit from the bus stop she had so conveniently bought a house next to? So I did.

I hopped off the bus outside of Blue Moon Pizza and headed inside, my heart revving up with anticipation. The little restaurant smelled of cheese and garlic and hope.

Devon was in a booth, earbuds in and fingers drumming the table. His floppy blond hair flopped. He looked up at me . . . and smiled.

I slid into the booth. "Hi," I said coherently.

"Hi," he said.

"Where's the rest of the band?"

"Oh, I think they went to the food carts," he said vaguely.

We sat there for a while.

"I haven't seen—"

"You haven't been—"

We laughed, and I said, "You first." Maybe that would give me time to think of something clever to say.

"I just wanted to thank you," he said. "For . . . you know."

"Getting a demon out of you?"

"Yeah."

"All in a day's work?"

"Sounds like some delightful days you've got there," he said with a wry grin that made me remember how much I enjoyed looking at him. I mean, talking to him. He looked back down and spread his long fingers on the vinyl tablecloth. I could see the calluses from the guitar. "Look, I know I did—Estahoth did—some obnoxious things when he was possessing me."

"Like kissing five girls? And holding hands with Reese right here over a cheese pizza?" Not like I'd thought about it or anything.

"Yeah. Those things."

"Forget it," I said suavely. "I know those things weren't you. You couldn't help it. Besides, it could have been worse."

He coughed on his water. "So, uh. How's things with your mother?"

"Ugh," I said. I looked around to see if anyone was nearby, but for the moment our table was isolated. "Can you keep a secret? I mean, more secrets than the ones we already have?"

"Shoot."

I took a breath and briefly walked him through last night's excitement. I mean, there were definitely more exciting things I wanted to talk to him about, but on the other hand, there were only two people total with whom I could discuss witchy things at all—Henny and her blackmail did *not* count—and I knew I was going to need some moral support this week.

"Wow," he said at last. "You don't get a lot of sleep, do you?"

"Sleep is for the weak," I said grandly. Then: "Why, do you think I did the wrong thing, confronting them?"

He shook his head. "I'm just worried about you, I guess."

I warmed at that. But, really, this was just a little nonsense at Ye Olde Witch Corral. Sarmine was always up to something, so . . . business as usual, right? I mean, there weren't demons involved this time or anything.

"So you have to fix the lives of all four victims," he said. "Have you identified the victims?"

"Two," I said. "It's tricky trying to sort out who has regular problems and who has witches interfering with their life."

He grinned. "Oh, I've had one of those."

"Witches? Or problems?"

"Well, there's this girl, you see."

I raised my eyebrows. "And she's a problem?"

He choked on his water a second time. "You look like your mother when you do that," he said.

I quickly lowered them. "Sorry. Didn't mean to remind you of the . . . possession incident."

He sighed. "At least when the demon was around I didn't mind singing in front of people."

I touched his arm before I could stop myself. "You sang at the Halloween Dance. You can do it again."

"You forget, that was a pretty exciting night."

Exploding phoenix. Demon-banishing. A kiss. "I could find some more phoenixes to explode," I offered. Of course what I really wanted to suggest was that I could come to every show and kiss him directly before he had to sing. Should I say that? Reese would say that, and then she would probably get kissed for it. I don't know, maybe I wasn't the sort of a person who could say it. Maybe I could just lean across the table and *do* it? I felt myself go red around the ears at the thought. "Er," I said. Maybe it was a good time to change the subject, before I found myself floundering on things I didn't know how to say. "How are your band things going? Do you have to sing soon?"

"Yeah," Devon said. He tried to smile but it looked sort of woebegone. "The Halloween Dance went so well we got an invite to try out for a Battle of the Bands this week. The audition is Wednesday after school, and the top three finalists play at the football game on Friday."

"That's fantastic!"

He nodded. "Sure."

"Stage fright still getting you?"

"Ugh," he said. He ran his hands through his floppy hair. "I feel so stupid for having this problem."

My heart went out to him. I mean, I know you can't magically fix anxiety or introversion or whatever his problem was, but—and then I stopped. What the heck did I mean, you can't magically fix it? Wasn't that the whole point of being a witch? And wasn't that what I was trying to do?

"I'm going to help you," I said. "I'm going to find some sort of self-confidence spell that will fix you right up."

He demurred. "I should be able to fix this on my own. And you've got a busy week already."

I didn't know what that meant, exactly, so like a birdbrain I said bluntly, "Do you not want my help?"

"I just mean," he said, falling over the words, "I mean you

shouldn't have to. I mean. . . ." He trailed off, looking over my shoulder. "Oh, hang on, that's Carlos from biology and he promised to lend me his study notes since I was sick last week. Hang on."

He got away from that booth faster than fast and I slumped down into it. I couldn't make it out at all. I guess I didn't have enough practice interpreting guy behavior—blame Sarmine for that. I mean, he was clearly sitting here with me, but at the same time, our conversation kept falling all over itself and imploding.

Maybe someone else could use a love potion.

I think my heart rate doubled at the thought. I mean, if Henny was forcing me to learn the spell anyway . . . would it be such a breach of good-witch ethics to make a little extra for Devon?

That was a rhetorical question. Yes, it very much would be a breach of ethics. It would be all kinds of wrong.

And yet maybe it was okay to . . . *imagine* what it would be like if I gave him the love potion. Imagination didn't hurt anyone, right? I picked up the Parmesan packets for the witch, fiddling with them. I slip a little potion into his soda . . . he turns to me and says, *Oh Cam, why are we talking about ridiculous things like biology homework? Let's go make out in the moonlight*. Yeah, about like that.

I crumpled up Sarmine's requested Parmesan packets and shoved them in my backpack. No, I knew perfectly well it was wrong. I was going to have to do all the hard work myself. And by "hard work" I meant pulling up my big-girl pants and, like, actually kissing him. Or actually asking him out on a second date, a real-er date. Something. Taking a stand.

Magic could solve some problems. But it couldn't fix your relationships with people, and it sure couldn't make you into a good witch. Else there'd be no such thing as wicked witches, I guess.

More and more students were coming in now. Laughing, chatting. There, a couple holding hands; there, a dude with his arm slung over his boyfriend's neck. Why was there such a gulf between me and everyone else? Other people seemed to know how to take the next step with their crushes.

Someone had left the door open; it was banging, rattling in the wind. One of the servers went to close it—and it tore out of his hands, smashing back against the wall. A tornado-like gust blew through the pizza place, snuffing candles and ripping menus out of hands. Several people shrieked, and then all the lights went out for a second, and I found my heart beating like anything. Someone was near me, breathing down my neck—no, that was just the wind—no, there was nothing.

The lights came back on. The wind was gone. The server shut the door.

Chatter resumed, mixed with nervous laughter, and then relieved laughter, as bodies processed that the danger was past.

Me, I stood, looking around for Malkin. This seemed exactly her style, down to that eerie feeling that someone had been near me. Had anyone been hurt in the confusion, anyone I could help? But I could not see anything wrong.

At that point Devon came back with some folded notebook paper and sat down. "Are you okay?" he said. His kind face was filled with concern.

I nodded, and then we were back to just looking at each other.

Screw it, I was going to say something. And now, before we were all destroyed in an epic witch battle. "Devon, I—"

"Devon!" chirped a voice, and I looked up to see Reese herself standing there. Reese is a blond, rich, ditzy, reasonably not-terrible sophomore whose main current fault is that she got to do way more making out with Devon two weeks ago than I did. "Ohmigod, that was crazy, right? Are you okay?"

Now that the demon's magic soul-sucking kiss had worn off, she was not forlorn over Devon anymore. But she still clearly liked him, and she unfortunately still perfectly well remembered having had a date with him right in this spot. Well, a date with the demon, if you wanted to be technical about it (and I definitely wanted to be technical about it). I don't think she and the other four girls remembered anything from Halloween night itself when the phoenix exploded—Sarmine tended to clean up loose ends like that—but I wasn't sure.

Devon smiled at her in a way that I chose to interpret as kind and not flirty. "Fine, thanks. Do you know Cam?"

She smiled absently at me. "Yes, we're old friends," she said. She was clinging to the arm of a tanned white guy who was brushing leaf debris off his sweater. Caden, looking much happier than I'd seen him that afternoon.

"Didn't your car get destroyed?" I said.

He laughed. "Dad was mad for about five minutes," he said. "Then he went and got me a new one, straight off the lot." To Reese he added, "Pretty sweet, isn't it?" and she giggled.

I snorted into my drink. Whichever witch had him was going to be sorely disappointed. Hard to bring someone down when their dad could replace whatever you destroyed.

"Must be nice," said Devon, whose thoughts were clearly running along the same lines. "I can't exactly haul speakers with my cargo bike."

"Ooh, speakers?" said Reese. "Are you playing this week?" She slid in next to him on the other side of the booth. "You don't mind if we join you, do you? It's so nice to catch up with you and Cam."

"I thought we were having a one-on-one, babe," said Caden. To me he added, "No offense."

"None taken," I said. I doubted I was his idea of a prime booth-mate any more than he was mine.

"Oh, just for a minute," said Reese to Caden. "Then we'll take your new car out for a drive." She took her gum out, leaned across the table, and kissed him.

Devon's expression flickered over to me and back. I didn't know what it meant, but I could tell you that *my* current feelings were a prime mix of embarrassment, annoyance, and envy.

Reese dominated the conversation for the rest of dinner. I mean, thanks to her I found out how many girls Devon had dated (three), how many pairs of jeans he had (two), and what the names of his former bands were (Owl Pellet, Betty & Veronica, Planet of the Bacon Monkeys), so hey, she wasn't entirely useless. Caden threw out a bored "yeah, whatever" every so often, and Devon? Well, Devon answered her ridiculous questions with his normal tact and courtesy, and tried vainly to include me in the conversation. I appreciated the effort, but at the same time, I really wanted him to tell Reese to get the hell out of Dodge and leave us alone.

But that wasn't Devon.

And since he was being so sweet and considerate to her (which was nice of him, seeing as the demon had just broken her heart and briefly borrowed a large chunk of her soul), I couldn't bring myself to be rude, either.

And I was too stubborn to get up and leave.

So we sat. We ate pizza.

And finally, finally, when I couldn't take Reese's inane questions a second longer, and after Caden had said, "Shouldn't we get going?" at least five times, Devon stood up and said, "Well, I've got homework, so. . . ."

"This was fun," said Reese. "We should all do this again."

Caden and I grunted.

We went to the register for the moment of check-splitting truth, and I was frankly interested to see what would happen. But what happened is Reese nudged Caden to pay for all of us, and he said, "Whatever, babe," and complied. So that bullet was dodged, I guess—and now I had some money for a change—but I also didn't learn anything.

Outside, I watched Reese and Caden peel off in Caden's shiny new SUV.

"That is a very big car your friend has," said Devon.

"Not my friend," I said.

"Your friend's boyfriend."

I looked sideways at him. "Not my friend, either," I said. Had he really thought Reese meant it when she said we were friends? She was, in fact, generally nice to everyone about 80 percent of the time. If you didn't ever run into her when the chips were down you would probably think she was the nicest popular girl on the planet.

There was an expression like light dawning and then he started laughing. "Dude, I wasted an hour of our lives," he said. "I am sorry."

My grouchiness melted away. "At least I now know that your favorite breakfast food is chocolate-chip pancakes," I said. "I mean, that's highly important information."

Devon unlocked his bike from the bike rack. "Did you bike?"

I shook my head. "Bus," I said. "But it'll be along soon, or I can walk."

He smiled at me, a little shy. "You can ride with me," he said, "if you don't mind."

Mind? Of course I wouldn't mind. But . . . "Like what, on the handlebars?"

"When my parents had the animal shelter, they would have me go pick up emergency supplies for them," he said. "Like huge bags of dog food. And obviously I couldn't have a license yet so they got me a cargo bike. Moving truck finally delivered it last week."

He pointed at the back and I realized now that his bike looked different than other bikes. It had some extra horizontal tubing sticking out in the back. Devon pulled a green foam cushion from one of the saddlebags and plopped it on, and suddenly the bike had an extra seat. "Hop on," he said.

I did as requested, feeling entirely awkward. It wasn't like when you see two people riding on a motorcycle. The extra seat was several inches lower than Devon's seat, so my face was level with the middle of his back. Plus, I hadn't been on a bike since the dragon squashed mine. It was hard to concentrate even on stable ground, and now here I was with the bike shifting underneath me, feeling as though I was going to make him fall over through sheer clumsiness.

"I don't have an extra helmet," he mused. "I wonder if mine would fit you."

"As kind of you as that is," I said, "I feel reasonably certain that Sarmine Scarabouche would find a way to put my scrambled brain back together if it did, in fact, scramble." After all, who else would dust her jars of rutabaga root? "And I doubt she would feel the same sense of urgency toward yours. You'd better keep it."

"Well then," he said. "Hang on tight." He grinned at me, and for a heart-stopping moment there was that devilish charm I had seen so often a couple weeks ago, when I wasn't sure which parts of him were Devon and which parts were the demon. I knew it couldn't be all Estahoth.

I took the excuse, wrapped my arms around his waist, and held on tight. He smelled of soap and boy. He pushed us off and away we went.

It felt like flying.

The strange wind had died down and it was a gorgeous, crisp-cold night as we flew down the hills. I was glad the pizza place was uphill from our street, because I could well imagine the embarrassment I would feel if I had to sit and do nothing while Devon got a workout. As it was, I could sit back and enjoy the ride.

"Not too fast for you, is it?" he called back over his shoulder.

"Perfect," I called back. The word felt like an admission. This was perfect, everything was perfect. I could forget about the nasty witch club and just sail along with Devon as life whisked by.

All too quickly, he turned onto my street, stopped in front of my house. I reluctantly let go of his waist and got off the bike, my legs shaky from using them to hold on. Kind of like horseback riding, I guessed. Then I wondered why I was thinking about horseback riding instead of about the fact that finally, *finally,* Devon and I were alone together. No Reese, no band members, no stray demons infesting his soul. The moonlight lit up his cheekbone and his neck. His hands on his helmet.

So far Devon and I had shared exactly one kiss. It was right after I'd saved his life and a phoenix was bursting into fire all around us. Pretty impressive stuff, but not entirely clear whether he wanted to go on kissing me as a matter of course or if he just felt awfully grateful to me and bowled over by the romance of kissing in a magical phoenix explosion.

He stood there, fiddling with his helmet. His blond hair fell down over his face.

"Cam, I . . ."

"Yeah?"

"Well. I mean." He buckled and unbuckled the straps. "I don't know what I'm trying to say."

"Now I know the demon's gone for sure," I said. "He always knew exactly what to say."

The minute I said it I wished I could take it back. I was trying to make a joke, but I saw his face fall as he turned away. The moment came crashing down around us. "I'm not him," he mumbled.

"Well, good," I said as cheerily as possible. "I mean, he was always talking about Elvis and eating people's souls and stuff. Better you don't know what you want to say than to, like, kiss every girl in school and stuff like that." This was getting worse by the minute. "I mean, not that exactly but you know he was nuts. All the girls running after him thought so. I mean, running after you. But not you, him."

Devon tugged his bike closer to him like it was a shield to hide from the crazy girl who couldn't stop talking. "Cam, I . . . I better get home."

The bottom fell out of my stomach. Reese hadn't ruined this night. I had. "Yeah," I said. "I'd better get back to the witch. Before I turn into a pumpkin." The night no longer seemed crisp and beautiful but cold and pathetic.

He swung his leg over his cargo bike.

"See you in algebra?" I said.

He smiled the same polite smile he had been giving Reese all night. "Definitely."

His foot came down and the bike left, going down the street, away.

I sat down on the curb. I didn't care how cold I was; I didn't want to go inside. I wanted to rewind the last five minutes and try again, this time with no stupid jokes. I huddled in my jacket, running through the ending over and over. Maybe I would sit out here until I figured out how to fix it. Or morning, whichever came first.

And that's when I smelled it.

Cigarette smoke, across the street. Someone lurking in the bushes.

My first thought was humiliation that someone had seen that little scene. But the second thought was anger. Stupid witch club.

"Well, I better make sure someone scooped up after Wulfie," I said out loud. I moseyed out into the street, pretending to look around. The bushes were silent. And then, I ran straight to the bushes and pounced on them.

There was some truly amazing swearing from the bushes, and all four foot six of Valda came stomping out of them, waving her cigarette. "What are you doing?"

"Me? What are *you* doing, spying on us?"

A pause, and then, "Nooooothing," said Valda in a shifty sort of voice. "Just checking out the competition. Making sure nobody was cheating."

"Nobody in this house is cheating," I said coldly. "Are you sure you weren't following me?" My eyes widened. "Or Devon? Did you draw *Devon*?" I seized her shoulders. "Did you make our date go all rotten through *magic*?"

She snorted. "You wish." She flounced free of my grasp and took a step back. "Maybe I like looking at bushes on a Monday night." She blew some smoke in their direction.

I took a step toward her. She took a step back. We could dance like this all night.

"Then why are you really here?" I said.

"Oh, that's an interesting story," she said around her cigarette. In the dark, I caught the flash of her fingers at her waist.

She was going for a spell.

Oh god.

I was about to have that epic witch battle.

I grabbed my fanny pack from my backpack and buckled it on. It was pretty dark, except for porch lights. Luckily the dark would hamper Valda, too—but she probably had muscle memory to go on, and I had no idea where Sarmine had put the ginger and thyme. If I had them at all. I stuck my finger randomly into one of the pockets and smelled it. Cinnamon. Another. Something disgusting.

Meanwhile, Valda had finished combining things in the palm of her hand. She jabbed at them with the cigarette, starting a little smolder. She must have hands of iron. She pulled out her wand . . .

Think, Cam.

I grabbed my water bottle from my backpack and dumped it on her hand. Her spell flickered out and streamed away. She shrieked at me, finally dropping her cigarette.

Good. That would make things easier to smell.

Aha. Now that was ginger. A pinch in my hand. A couple more pokes . . . did I even know what thyme smelled like? Then the next pinch took me back, very strongly, to the smell of the witch's chicken noodle soup. I dumped it in my hand, hoping that I wasn't confusing it with oregano or tarragon or heaven knows what else. A hair from my head. A drop from the dragon's tears vial.

Valda was still drying her hands when I touched my wand to my palm and flicked it toward me, inhaling the slightly damp powder.

The moonlight picked out the whites of her eyes, growing big and round.

I felt something strange surging through me. Animalistic. Like I didn't care about anybody else. Valda backed away and instinctively I lashed out my wand, stopping it a millimeter from her throat.

"You will tell me why you're here," I said. Menace rumbled through the words.

"I—I urp," she managed. "I'm following Malkin. Take your wand away."

"Malkin?" I said, not budging. "Was she here? Was she at the *pizza place*?"

"She's been all over town. You don't understand. She always has ulterior motives. Take that wand away, *now*." Valda put her fingers between my wand and her neck, glaring up at me and my aura of menace. I didn't think she should be able to do that, and then I realized that my menace was fading. I was returning to my normal self, and Valda was no longer intimidated. I pulled the wand away as she laughed. "Beginner, aren't you?"

"You talk big for someone who was vanquished by a water bottle," I said. "What do you mean, ulterior motives?" Another porch light snapped on, next door. I held my wand steady.

Valda rubbed her neck. "Malkin wouldn't have stopped her hunt for the lindworm just for this contest," she said. She was tugging on something behind her back. "She's hiding . . . something . . . and I want . . . in on it. . . ."

Suddenly the thing was free. It was a broom, and she was astride it. It lurched down the street, straining under her bulk. I chased it down the street, but it finally grunted up into the air and then she was zooming away, too fast for me to follow.

4

A Lovelie *Spell* to Open You to Possibilities

Late that night I sat in bed, staring at the wand in my hands. I had finished my homework and remade my bed for the cold weather with additional spare blankets from the hall closet (the witch does not believe in running the heat at night) and now I was trying to figure out how I could be more like Malkin.

Well, not entirely more like Malkin. But I did need to disguise my wand, in case any more epic witch battles decided to happen at school. The wand was plain black wood with a shiny tip, which the witch had told me was abalone. The wood felt warm in my hands, the difference between the wood and the cool shell rather striking.

It had been my father's, Sarmine said. I was too much like him, she said. Too kind. Too tenderhearted.

My fingers closed on the wand. I hated to mess with my father's wand in any way, but I couldn't take it out at school without it being obvious. But perhaps a simple fix would make it more subtle. I searched through my desk drawer until I found a black pen cap that would fit over the abalone end. Much better.

I tucked the wand into my backpack and turned out the light, wishing I could solve all my problems as easily as disguising the wand.

Foremost in my mind was the fact that I had well and truly borked my date with Devon. My natural instinct was to corner him first thing tomorrow morning and apologize. It was better to be blunt about things than to let them fester.

On the other hand, the things that had come out of my mouth

so far hadn't really helped. Maybe at this point I should try to just move forward. And never mention that demon again. Who knew he would still be causing trouble, even *after* being sent home?

I banged my head on my pillow, which did nothing for the quality of my sleep or the pillow. All I needed was some actual alone time with Devon. Like, the two of us, and no way for him to escape. And then I would turn the Power spell on him until he succumbed to my will and confessed his true feelings for me. . . .

More head banging. No. Bad witch.

I rolled over and stared at the ceiling. That Power spell *had* been good tonight. I had held off Valda. Only for a moment—but that was long enough to see that it might be useful for standing up to the witch club. I would ask Sarmine what I had done wrong to make it fizzle out so quickly.

That only left the problem of the love potion. Clearly, Esmerelda was going to make Henny pretty miserable this week. I didn't think Henny had enough gumption to stand up to her. So I would, in fact, need something pretty big to counteract her getting trashed daily in art class—something like Leo the football hero falling in love with her. Now, on the one hand that wasn't fair to Leo. On the other hand, it probably wouldn't make him miserable to fall in love with Henny for a few days—especially if the love potion wore off as quickly as Ye Olde Spell of Power had.

I tabled the ethics part of the love potion for my subconscious to work on and went back to the fantasy part of it. There was nothing unethical about entertaining the idea in my dreams, right? The little scene with Devon a couple hours ago could have had a much better ending. I give him the love potion, and then—

Oh, Cam, he says. *Why are we talking about demons? Let me bike you to this quiet park nearby, where we can gaze at the moon. . . .*

I tell him sternly that there better be more going on than moon gazing; he assures me that moon gazing is a euphemism—

I fell asleep very quickly after that.

☾

Tuesday morning I brought down my wand and fanny pack and sat down on the bar stool. "I need to make a love spell," I announced.

Sarmine's face lit up. She had actually beat me down this morning, and was fully dressed. Maybe she was trying a course of self-improvement, too. I imagined Sarmine having lists like mine. They would probably start with "Get out of bed at a reasonable hour" and "Try not to be so terrible to Camellia" and quickly devolve into "Destroy those neighbors down the block who run their sprinklers all summer."

Sarmine set down her coffee and cracked her knuckles. "This is more like it. Love spells are one of the nicest kinds of havoc you can cause."

I had a pretty good guess what Sarmine meant by "nice," especially when paired with "havoc."

"No, no," I insisted. "I need to figure out an ethical love spell."

Sarmine snorted. "*Ethical* love spell?"

"Yes." I had woken up with the idea bright and fresh in my mind. That was the whole point of the student-mentor relationship, right? I could ask the expert.

"This is going to need some fortification," Sarmine said. She found the whiskey and poured a slug into her coffee.

"Isn't this a little early for spirits?" I said.

"It's a little early for discussions of ethics and morality, I'll tell you," Sarmine said. "I don't see how anyone can be expected to work out how nice to be to a measly *human* when it's not even time for brunch."

"Now look," I said. "Henny is miserable, because Esmerelda is busy squashing her self-esteem into soup and it's only Tuesday. However, there's a guy she has a crush on. Also she mightblackmailme." That last bit came out in a mumble and Sarmine pounced on it.

"She *what*?"

"She saw me using unicorn hair sanitizer on Jenah."

"And you let her believe what she saw? Really, Camellia, you could have done any number of things. Erased her memory. Erased her believability. Defenestrated her."

"Well, I didn't," I said crossly, "partly because if I want to win the bet she needs to be *happy* on Friday, and throwing her out the window is more likely to leave her miserable about her full-body cast."

"The hospital would give her Percocet," Sarmine pointed out.

I ignored this. "*Anyway,* she wants a love spell, but I'm not going to do a real love spell without the explicit permission of the victim, which obviously I'm unlikely to get. But then I had a brilliant plan, which was to ask you." Sheer buttering up. "I thought, maybe you would know of something I could give her instead. That would satisfy her and not compromise my ethics."

Sarmine snorted. "You will never get anywhere if you keep trying to please everyone, Camellia."

"Is that a yes?"

She waved a hand at me. "Yes, I know the spell you want. I've used it a hundred times." She eyed me. "I mean, for other people." She thumbed through the college journal until she found it. "A Lovelie Spell to Open You to Possibilities. Again, not my spelling."

"Like love possibilities?"

"If you are a teenager, then mostly yes," she said dryly. "In general you will . . . be aware of other potentials floating in the air."

This sounded awfully woo-woo for Sarmine, but I'd take it.

"Awesome," I said. "So then if there was a possibility that this boy could like Henny, then he would be open to the idea and would notice her when she came up to talk to him."

"That's the idea," said Sarmine.

"Any catches?" I said. "How come you used this and not a classic love potion? I mean, if you're not so concerned about ethics."

"Because, Camellia, where would be the fun in that?"

She had a good point.

"Besides," she said. "A classic love spell is problematic to apply. Because you want the crush to fall in love with the person paying you good money to work this spell, and not with you, the witch."

"I thought you weren't so big into people finding out we were witches."

"I have a love-hate relationship with fame," said Sarmine.

"Mm. And people paying you?"

"Obviously, Camellia, even witches have student loans. I worked my way through college via love spells."

I started to say that that sounded a little naughty, but the look in her eyes dared me to make a joke. Some things you didn't joke about to Sarmine Scarabouche. "So, uh, did you work a spell for anyone who asked?" I said. "Because that seems a little like, the person didn't get a chance to say if they wanted that. It's a little . . . uh . . . not right."

Sarmine looked uncomfortable. "I usually researched the potential match ahead of time," she said. "If I decided they weren't a good pair they got the Open to Possibilities potion and a speech about how you can't force people to fall in love against their will."

"And if they were a good match?"

She spread her arms. "Then all they *needed* was the Open to Possibilities potion," she said. "And the speech about how it won't work if you don't go up and actually talk to them."

"You are secretly a softie, Sarmine."

"I am not," she said indignantly. "The strong love potion is tricky to administer correctly. The last thing I wanted was a bunch of moony-eyed frat boys following me around."

The look in her eyes dared me to call her a softie again. I refrained.

"Okay, then show me the Possibilities potion."

She passed me the book.

The spell was handwritten in Sarmine's journal in reverse lettering.

"Ugh, why are witches so . . . witchy?" I said. There was a little mirror by the front door and I held the book up to it, reading through the spell. "I can't even work through the problem until I transcribe it."

"You claim to have learned about the scientific method and all that nonsense at school," she said. "This is your chance to shine." She took another sip of whiskey-enhanced coffee. It must be putting her in a jovial mood, because she said, "Tell you what, if you work the spell out before school, I'll let you have the proper ingredients from my own stores."

This sounded pretty good, because I had no idea how I was going to track down "tears of the lake dryad" if that was one of the ingredients that was actually used. "It's a deal," I said.

I took the mirror off the wall and sat down on the couch to transcribe the spell. Wulfie bounded over with a tennis ball and I absently threw it for him as I studied the thermometers. They didn't look too different than I was expecting. Esmerelda's bubble was all the way down on the bottom. Poor Henny must still be upset. Malkin's was a little bit down—perhaps she had Caden? Although Caden had been pretty stoked about his new car and his date with Reese last night, so . . .

"By the way, I worked the Power spell yesterday," I said as I transcribed.

"Well done," said the witch. That was a significant amount of praise from her.

"But it fizzled out quickly. Do you know why?" I walked her through what I had figured out with the spell and what I had done to work it. I did not tell her that I had been momentarily enraged at the thought she was tricking me. As long as it seemed like she was playing by the rules, I would try to believe that she was worthy of trust.

Sarmine pulled yesterday's spellbook off her shelf and followed along. "Hmm," she said at last. "When you mixed the dragon tear in, did you get the herbs and hair fully coated?"

"It was dark?" I hazarded.

"So, you're probably not getting your full potential out of the ingredients. You would do much better to combine everything in a nonreactive bowl, and heat it with a touch of unicorn sanitizer to bring out the essence of the ingredients."

"Unicorn sanitizer is unicorn hair steeped in vodka," I pointed out. "Wouldn't the unicorn hair or the vodka change things?"

"Only for the better," said the witch.

"Also the book said to breathe the mixture in. I have a feeling that snorting vodka is painful."

The witch waved this aside. "I'd drink it. Just burn the vodka off with a match if you're concerned about that."

"Thanks," I said. "How come that's not in the original spell?"

She raised her eyebrows at me.

"Right," I said. "Witches are paranoid and never share all the information with each other, and it is a supreme honor that you are teaching me this." I paused. "I mean, actually, it kind of is. Thank you."

A suspicious look crossed her face. That made two of us. But all she said was, "You're welcome."

☾

A half hour later I had the spell worked out and ready to go.

"All right," I said at last. "The recipe is one tablespoonful of syrup, one drop pomegranate juice, one finely ground rose petal, and one drop pixie dew. What does it mean by just, 'syrup'?"

"I have used maple syrup, corn syrup, and molasses, all to good effect and all with slight variations in results," said the witch. "But for the most romance-oriented version, you want local honey." She placed the items on the bar. There were about three tablespoons of honey left in the honey bear, so I decided to use that as a storage and transport container. That meant I would need to increase the other ingredients by three. So three drops pomegranate juice, three rose petals, and three drops pixie dew.

It crossed my mind that my subconscious was trying to make

sure I had an extra dose to give Devon, but I told my subconscious to take a hike. There was nothing suspicious about just happening to have three doses made up and ready to go. Who knew what might happen this week?

"And the pixie dew?" I said.

"Is gathered at a full moon by gently scraping the backs of the pixies," Sarmine said, rolling her eyes. "No pixies were harmed in the making of this love potion."

"Good." Pixies looked like little frogs to humans, with wings that only witches could see. So pixie dew was basically magical frog sweat, but pixie dew sounded a lot nicer. Witches also drink a fermented sparkling pixie juice for magical occasions and I won't tell you what that's really made of. Sometimes it's best not to know.

I added everything into the bear and stirred it with a long swizzle stick. The pixie dew had lent it a slight anise scent. I started to lick the honey off my fingers and then stopped myself, shuddering. Bad habit for a witch. I washed my hands, then tucked the honey bear into a side pocket of my backpack so it would stay upright.

I was ready to play Cupid.

☾

The plan was to meet Henny and Leo at lunchtime. According to Henny, Leo had been in the computer lab every day for two straight weeks, so fingers crossed he wouldn't break that streak today. Maybe I could slip the honey into his soda or something. I discussed this with Jenah at our locker before school and she looked dubious.

"I don't think he drinks soda," she said. "He's one of those superhealthy athlete types."

"Hmm," I said. The hall clanged with lockers opening and closing, with the rise and fall of voices.

"But maybe you could ask him to take it," Jenah said. "Pretend it's for an experiment. Give some to Henny, too. I mean, she's already in love with him, so that won't hurt anything, will it?"

"No."

"And then what?" Jenah said. "You stand back and run? Make sure they don't look at you as you hightail it from the room, or you'd have both Leo and Henny mooning over you?"

"Ugh, no," I said. "This is not one of *those* love potions. I decided that was wrong."

"Darn," said Jenah. "I mean, good, that sounds ethical and all that. Just, the other way sounded kind of fun." She turned to shut the locker and that's when I noticed the brace on her wrist.

"What happened to you?"

"Eh, I was outside raking leaves before my grandparents come on Thursday," she said. "And—"

"And did a strange, sudden wind bowl you over?" I said.

She wrinkled her nose. "No, I tripped over my own rake."

"First the lasagna" I countered, "and then the rake. Are you sure it was an accident?"

"Well, I don't know everything magic can do," Jenah pointed out. She turned away, leading us to algebra. "But I can tell you one thing. If some stupid witch thinks she can make me feel miserable just by banging me up, she's got another think coming."

I squeezed her arm—gently. "Your positive attitude will destroy them," I promised. But inside I was worried. It was only Tuesday. I didn't want to see Jenah—even a cheerful, positive Jenah—in a full-body cast.

In algebra, Devon smiled politely at me and made noncommittal answers to my questions about band practice. In French, I found I didn't know the conjugation for *craindre* quite as well as I had thought. In English, the witches were still driving Macbeth nuts.

Finally it was lunchtime. My heart revved up as I approached the computer lab. I was about to be a witch for real.

But what kind of a witch?

Henny was in the lab, sketching on her tablet, trying not to look suspicious. Frankly, she was failing at that last part, since she looked up immediately when I came in, then waved, then realized she shouldn't wave, then dramatically shushed me with a finger, then turned back to her tablet.

Maybe Sarmine was right that I should make her lose her memory. She certainly didn't seem like someone who could keep a secret.

I studied the room. It was quiet except for the hum of the computer fans. The teacher was hunched over his own screen, earbuds in, playing some computer game and eating a sandwich. Henny was near the front. And then there were three boys, none of whom I knew.

I raised my eyebrows at Henny. She pointed, very unsubtly, at a boy sitting in the far corner of the room, hunting and pecking on one of the school laptops.

Leo.

I took a deep breath and went slowly to the back corner, rehearsing what I was going to say. I was doing a project on allergies for biology. Did he have any? Good, try this. Did he not? Good, he could be my control. Too bad it wasn't actually allergy season, but it was the best plan I had.

Leo had dark hair and olive-brown skin, like he might have some Middle Eastern ancestry. He was broad-shouldered and extremely fit and he looked a whole lot more like he should be hanging out with some jocks crunching aluminum cans between his fingers than studying in the computer lab for two weeks straight.

Can't put it off any longer. Gonna do this.

I plopped down in the chair next to him. He jumped a half inch, swiveling his laptop away from me. I had never made a football player nervous before and it made me feel flush with confidence, even if it was probably only due to the contents of the laptop and not anything to do with me. "Hi," I said in a low voice. "I'm Cam." The teacher glanced up, then went back to his game.

"I know," Leo said, confusion on his face. "You're in my AP biology."

"Really?" I said. I thought back to class. AP biology's my fave, but I didn't realize I was that out of it. I mean, it's a good class because it's only upper-level students who want to be there, and we focus pretty hard on the lectures and lab, and he's not my lab partner, so . . . I snapped my fingers. "That's right," I said. "You're in the back, right? You guys were having problems finding the frog's spleen the other day?"

"It was a mutant frog," he protested.

"Aren't they all," I agreed cheerfully.

Across the room, Henny was giving me a dirty look as she sketched on her tablet. I figured that meant I wasn't supposed to be getting chummy with her crush.

"Well, look," I said. "I'm doing this project for biology"—oh wait, that lie was suddenly not going to work since he was *in* my biology—"I mean, I'm gearing up for the science fair, and I'm testing the compounds in this honey mixture. It's supposed to be good for pollen allergies, and I wondered if you'd be willing to be one of my guinea pigs. Do you have allergies?"

"Not this time of year," he said. But he was looking intrigued. "I'll try some if you want. I know you're the best in that class." He casually turned his laptop even farther away from me.

What he didn't realize was that he was turning it toward the window. And since the blinds on that window were drawn, there was a faint reflection.

Now I was getting curious. Who was this football player who didn't act like a football player, and what did he not want anyone to know about?

"The honey is supposed to safeguard against specific plants," I improvised further. "I've got a whole questionnaire to fill out, and then we'll expose you to a small quantity of allergen. Do you know which pollens you're allergic to?"

Everyone raises or lowers their eyes when trying to recall things from memory. He raised his to the ceiling, and I turned mine to the window, trying to make out the blurry, backward shapes of pictures and text. It looked like pictures of wolves, I thought. So what? What was there to hide? Carefully I pieced together the backward text.

How to Tell a Shapeshifter.

5

How to Tell a Shapeshifter

"Holy cats," I said, shocked. The other two boys swiveled to look but I waved them off, scooting closer to Leo. Leo slammed the laptop closed. "Wait a minute," I said, more quietly. "Are you googling what I think you're googling?"

He leaned back and tried to act casual. "Project for English class," he said.

At least we were both lying.

But this was serious stuff. "Don't mess with me, Leo," I said in a whisper. "Have you ever gone to bed a human and woken up, I don't know, a cockroach?"

"Of course not," he said, but the defensive way he said it made my eyes get really wide.

So look, I don't know much about shifters. But I definitely know they are witch world things and not human things. Leo might not be *exactly* one of us, but he was very *sort of* one of us. I crammed the honey bear into my backpack and took him by the shirtsleeve. "You need to come with me now. I am not even kidding."

And I wasn't. I mean, the last thing I needed was other magical things going on in this school. That's how you get things traced back to you and then all your secrets come out. Henny eyed me as I pulled Leo out of the room but I mouthed "need privacy" at her and she nodded warily in response.

For his part, Leo looked rather entertained to be pulled somewhere. I mean, he's apparently one of the top football guys and all. So I expect he mostly gets girls hanging on him and not girls ordering him around. But I wasn't here to hang on him. I wanted to find out how much he knew.

I dragged him all the way out to the new food carts at the corner of the high school lot. It was chilly enough that the picnic tables weren't crowded, even though it was lunchtime. I found one off to the side that was only partly covered with the remains of somebody's lunch and sat down. "Okay," I said. "Spill."

He was looking all tough now. "I don't have anything to spill." He nodded at a couple passing football players. "Hey. Hey."

Urggh. Not this act. "You mean, you don't know who I am or why you should trust me."

He shrugged, still looking around.

I hunched over. "Look," I commanded him. "I'm on your side. I'm not one myself. But I know more about this stuff than you do. Witches. Shifters. Spells. For starters, I mean, you were *googling* it? You weren't even on WitchNet."

"WitchNet?" He laughed.

"Hey, I didn't name it," I said. "Do you want help with this thing or not?"

The football players drifted off and we were momentarily alone. Leo dropped the tough act and looked at me intently. "Cam," he said. "I know you know where a frog's thorax is and stuff. But why do you think you can help me on this? I mean, if there was anything to help me on. Which there isn't."

Ah, boys. You had to show them for them to believe anything.

I pulled the unicorn sanitizer from my backpack and spritzed the noodle-covered table. The anime stars flashed and popped. The noodles vanished. The table lost its graffiti.

"Wow, that's, uh . . ." said Leo.

"Really clean?"

"A really nerdy spell." But he was grinning—making it an in-joke between us. "Kidding. I'm impressed."

"I should get something cooler to prove my skills," I said.

"Can I see?" He held his hand out for the bottle, and then suddenly pulled his hands away. There was another jock stopping by our table—this one accompanied by a certain cheerleader I knew all too well. "Hey, Parker," Leo said casually. "Sparkle."

My best childhood friend barely nodded at me. I had half-hoped that everything that had happened on Halloween would make her behave in a more friendly way to me, but apparently not.

"Ready for the game this Friday?" said Parker.

"You know it," said Leo.

The guys high-fived and finally Parker and Sparkle wandered off.

Leo leaned across the table. "You don't have to show me anything else," he said. "I believe you. I mean, I'm already primed to anyway."

"After whatever has recently happened to you," I hazarded. Now we were getting somewhere. The November wind was brisk around the table. I pulled on my jacket and looked for my hair wrap. "Go on."

"I didn't know I was a . . . a shifter," he said. "It just happened one night. I was out alone and this noise startled me. And . . ." He looked embarrassed. "Well, this makes me sound jumpy. I mean, I know I'm this big tough football player and all."

"Clearly," I said. He did in fact have very broad shoulders.

"But when I jumped and turned around . . . suddenly I was a rabbit."

I choked back a laugh. "And then what?"

"Well, it wasn't anyone. Some friends from the football team. So naturally I ran—"

"Like a rabbit. . . ."

He threw me a dirty look.

"Sorry. Go on."

"I ran all the way home. I didn't even know I was a rabbit at first, you know. I was low to the ground and scared out of my wits, which is I guess how rabbits feel most of the time. By the time I got home I was exhausted. Rabbits aren't made for endurance running. So I was hopping around my yard and I started to think that, however unlikely it was, I must be a rabbit. And then I wondered how I was going to—"

"Not be a rabbit."

"Yeah. And of course my heart's going a million miles a minute, not just from the initial scare but now the idea that I might be—"

"Stuck. As a rabbit."

"If you don't mind not mentioning it so much, that would be awesome."

"I'm sorry. So what happened?"

"So finally I calmed down. And I thought hard about how tall I was supposed to be and how broad I was supposed to be. . . ."

"Yes, I do see that."

"And how calm I was supposed to be and then I was suddenly me again."

"Did you have all your clothes?"

He looked at me like *you did not just ask that,* and I grinned. It was awesome feeling like I had the upper hand on a football player.

"Not a stitch," he admitted.

"So . . . is it just rabbits then?" I said. "Maybe you're some kind of were-rabbit?"

"Once and for all, please stop mentioning rabbits. I am not a were-rabbit. Or a were-anything. At least not as far as I can tell. Because I started turning into other things too."

"Like a hare," I mused. "Or a bunny. . . ."

"I'm going to bunny you in a moment."

"So what did you turn into?"

"Well. I was feeling sort of . . . placid one day and I suddenly became a cow."

"This is amazing. Go on."

"And then there was a little tickle in my throat. . . ."

"And you became a horse."

"No, a giraffe. Are you taking this seriously?"

"I take everything seriously."

"Well, so then I started worrying about the football game."

"Where you charge down like a young lion, or a bull, or—"

"Exactly. I don't want to be thrown into jail for goring somebody. I want to finish my senior year and go to college."

"You could always be the mascot."

He stood up. "That's one crack too far," he said. He was very tall.

I stood up, too. "Gallows humor," I said. "I can keep apologizing for it but really it's the only way I can cope with the wicked witch some days."

"Wicked witch?"

"You told me your secret, I'm telling you mine," I said. "We'll be even. It's not just a few fancy tricks with a squirt bottle. I actually live with a wicked witch, and I'm training to be one, too, except not the wicked part."

"Is that for real?"

"Is the rabbit part for real?"

He sat back down. He looked excited. "So maybe you can help me," he said. "I want to stop it."

"I'll ask," I said. "But I don't know if you can stop it. Maybe you can learn to control it."

"That's what I mean."

"But can't you ask *your* parents? Surely this trait didn't come out of nowhere. Not like the frog with no gallbladder."

He shook his head. "I'm adopted," he said. "I've got two dads."

"Well, was it a closed adoption or whatever it's called?" I said. "Don't your dads know where you came from?"

He shook his head. "From what they've said, they wanted a kid, but at the time no one would adopt to them through the official process. My mother was the friend of a friend. They only met her a couple weeks before I was born. I gather she was maybe here illegally, or she was a refugee, or something, I don't know. It was all very hush-hush but she said she couldn't keep me safe, and she would rather see me safe than with her."

"How thrilling," I said. "Like a spy novel."

"Well, I wish it were a little less thrilling and more mundane," he said. “I love my dads, wouldn’t trade them for anything, don’t get me wrong. But they’ve said a million times that if my mother had been able to stay in my life, they would have been happy to include her. She could have visited me whenever she wanted. And I know she wanted to. But she . . . couldn’t.”

“Do you think that her fleeing is related to you being a shifter?” I said.

He nodded. “I am definitely starting to wonder. Occam’s razor and all that.”

“Occam . . . that was just on a biology handout.”

“The simplest explanation is usually right,” he reminded me. “My birth mother disappears under weird circumstances. I *am* a weird circumstance. Ergo.”

“They *must* be related.” Frankly, the weirder circumstance was that he remembered some biology terminology that I didn’t.

“So that’s when I started coming to the computer lab every day. I thought maybe I could do some research on any leads to my mother, as well as on this whole shapeshifting thing. I didn’t want to do it at home in case my dads saw what I was doing. I don’t want to hurt them, plus, I’m reasonably sure they don’t know about the whole shifter business. I mean, none of the ‘so you’re a man now’ talks we’ve had exactly included ‘and by the way, if you start growing a bunny tail you will tell us, right?’ ”

“Wow,” I said. “Wow.” I sat back, trying to process all of this.

“So you can help me?”

I nodded. “I don’t know how, but I’ll try,” I said. Add him to the list of students I was already helping this week. Henny, and now—oh, wait. Henny’s love potion. I had completely forgotten.

I looked at Leo—innocent, quarterback, *bunny* Leo. Now that I knew him, it seemed harder to slip him the dose. “I guess I forgot. . . .” I said, hesitating.

“The honey,” said Leo, snapping his fingers. “Do you want to do that now?”

I pulled up my phone to check the time. "I, um. I would have to make notes. And sit with you for ten minutes to check for allergic reactions. And gee, look at that! The bell's going to ring for the end of lunch in two minutes."

"After school then?" he offered. "It's the least I can do if you're going to help me with my shifting problem."

"After school," I said, thus continuing my exceptionally ethical method of pushing complicated problems out to let future Cam deal with them. "It's a plan."

☾

I went to fourth-hour American history, aka the class where we watch bad videos and I think about anything else I want. Today's topic: *Good Witches, Love Potions, and the Blurry Lines Between!* Scintillating stuff.

The problem was that I *needed* to give the love potion to Leo, but I still wasn't sure I *should*. My friends and family weren't helping, either—Sarmine obviously considered this to be a bend-over-backward, overly considerate sort of potion, and Jenah thought love potions were funny. Finally, after much thought, I pulled out my ethics list and added to it.

Good Witch Ethics

1. Don't use animal parts in spells.
2. Don't cast bad spells on good people for no reason.

I sighed. It was pretty clear to me that what I wanted was a way to make slipping Leo a dose of the Possibilities potion okay. It wasn't a bad spell—right? There was a reason—right?

Making a list I was okay with was going to be harder than I had thought.

☾

I was near the end of fifth-hour AP biology—and yes, Leo was correct that he was in that class with me, way in the back—when a student knocked and entered with a note for the teacher.

Ms. Pool motioned me to the front and handed me the note. "The nurse's office needs you." She must have seen my confused expression, because then she patted my shoulder, with the awkward air of someone who is not sure if shoulder-patting is the correct social protocol. "Your locker mate had a fall."

I hurried out of the room, worry and anger flooding me. There was no doubt in my mind now that Jenah was one of the victims. One of those horrible witches had done something to her. But what?

I opened the note, searching for more information. The note asked me to fetch Jenah's jacket and phone from our locker so she could call her mom to get her. I changed course, confused now. One, Jenah never left her phone in her locker, and two, it was her dad who had the job where he could come pick her up.

I'm only a little slow on the uptake, so by the time I had half-heartedly searched our locker I had realized it was a ruse. Jenah wanted to tell me something. This was code.

But even if fetching me was a ruse, Jenah wouldn't be in the nurse's office without something having happened to her. I jogged to the nurse's office, pulling out my own phone for a prop. Who was her witch? I would be crushed if Sarmine could do such a thing to my best friend. I wasn't going to consider that. Was it Valda? *Malkin?*

I rounded the corner into the nurse's room to find Jenah sitting on the bed with her leg elevated. Several industrial-sized bandages were taped up and down her left shin, her ankle was taped, and she still wore her wrist brace from that morning. But her eyes were alert and she was here.

"Ohmigod, Jenah," I said. "What happened?"

"I twisted my ankle," Jenah said sadly. "It hurts to walk." She turned puppy-dog eyes on me and my prop phone. "Thanks for getting my phone. I can't remember Mom's number." I handed it over to her and watched her pretend to text somebody. A few seconds later she announced, "She's coming right now."

The nurse signed her out and agreed I could help her to the front steps. I eyed Jenah suspiciously as we left the office. She really did look banged up, but there was something more going on. She balled her bloodied tights into her jacket pocket as we limped down the corridor. The hallway was strangely quiet between classes. I could hear the squeak of our shoes.

Jenah leaned into my ear. "Is one of the witches short and kind of frumpy? Smokes?"

Valda. I nodded.

"Word from the Granola Crowd is there's a new lunch lady this week who smells like an ashtray. She started yesterday."

"Right when you got bowled over by that bike," I said. The too-quiet hallway magnified our words.

"And today at lunch, I almost slipped on some water that appeared out of nowhere. I didn't think about it at the time. But then, I was at the top of the stairs, right before fifth hour. And this time—the puddle got me."

"I am *so* sorry, Jenah," I said quietly as I helped her limp down the hall. "This is all my fault."

But she was beaming. "Ohmigod," she said. "This means I really get to help you fight witches. I really *am* in the thick of this."

"May I remind you that witches aren't all rainbows and butterflies?" I said to her. "Look at your ankle."

In my ear she said, "Acting skills. So I could tell you what I saw. You don't have a phone for me to text you."

They were, in fact, impressive acting skills. She wasn't overdoing it. But the rest of her scrapes weren't faked. "You could have been seriously hurt."

"I know how to pratfall," she said in a wounded tone. "I really did slip, but the rest was for maximum effect. Playing to the crowd. Think of the emotional capital you can accrue from worried people remembering how much they'd miss you if you weren't around. Not to mention getting a couple hours off school." She stopped next to the front door. "Hang on, let me get out my actual phone to text Dad."

I let her lean on my shoulder while she retrieved it. There was a glass display box next to the front door where Mrs. N rotated people's artworks in and out. I wondered if Esmerelda would put up everyone's drawings of her in her pink bikini.

"This is really the best thing for you, Cam," Jenah said.

"Why?"

"Because you can count on me not to get depressed about it. I'll keep an eye out for Valda—I'll even tackle her if I get the chance—but it would take more than a flight of stairs to get me down. There's no way I'll contribute to your losing."

"Unless Valda decides to redouble her efforts," I said. There didn't seem to be any pink bikini drawings in the display. They were all line drawings of faces and bodies, most of them startlingly ugly. But somehow . . . familiar?

Jenah leaned forward. "Do you think she'd try to murder me?" There was a little too much glee in her voice.

"Jenah," I said slowly. "Do these drawings look like anyone we know?"

She peered in. "It looks like they were practicing caricatures," she said. "Of . . . Ohmigod, these are all *Henny*."

They were, unmistakably, Hennys. A whole case full of Hennys, her features wildly distorted, each drawing uglier than the last.

"Forget Valda," Jenah said, her fists balling. "I'm going to bring down *Esmerelda*."

☾

After school, I grabbed my jacket and backpack and went straight to the food carts to meet up with Leo. Hopefully this wouldn't take too long—I still had the witch's afternoon chores to do. He was not there yet, so I sat down at our sparkly clean table and updated my logic puzzle list.

WITCHES	VICTIMS	HOW TO MAKE THEM HAPPY
Esmerelda	Henny	Love potion (Is this ethical?)
Valda	Jenah	Just keep her from getting killed
Malkin	Caden	Car fixed; stay on lookout
Sarmine		
~~(not S or E)~~	~~Caden~~	~~?? Fix his car?~~

If Valda had Jenah, then Malkin must have Caden. Maybe that's why that windstorm had blown through the pizza place. She had been there, trying to do something to him. Except—ooh. I straightened up. *Maybe my presence had stopped her.* It seemed unlikely, but honestly, I could use every drop of encouragement. I smoothed out the creases on the paper, pondering the final blank. Sarmine had agreed to help me win—did that mean she was ignoring her student or actively helping them? I couldn't imagine her up at the school, helping someone with their Spanish homework. She was bad enough at helping me with witch things—oh. *Oh, wait.* What if Sarmine had *me*?

I toyed with this idea. Malkin could well have put me in that deck of cards. It might even explain why Sarmine was helping me in the mornings. And probably, knowing Sarmine, helping me with a double-edged sword—if I stopped following her directions, she wouldn't hesitate to bring me down and win the game after all.

The wind teased around its corners, trying to take my paper. I pressed it down and wrote my name next to Sarmine, with a big question mark. Should I flat-out ask her? But no, if she really did have me, then I now knew something that she didn't know I knew, which would make me one up on her. Or something like that.

True Witchery was confusing.

I glanced around. Still no Leo. Maybe I could put the love potion ethics question off a little longer. . . .

A tall, clean-cut guy in a letterman jacket sat down across from me. It was a shame our colors were forest green and orange, I thought, but he wore it well.

"You appeared out of nowhere," I said. I had half-thought Leo would change his mind and ditch me—I mean, c'mon, he was a popular guy and I was a liability who knew his most embarrassing secret—but there he was there at the cleanest table on the planet, smiling and waiting for me to give him a love potion.

"Like a panther," Leo agreed. "Science project. Lay it on me."

I took out the honey bear.

I measured one tablespoon onto a plastic spoon. He held out his hand—but I could not move mine.

Think of Henny, who must have had the worst day imaginable, I told myself. Winning Leo would convince her Esmerelda was wrong.

It'll wear off quickly.

It won't *make* him do anything.

But no. I couldn't go any further.

I kept saying I wasn't going to be like the witches. Well, here was my test. This was the slippery slope. It was one thing to try to stop the malice that the wicked witches were working. It was another to perform a spell on somebody without asking them first, no matter how great an idea it seemed to be. They should get the choice to say no.

"I'm going to tell you something," I said.

"Yes?"

"It's embarrassing. I think I need a bubble tea to get through it."

"We can do that."

I stuck the spoon back in the honey, shouldered my pack, and we walked twenty feet to the bubble tea cart. I got mango, and he got kiwi. I was getting out my ten when Leo handed over a credit card, saying casually, "My treat."

"I did not know football players drank bubble tea," I said.

"That is one of the many things that you don't know about me."

"You forget, I already know some of the many things."

"I suppose you do."

We took the bubble teas back to our clean table. I immediately put several tapioca bubbles in my mouth in order to avoid talking.

He watched me in silence. "So what's the embarrassing thing," he said finally, "and can it possibly be worse than mine?"

Chew and swallow.

Have to confess sometime.

"I was going to give you a love potion," I said.

He stared at me blankly and I realized what was going through his head.

"Oh god, no, not for me," I said quickly, cheeks reddening. "I like someone else. I do not need any love triangles in my life."

"Ah, well, my loss," he said easily.

I didn't know what that meant so I sailed on. The worst was out now. "The embarrassing thing was that I was going to do it at all. Or that I'm capable of doing it, possibly. That's also kind of weird."

He leaned in. "So who asked you to give me a love potion?"

"I can't tell you that," I said. "Witch-client confidentiality. But I can tell you it's not a real love potion, if that makes you feel better."

"Should it?"

"It's like a . . . being Open to Possibilities potion," I said. "So you'll be more aware if potential crushes or crushees are around you. You'll consider shaking up your love life."

"And how do you know I don't already have a girlfriend or a boyfriend?" he said. "Might be hard on them."

"Do you?"

"No," he admitted. "It's been tough to think about my love life when I've been dealing with all this . . . shifting."

"Well, I don't think it would mess up what you already have going on," I said. "I read through all the witch's notes on it and it's basically an opening up to possibility. So if you already love—er, *like* someone, you'll probably just go on liking them."

Leo wrapped his hands around his knee and leaned back, considering. He was really a good-looking guy. The moody, overcast light bathed his high cheekbones, his heavy brows. I could see why Henny liked him, or at least liked looking at him. "You must have a pretty good reason for trying to help this person who likes me," he said.

"I didn't actually know her before this week," I said honestly. "But let's just say that somebody is deliberately trying to ruin her life. And I'm against that sort of thing."

He nodded. "You're a helping person. I like that." There was silence for a minute, and then he said, "I tell you what. I'll take your spoonful of honey."

"You will?"

"If you take one, too."

6

A Lovelie *Spell*, Take Two

I gulped. This seemed like one of those crazy romantic-comedy pacts that get people into deep trouble. "Why me?"

Leo looked at me seriously. "Should you be messing with people's lives without knowing what you're doing?"

I swallowed. "No," I said in a meek voice.

He didn't say anything after that, just kept watching me while I realized that now was my moment to toughen up, be brave, be ethical, be a good person, et cet, et cet. It was rather odd that I had reached a turning point where taking a love potion would prove my morality, but clearly that is where we were.

"I will," I said.

I retrieved a second plastic spoon from the food carts and measured us each a spoonful.

"Bottoms up," he said.

The honey was rich and flowered on my tongue. It tasted the way I imagine mead tastes when I read about it in books. Like it was honey, but there was something else there, too, the potion part, making me feel . . . well, quite specifically, like I was a little more open to possibilities. I don't think I would have noticed it if I hadn't been expecting it—I probably would have thought exactly what Leo said, which is—

"That is some darn good honey."

He looked at me, really looked at me, and for the first time he laughed. Just a smirk-snort thing, like he was pleased with himself for noticing something. Something . . . appealing?

"Remember that this is the honey talking," I cautioned him. "Nobody needs to be open for possibility right this very second."

"Right," he said. He put his face back into a serious expression. "Love potions are no joke." The smile crept upward again.

I stood up from the picnic table before anything weird could happen. Well, weirder than love potions and bubble tea with a football player. "I'm going to go home and research your problem," I said as I shouldered my backpack. "Find out a way to stop it."

The smile vanished and he stood, too. "Don't tell anyone yet," he said. "I thought about it this afternoon and I'm not ready for more people to know."

"Okay," I said. "But it might be interfering with your life. I mean, you can't keep worrying about what you're gonna become whenever your emotions take over."

"That's why I'm nervous about the football game," he admitted. "First one since this started happening. I mean, I sat one game out—pretended I had a pulled muscle. I can't keep doing that."

"It seems like it often happens through fear," I mused.

"But not the only time. It's just the most obvious trigger."

"I wonder if we could—" I started, and then stopped cold. A dead, ominous hush had fallen on the parking lot. The wind was gone; the flag on top of the bubble tea cart was limp. "I don't like this," I said. It was the calm before the tornado, the flat before the implosion. Leo looked around with a wary expression.

Power. Near.

Malkin.

Somewhere. Moving closer. Any second now—

"Leo! Down!" I pushed him toward the picnic table. We dived under it right as the hurricane hit. It swept through the food cart area, ripping the banner off of the bubble tea cart, knocking over the tables, blowing the plastic chairs straight across the parking lot and slamming them into cars. Luckily the picnic table was bolted into concrete. I heard shrieks from other students and I shouted behind me at Leo, "I'm going out!"

If he responded, I didn't hear him in the gale. I nudged out on my elbows, trying to get the spices from my backpack while staying somewhat protected. Branches cracked around me, sticks and leaves flew past. One pinch ginger, one pinch thyme . . . I didn't have a bowl and match like Sarmine suggested, but I added a spritz of unicorn sanitizer to get everything well-mixed in my hand.

I knew my feeble spell would never stand up to Malkin, even with the unicorn-hair vodka.

That didn't matter.

I touched the wand to my palm, closed my eyes, and licked the ginger-thyme-unicorn sanitizer off of my hand. Ginger and thyme do not go well together, and the burn of the few drops of alcohol didn't help. Still. Focus on the power, Cam. Imagine it filling you. You are ten feet tall. You are the equal of Malkin.

"Give up," I shouted, and my voice whipped away in the wind.

Big words coming from me. I really wasn't sure if my tiny spell would have any effect at all.

But a small, localized area around me calmed. It went from a hurricane to an everyday brisk wind. I hurried to where several students had fallen in the parking lot, bringing the calmer wind with me. Someone was flat on the ground, trapped under a tree branch. Was that Caden? As I neared the group, the other kids were able to stand, to brush themselves off and wipe the grit from their faces. One of the guys pulled the tree limb off of the guy on the ground, and he stood up, shaken.

It was not Caden.

I whirled—was he somewhere else around here? Had something worse happened to him?

But around us the rest of the winds were calming. I did not for one second believe my spell had done it. Malkin must be moving on.

The trees stood up again. The brittle leaves fluttered to the ground. My heart rate slowed as I looked around for Caden, and then—

Leo.

I ran back to the picnic table. He was not there. I whirled, seeking him in the devastation. No tall boy. No cow, either. No giraffe. No nothing. "Leo!" I shouted. But there was nothing, not even a flash of fluffy white tail.

What with the extra excitement, I just missed the bus. I ended up jogging the four miles home. Okay, so it's mostly downhill. I was still pretty tired when I got home. Wulfie was out in the front yard, running back and forth and mostly being well behaved. Sarmine was inside, cooking her favorite beetroot lasagna for dinner. I collapsed on a bar stool and chugged a glass of water.

"You missed your stirring chores," she told me over her shoulder. "I had to tend to the cauldron in the RV garage myself."

"Bus woes," I said.

"Your face is all scratched up. Did you get hit with something?"

"Witch woes."

"Hey, crack the front door for Wulfie, will you?" she said. "He's been out there a while."

I went back and did that, then stopped to look at the thermometers on the coffee table. Malkin's was a little down but not too terrible. Whatever Malkin had been trying to do to Caden at the food carts, she had missed. The rest were slightly above grade. Sarmine's was quite buoyant, in fact. I felt a renewed sense of warmth toward my mother, despite the beetroot. She was playing me fair.

"Did you discover anyone yet?" said Sarmine.

I pulled out my list and smoothed it out on the counter. "Esmerelda—Henny. That's the love potion girl."

"Did you try out the love potion?"

"Yup, but I dunno if it works yet."

Sarmine sniffed. "If you performed my spell correctly, than naturally it will work correctly."

"I mean I don't know if it'll make him fall in love with *Henny,*" I explained. "Okay, and Valda's got Jenah. That sucks, frankly, but on the other hand it's better because Jenah knows what's coming, so she can steel herself."

"Well observed," said Sarmine. She placed the lasagna in the oven and began cleaning up the kitchen. "Anyone else?"

"Yeah, Malkin has this kid named Caden."

"Oh?" said Sarmine, not turning around. "What did she do to him?"

"She disintegrated his car," I said, and then the penny finally dropped. There were now at least three dead cars. Maybe more I hadn't seen. That meant that Caden wasn't necessarily the victim. And in point of fact, Caden had rebounded quite nicely from the first attempt, when he had been given a new car from his dad's dealership. And if more and more cars were dying under mysterious circumstances . . . well, that would be awfully nice for a boy whose dad owned the biggest set of dealerships in town, wouldn't it? I peered more closely at Sarmine's thermometer, at the bubble bouncing near the top of the water. "You wouldn't . . . you wouldn't know anything about that, would you?"

"About what?" said Sarmine.

There was a screech from the street and then a howling noise.

Wulfie.

Sarmine ran for the door, her face ghastly white. I ran, too.

I got there first and flung open the door. Wulfie was on the other side of the street, running around in tight circles and howling mournfully at the sky. Our neighbor's massive orange SUV had skidded to a halt in front of us. He leaned out the window, yelling at us. "Your dog just ran across the street, lady! He'd better not have scratched my paint."

Sarmine drew herself up in righteous fury, but before she could utter a scathing rebuke, the man tore off down to the end of the block, honking at a kid on his bike to get out of the way. I hurried across the street to catch Wulfie.

The witch was shaking with anger. "That does it, that absolutely does it!"

"Sarmine," I said warningly. But she was already stalking down our sidewalk to the street, presumably headed straight to our neighbor's house.

"Aaaaggh," I said coherently. Wulfie had stopped running in circles and had darted into some thornbushes. He was huddling in fear from the scare and from Sarmine's anger. I tried coaxing him out, but he was not willing to budge. Finally I stuck my arms in, heedless of the thorns. I scooted him back into the house, where he scrabbled frantically at the floors and shed a million werewolf hairs all over everything. Sarmine would have a fit, but then Sarmine was the one who was off on a vengeance mission, heedless of anything else, as usual.

I took off down the street after Sarmine. The orange-SUV guy lived at the end of the street, so the massively oversized jeep was already parked in his driveway and he was nowhere to be seen.

"Tears up and down our street at fifty miles an hour," Sarmine spat as I arrived, panting. "It's only luck that none of the kids have been obliterated." She was mixing a powder up in the palm of her hand. "Can't even fit it in his own garage."

"Sarmine," I pleaded. "There are rules. You can't just—"

She touched her wand to her palm. "Excaliminivandervagon," she said, and flicked.

"Nooooo," I said, lunging at her in slow motion.

Time seemed to slow then, or perhaps it was my witch blood seizing the opportunity to demonstrate another of its capabilities. I watched in horror as the witch's powder flicked out like powdered sugar—except more green and sparkly—coating the orange SUV. There was a noise like a beached whale groaning.

And then with a creaking clunk, the SUV toppled over on its side. Its wheels spun gently in the November wind.

"Oh god," I said. "Run," I said.

"Nonsense," the witch said crisply. She was calmer now that the destruction had occurred. She marched straight up to our neighbor's door and rang the bell.

A vaguely doughy, sort of ex–frat boy, thirtysomething guy peered out, five o'clock beer already in hand. That was fast. "I'm not buying whatever it is," he said, and started to shut the door. Which: totally obnoxious. Even *I* knew he was our neighbor, so you would think he would vaguely recall our faces from having almost run over our pet-slash-preschooler moments before. I couldn't tell from Sarmine's face whether this pissed her off or pleased her to have confirmation of his obnoxiousness.

"I simply wanted to let you know that your car has fallen over," she said pleasantly. "Good day."

She turned and walked crisply down the sidewalk, her heels clicking in a crisp way that was probably magically enhanced. I followed, stunned. The neighbor followed, also stunned. As he stopped in his driveway, a small trail of smoke rose up from the tipped-over hood. The car made a noise like a sigh of giving up. Then its hood popped open and all of its internal organs belched out onto the driveway.

An incoherent mumbling that sounded like *what did you why did you how did you* started, and then that escalated into a full-on pissy fit.

Sarmine stopped at the end of the driveway and eyed our neighbor. "If you think a teenage girl and a little old lady could push that massive gas-guzzling elephant on its side, then you're stupider than you look," she said, almost pleasantly. "And yet, I'm not sure if that's possible."

He began to turn a funny shade of red-orange.

"As a general tip," said Sarmine, "you might consider driving the speed limit on this pleasant residential street that we all live on." She eyed the dead car with its puked-up car parts and gently spinning tire wheels. "Or, ride a bike. You might consider that. Good day."

She stalked off toward home, and with a final glance at the guy's apoplectic face, I hurried after her. "So, uh. I think you might in fact know something about all the destroyed cars?"

"Camellia," she said under her breath. "I need you to find me a bug."

"A bug? What kind of—"

"Immediately!"

I scanned the sidewalk, quickly found a ladybug, scooped it up with a leaf. Sarmine was still walking home, hurriedly rolling something in a twist of paper as she walked. Our neighbor was stalking down the street after us. "Hey, lady," he said in an angry voice. "Wait up."

"He wouldn't do anything to us in broad daylight, would he? On our own street?"

"Never underestimate a man who drives a car the size of a house," said Sarmine. "Now squish the bug into the paper here."

I stopped holding out the leaf, drew back. "But . . . I don't . . . I can't—"

"Camellia," hissed Sarmine. "This is no time to get prissy. Squish that ladybug. Do it!"

Our neighbor was getting closer. But . . . "I can't do it," I said. "I'm not going to kill things for magic spells. It's not right!" I turned around to see the angry red face behind us, only a few steps away.

Sarmine seized the leaf with the ladybug in it, and squished it firmly into her twist of paper. She muttered some words, and then turned and flung the paper directly at our neighbor's feet.

A hundred ladybugs climbed up his shoes. Up his socks. Up his legs.

"What the—"

A thousand ladybugs slithered all over his body. He danced around, squealing. Then staggered for home, trying frantically to scrape them off of him.

"That will take care of *him* for a while," said the witch. "And his SUV."

"Aren't you afraid he'll, you know, report us to the police?"

"And say we sicced some ladybugs on him?"

"Good point."

"Where's Wulfie?"

"I put him inside," I said.

"Hmm," said the witch as we crossed the doorstep back into our home. "I have a spell to take scratches out of hardwood floors. I'll text it to your phone for you to study. I expect the floor restored to its pristine state by the end of the week."

"You're welcome for rescuing Wulfie," I said. He was now curled up on the couch, nose draped over his favorite stuffed bear.

"You're welcome for attempting to restore order to our block."

"Well . . ."

"And furthermore, Camellia," she went on, "this is nonsense about you not being able to squish bugs. I refuse to raise my daughter to be that squeamish."

"I'm not squeamish," I said. "It's just *not right*. I've told you several times now."

The witch dismissed this with a wave of her hand. "The world out there is not kind to prissy witches, Camellia. They will eat you alive. Other witches, I mean."

"Look," I said. I was trying not to raise my voice. "I admitted that I have witch blood and all that. I agreed to try some spells. But I absolutely did *not* agree to kill anything for it. If I'm going to be a witch, then I'm going to do good things with my magic."

The witch raised a pointy eyebrow. "Such as?"

"Well. Making people's lives better."

She dismissed this with a wave and went to pull the lasagna out. "I believe I made everyone else on the block's lives better today when I destroyed that horrible orange thing."

"No no no," I said. "You are not going to twist my words around. I mean a proper good-fairy sort of witch. That's how I got muddled up in this bet this week, after all. Unlike basically every witch I ever met, I'm going to do good things for people. Ask them if they want help. Ethical spells." I trailed off. "You know. Helping people," I finished lamely.

"People," said Sarmine, "are morons." She set the beetroot lasagna carefully on the table and served me a large helping. "I know you're determined to believe the worst of me, Camellia," she said, "but I do believe in making the world a better place." She stared me down. "The difference between us is that I'm not going to pussyfoot around in order to do it."

"The ends justify the means?"

"Perhaps."

"And you're some sort of benevolent dictator, who best knows how to run things?"

"Why do you think I keep trying to take over the world?" A glimmer of amusement was in her eyes. Sarmine would never laugh at herself, so I assumed she must be laughing at me.

I sighed. At least Wulfie was all right. I scooped him up and petted his fur. He licked my hand. "Backyard for you for a week," I told him. He whined. Poor thing. If I hadn't missed the bus I would have been home watching him. "Sarmine," I said slowly as I sat down at the dinner table.

"Yes?" she said over bites of her lasagna.

I tried a bite and made a pleasant face. "Very nice," I said with as much enthusiasm as I could muster.

"Thank you, Camellia," she said. "You are welcome to take the leftovers for lunch if you wish."

"Very kind of you," I assured her, "but I wouldn't dream of depriving you."

"Mm."

"So," I tried again. "Sarmine. *Mom.*"

"Yes."

"Well." There was no way to make this any easier. "So Devon has this bike. And it's extra long and he can carry stuff on it. So he doesn't have to take public transit everywhere but he can still get around, without burning fossil fuels, right?"

Sarmine steepled her fingers. "You want a bike."

"I used to have one. The dragon sat on it last winter solstice, after you gave her a saucepan of fermented pixie juice."

She nodded, considering. "I suppose you have worked rather hard this year."

"You suppose?" I said. She raised her eyebrows and I shut my mouth.

"Your sixteenth birthday *is* approaching in February."

I will note at this point that witches definitely do not celebrate any sort of winter holiday-giving. Sarmine occasionally joined some other witches at the solstice for some sort of sitting-on-a-hill-drinking-martinis thing, but there was definitely no gift-giving. Birthdays, however, they were fond of. But Sarmine's idea of a good present was rarely my own.

"I had planned to procure you two ounces of powdered hen's teeth."

I rolled my eyes. "I have saved every little powder and spellbook you've gotten me over the years but none of them were something that I could use to go out and see my friends, you know?"

Sarmine looked offended. "It is an extremely complicated undertaking to procure powdered hen's teeth. In the first place, there's only one witch in the continental U.S. that farms hen's teeth, and he makes you meet with him *in person*."

"Oh, I am sorry," I said. "You mean you would have to *talk* to him?"

Sarmine shuddered.

"Well, look," I said. "Take this as the gift it is. You can actually go down to the bike shop and purchase me one bike. No weirdo hen's teeth farmers required. And then, I won't try to borrow the car next year when I learn how to drive."

She nodded thoughtfully. "I have in fact been thinking I should get rid of that car. It goes against everything I stand for."

"It might not be around much longer the way cars are exploding all over the place," I said dryly.

"True," Sarmine conceded. She stretched. "Very well. Your sixteenth birthday present will be a bike."

"Yes!" I said. "Can we go to the store now? I mean, as soon as we finish this lovely beetroot?"

Sarmine shook her head slightly. "Not a *new* bike, Camellia. You must remember that it is far better to reduce, reuse, recycle than to purchase new."

"Uh, okay," I said. "Is this a working bike? Are we going to find one here in town? Or . . . no, you have something in mind, don't you?"

"Let me show you," she said.

We finished dinner and got in the station wagon—surprise number one, because the witch really does try to limit vehicle usage—and drove to a storage facility—surprise number two.

"I had no idea you had a storage unit," I said as we walked up to it. The winter sun had set and it was dark except for the facility's lightbulbs, half of which were burnt out. It was definitely not one of your high-end storage facilities, not that I had any experience with either kind. I half-expected someone to jump out at us.

"Certain compounds are too volatile to be stored on premises," Sarmine said.

"Bikes are volatile?"

"And certain things I have no room for," she admitted.

"I thought one of your regular rants about McMansions was how people should reduce their possessions and live minimally and so on?"

"Did you want a bike or not?"

I shut up.

She heaved open the garage door and the smells rolled out as the air was disturbed. Dust. Old books. Oregano. Lemon. Compost.

She rubbed a few ingredients from her fanny pack together on her palm and tapped her wand against it. The wand clicked on like a flashlight. She swept the inside of the facility with the light to reveal what must be the holy grail of treasure-hunting, to a witch. Rows and rows of boxes—some wooden, some metal, some cardboard, all neatly labeled. It was too dark to see much, but the label on the metal box nearest me said, *1961, Wich, Kan.—Blk Recluse, petrified. 1 doz.* There were hundreds of boxes like that.

"How do you keep this all safe?" I said, starting to go in.

Her arm stopped me. "It is extremely well warded, Camellia. If anyone besides me goes in I can't be responsible for how it protects itself."

I stopped.

Sarmine petted the side of the storage building and then stepped inside. The flashlight disappeared into the gloom and there was the sound of someone going down a long flight of stairs. A distant splash. That seemed pretty impressive for an eight-by-ten storage facility, but maybe one of her treasures was a secret portal to a cave somewhere. Probably somewhere disgusting with leeches and river monsters, and not anywhere nice we could go on holiday.

The stairs noise reversed itself and a minute later she came out, wheeling a burnt-orange-and-avocado bike. By that I mean that one of the remaining, paint-flaking colors was burnt orange, not that the bike had been in a fire. But it could hardly look worse if it had. One tire was missing and the handlebars were bent. Rust ran up and down the frame. A spider was living in the bell. It did not look as though it had been ridden in at least twenty years.

"*That?*" I said. I was feeling a little hurt, even though I did know what the witch was like. This was the kind of bike you'd give someone as a hand-me-down to tide them over if they were desperate. It was not any kind of sixteenth birthday present.

The witch ignored me. "Let's get it adjusted to you," she said, tinkering with the seat height.

"If you haven't noticed, I can't go anywhere without at least two tires," I said bitterly. "And maybe some air to pump them up. And with the handlebar like that I'm only going to go in circles anyway."

Sarmine sighed a put-upon sigh.. "And now I'll teach you how to use it," she said.

"Step one. Pedal the pedals. Oh no, wait, step one, put on a freaking tire."

"Language, Camellia," she said. "Now, you see these shifters here."

I nodded.

"This side controls the bike on the ground. And this side controls the bike in the air."

7

Bikes and Boys

I goggled for a full minute. "This thing actually flies?"

"You will have to first learn the technique for making it invisible, Camellia," the witch said. "I can't afford to have you flying all over the city and make our presence known. Someday we witches will be able to come out of hiding and rule the world as it should be ruled. I live for that day. I long for that day. But today is not that day."

I sat down on the bike and put one foot on a pedal. I did want to try taking it for a spin. But . . . "I'll still need a tire."

"Correct. You will need to be rolling to get off the ground. For that you will need to replace the front tire. You cannot try the shifters while you are stopped because that would damage it. But yes, Camellia. This bike will fly."

I threw my arms around the witch, surprising both of us. "This is even better than a cargo bike." I couldn't wait to show Devon. He knew about all the witch stuff. So I could totally show him.

The minute we pulled into the driveway, I hopped out of the car, lifting out my new-to-me bike. "I'll be back soon," I hollered to Sarmine.

"Did you hang up the snakeskins?"

"Do it when I get back," I said. I wheeled my new bike down the street. I'd been telling Henny that people didn't like her comics because she never made them interesting. Well, just like Leo said about the honey spell: if you're going to go dishing things out to people you should be willing to take it yourself. That included advice.

I was going to go ask Devon out.

The missing-tire wheel made a clankety clank on the asphalt as I walked. Cool, he would hear me coming. It was full night now, even though my phone said it was only five to seven. There were porch lights, though. Several of the neighbors still had their jack-o'-lanterns out—now drooping at the mouth and falling in. Straw bales. Corncobs. It's a very family sort of street.

I stopped on his block, trying to remember which house was the one that sold last month. I was pretty sure I had the right one, but I had never technically been told the address or invited over. But I was bringing a bike, and a request for help, and Devon liked bikes and maybe would also like helping me? It was worth a shot.

I rolled into his driveway. I had hoped that Devon would be outside and then I would know for sure it was his house and I also wouldn't end up in any embarrassing parent interactions, but after all it was November, and he wasn't. So I stood in the glow of the porch light and rang the bell.

The door opened to a hallway full of cardboard boxes and a man I presumed was Devon's father. He was wearing paint-covered jeans and an old flannel shirt, and he looked as if he were busy thinking about something else that was not the doorbell. He looked nice; sort of rumpled and kind. He didn't look a ton like Devon, but I thought they might have the same eyes, especially when it came to the absentminded look. He smiled at me. "Are you here to pick up Devon?"

Pretty much exactly, I thought. "Um," I said helpfully. "I'm Cam. Is Devon home?"

"Sure, kiddo," he said. He hollered over his shoulder to his son. To me he said, "Have you had dinner?" The garlicky aroma coming from inside smelled way better than beetroot lasagna, but I assured him that I had eaten.

Devon came running up to the door. He had his backpack with him, and lit up when he saw me, though he looked over my shoulder. "Cam!" he said. "I didn't expect you."

"I know," I said. "So actually the wi—I mean, my *mom* gave me her old bike, but it needs help, and I wondered if you would look at it with me. Since you, um, know about bikes." I was not sounding particularly eloquent so far. Still, I hoped Devon would see that I *did* value him, for something that was definitely not demon-influenced.

"Sure," he said, and put down his backpack and came out to the front porch. His dad had helpfully faded away. Devon looked at the missing tire and bent handlebars. "Wow, that *is* old," he said. "And, um . . . green."

"I can't decide if the seventies look is a point of pride or if I should take some purple spray paint to it immediately," I said.

"It's definitely retro," he said.

"Too retro to ride?"

"Nah," he said. "I can help you with it." He lifted the garage door from the outside and let it roll up. It, too, was full of boxes. I wondered if they had had a bigger house when they had been out in the country, or if they were just the sort of family that collected lots of things. Or if it was just moving chaos. "I don't know if we have any spare tires," Devon said, turning on the light. "Everything's still a disaster. I do know where my pump is, and there's a pretty good bike store not too far from here."

"Hey, that would be great," I said.

Now was the moment. He was looking at me with his kind eyes. Like he was actually happy to see me. Like we could move on from last night.

It shouldn't be that hard to ask someone out who's already kissed you, right? I mean, I think you have a better than average chance that they like you, even if you've since insinuated that their thriving social life was only due to demonic possession.

"So, I thought maybe after you helped me, I could take you out for ice cream," I said. "For a thank you." So it wasn't suave. I had made a step forward.

His eyes fell. "I'd love to," he said, "but—"

Which is of course when the battered old minivan pulled into the driveway, honking up a storm. A girl stuck her head out the window and called in faux British, "Hurry up, you git!"

"Nnenna!" he said. "Coming!" He looked at me. "I'd really like to," he repeated, "but we have emergency band practice."

"Your mother was a hamster . . ." she said irrepressibly, apparently gearing up for a round of *Monty Python* taunting.

Devon held his hand up, laughing. "Ten seconds."

I recognized the girl then as his drummer. I had seen her briefly at the school dance. She was a fine-boned black girl with piercings, and she made me feel—which was not in the least her own fault and had everything to do with me—about two inches tall. She cocked a salute at me as she waited for Devon to grab his stuff and get in the van. There was a kind of *studying* feel to it that I didn't much like, as if she were assessing the current situation.

"Look," said Devon. "Leave your bike with me. I'll look at it when I get home tonight."

"I don't want to be any trouble. . . ."

"No trouble." He took the bike from me and wheeled it into the garage, then closed the door. He leaned in. "Look, I—"

Nnenna honked the horn again. "Band practice waits for no man," she said.

"Going." He hopped in the van, and Nnenna peeled out.

I couldn't even tell if he waved as he drove off.

☾

I tried to review the *Macbeth* study questions that night while I stirred the witch's brew, but my thoughts kept floating back to the witches' plans. When they didn't float back to Devon.

Firmly I admonished myself to stay focused on the witches and on my homework. Devon was a distraction. If I was going to stop the witches—not to mention maintain my GPA—I had to keep on task. After I showered and got into bed, I pulled out my logic puzzle list.

WITCHES	VICTIMS	HOW TO MAKE THEM HAPPY
Esmerelda	Henny	Love potion ~~(Is this ethical?)~~ It is if you ask first.
Valda	Jenah	Just keep her from getting killed
Malkin	~~Caden~~	~~Car fixed, stay on lookout~~
Sarmine	Caden	Sarmine's taking care of it

After that I flipped the paper over and added to my ethics list.

Good Witch Ethics

1. Don't use animal parts in spells.
2. ~~Don't cast bad spells on good people for no reason.~~ Ask people before you work a spell on them (unless in self-defense).

One step backward on the logic puzzle. One step forward in living up to my ethics list. Frankly, the list I needed right now was the list of how to make things work with Devon. But I didn't think I'd learned enough in that area to start making any lists. Maybe I should have Jenah make one for me, because even though she didn't really date, she understood people. Jenah could probably get any guy in school just by lifting a finger. Maybe I *should* ask her. I hadn't really shared anything about the boy problems I was currently facing. I knew that's what best friends were for, just . . . sometimes it was hard to open up about certain things.

My thoughts never stopped running in circles, but my body was so exhausted that when I finally did put my head on the pillow, I went thunk.

Wednesday morning started off a lot better. This is because when I took Wulfie outside to do his business—staying with him this time—I found a note taped on our door. It was from Devon. *Bike around back,* it read. *Didn't want to wake you.*

A happy shiver ran down my spine, and not just from the frosty air. People do not fix bikes for you in the middle of the night if they don't at least like you a little bit. I went around to the fence and found that he had unlatched the gate and rolled the bike inside.

I was actually going to have a bike again. And not just any bike.

A flying bike.

I whistled as Wulfie and I went back in. We found Sarmine in the kitchen, peering into the coffeemaker as if angels would stream down from the heavens and remind her how it worked.

"Allow me," I said, rubbing the chill off of my hands. I measured coffee into the machine and poured the water in. She didn't quite say thank you, but she did have a look on her face that was more grateful than I usually saw. Hey, you take what you can get. I rustled up some breakfast for myself, poured a bowl of kibble for Wulfie, and handed Sarmine the first cup of coffee as I sat down at the bar.

"All right," I said, picking up my spoon. "I know what spell I want your help on this morning."

She drank a long draft of what must be scalding-hot coffee, and then clutched her coffee cup as if it would protect her from having to get up and actually help me do anything. "Yes?"

"Ye Olde Invisibility Spell," I said. "So I can fly this bike of yours."

She raised her eyebrows behind the mug. "Nothing about stopping the other witches this morning?"

I gestured at the glassware on the coffee table. "Everything's bobbing along," I said. "Knock on wood, I'm on track. Jenah is on guard against Valda, and is going to help take down Esmerelda. Back to square one with Malkin, but I can't do anything about it here. Frankly, an invisibility spell would be pretty darn helpful for tracking her down—even without a flying bike."

Sarmine poured more of the coffee into her mouth. She looked like she might try that next with the glass carafe. She really was not a morning person. I wondered if she was regretting her rash promise to teach me spells every morning before school.

"I don't really need to teach you a spell as such," she said, and stopped to yawn.

I found myself getting grumpy. Sarmine was good at getting under my skin. "Look," I said carefully. "You said this was my early birthday present, and that I could ride it if I made myself invisible. And now you say you're not going to teach me a spell?"

"Stop getting wound up," she said. "All I'm saying is that the invisibility tools are out there in nature. Anyone can do it. You don't even need witch blood."

"Oh!"

The witch downed the rest of her cup and crossed to the whiteboard. "The method of invisibility I am about to show you has one excellent plus side," she said, and she drew a diagram. "Anything you bespell will have an invisible force field around it. For example, if you spread some invisibility ointment on a towel and cover yourself, the towel is unlikely to twitch aside and show your shoe." She eyed me. "The force field extends for a short distance around the object, covering what is supposed to remain covered."

This was too good to be true. "So you could bespell the bike itself," I said slowly. "Would it cover all of you if you were sitting on it?"

"Very good," said Sarmine. "Yes, it would." She waited patiently. Sarmine likes the Socratic method of teaching, whereby I work things out for myself and she sits around and looks bored with how dreadfully long it's taking me.

"But if you could do that . . . you *would* have done that," I said. "So I'm missing something." Sarmine had said the force field was the plus side to this method of invisibility. . . . "What's the downside?"

"The invisibility doesn't last very long," she said.

"Ah." That sounded like a witch trick if I ever heard one. Amazing, incredible, just the sort of power you need! Fails when you least expect it! "Why?" I finally said, after trying to come up with a supposition and failing.

"Because it's run on invisible eels," she said simply, or as simply as you can say a statement about invisible eels.

My dreams of riding a flying bike to school were rapidly decaying. "And, pray tell, how do you use these invisible eels?"

She lit up. "Well, they're quite small," she said. "About the size of minnows. They're quite delightful. In fact, I have a whole pitcher full of them to show you. I went out fishing for them last night after I gave you the bike." She pointed to a glass pitcher of water sitting on the bar. It was full of water but otherwise empty.

Except, I was pretty sure it wasn't otherwise empty. "Invisible eels?" I said.

"At least a dozen," she said.

I was glad I hadn't decided to drink from that pitcher. "So how does it work?"

She stuck her hand in the pitcher, searching. Her fingers flickered back and forth. And then she, and the pitcher, disappeared.

"That is so cool," I said.

"It is rather delightful, isn't it?" said the disembodied voice of Sarmine. She reappeared, her hand coming out of the water. She gave me the slight smile that was the Sarmine version of beaming as she dried her fingers on the kitchen towel. "Rite of passage for witch kids. Spending long, hot afternoons down at the river catching eels."

"Of course, holding onto an eel would be hard to do on a bike," I mused, and Sarmine gave me the good student nod of approval. "Is there another method?"

"Definitely," said Sarmine, and she ticked the three options off on her fingers. "Tickling, mashing, or ingesting."

"*Ingesting?*"

"That is the one I recommend," said Sarmine. "And swallow them live—they last so much longer that way."

"Swallow. A live eel."

"It confers complete invisibility for approximately four hours," she said. "Plenty of time to fly around and see things. Then you slowly become visible again over the next three to five hours while your system finishes breaking down the eel. I usually recommend being home then so no one notices your translucency."

I shook my head, my hopes falling. "I can't use eels."

"Eels are a dime a dozen, Camellia," she said. "You can find them in any stream, if you know how to tickle them up."

"I've told you, it's not right to use living creatures for my spells."

"You eat fish! How is this different?"

I didn't know, but I felt sure that it was. It didn't matter that Sarmine could talk rings around me. I was going to stick to my guns regardless, and by guns I definitely meant my morals, because I don't approve of guns, either. Sarmine probably did. Like witch guns or something.

"If you don't care to swallow them, you can mash them up into a paste and rub the resulting ointment thoroughly over the object," Sarmine offered. "Or dry the eels and incorporate them in a reconstitution spell. The advantage to the paste is it lasts approximately twice as long; the disadvantage is that the fishy smell permanently saturates your object. Hard to stay unnoticed if you reek of anchovies."

I pushed the pitcher back to her, feeling sick to my stomach. "I will not use your eels," I told her.

The delight in her face fell. "Really."

"In fact, I think you deliberately introduced this lesson today to 'toughen me up,' as you're so fond of saying. Now that I think about it, you didn't offer to give me a bike until *after* I made my stand about the ladybugs." My anger was rising but I tried to stay calm. If I flew off the handle at the witch her punishment would be swift.

I couldn't afford to miss a chunk out of this week. "I've told you over and over, and you need to respect my decision. I'm not going to use animals in spells."

"You used pixie dew in your so-called ethical love potion," the witch pointed out.

"I mean I'm not going to take anything they need to live," I said. "I'm not trying to be vegan, just vegetarian."

"Fine," she said. "Then no more ingredients for you." She picked up the pitcher and returned it to the counter.

The witch was so maddening. "Is there any other invisibility spell I can use?" I said.

She poured herself another cup of coffee. "You know how vegan marshmallows don't taste as good as the real thing?"

"I suppose," I said. I couldn't remember the last time the witch had bought marshmallows, period. Oh yes, I do remember. She needed them for a spell once. It was definitely not a spell involving me getting to eat any of them. "Are you saying that there's another spell that doesn't work as well as live eels, or that it literally tastes worse than live eels?"

"Both," she said. "As I've said before, Camellia, the spells are the spells. I do not go off into my little laboratory and come up with a spell designed to annoy you. You want some other spell, you'll have to make it."

I looked at the eels swimming around in the pitcher. Or, rather, looked at the pitcher of water and imagined the eels swimming in it. "I suppose. . . ." I said hesitantly.

She tapped her fingers, waiting for me to give in to the inevitable.

"I suppose I could carry a jar of them around with me," I said. "And then return them to the river so they can live happy, eelish lives."

She snorted. "If you want to go through all that. First off, how are you going to steer and tickle eels at the same time? And second, good luck carrying around a tank of eels on your bike."

"I could use a Mason jar," I hazarded. But then I realized the problem with that right as I said it. "Oxygen, right. But if I poked holes in the lid it would work for a while, and then I could return them to the stream?" I sighed. It would be a lot of work just to take a bike ride. I could see that it would be much easier to either a) swallow a live eel, or b) rub your bike daily with eel paste.

The options made me mad all over again. "How am I supposed to be a good witch when you won't even help me?" I thumped the counter. "Other people's parents help them be good people," I said. "I am *trying* to figure out the right thing to do, like stopping Valda from killing Jenah and fixing Henny's love life, which, right, brings up a whole slew of questions you don't even care about, like not dosing Leo, who's got enough problems with becoming a bunny every five minutes, and—"

The witch pivoted slowly to look at me. "Becoming a what?"

"Um. A bunny? He's not a were-bunny, though. He's a shape—"

Sarmine grabbed my hand and pulled me up the stairs into her study. She slammed the door, closed the blinds. "This room is shielded," she said. "Are you saying you met a shapeshifter?"

"Yes?"

"Have you told anyone else? Who else knows?"

"Well, Jenah," I said. "I mean obviously I don't think he wants people knowing. I don't even think he's told his dads." My heart was starting to race. What was up with shapeshifters?

"This is serious, Camellia," she said.

"I am seeing that," I said. "But why?"

By way of answer she crossed to her bookshelf and pulled out a book. She dropped it in my lap. Its title: *Thirteen Ways to Force a Shifter to Shift.* I opened it up to the first page. The black text read, starkly, "Way 1. Torture."

8

Being a Wicked Witch Isn't *All* Fun & Games

I slammed the book closed. "What is this? Who is he?"

Sarmine paced her study. "I'm going to tell you one of the less pleasant aspects of witch history, Camellia," she said. Seeing as there were already plenty of unpleasant aspects to being a wicked witch, I got even more nervous. "Shifters are an endangered species. It's a recessive trait, and there are hardly any left."

I knew what recessive was from the genetics part of AP biology. It was kind of like the way blue eyes worked. It meant that if both parents were shifters, their children would definitely be shifters. But it also meant that the unexpressed shifter genes could be lurking in regular folks, and if two seemingly normal humans had a baby, there was a chance they could suddenly end up with a shifter on their hands.

"But if those genes are out there, they can still combine," I said. "It's hard to eradicate recessive genes."

"It gets easier if they all end up slaughtered."

My heart sank to my stomach. "Why?"

Sarmine shook her head. "Consider the spells we've done together, Camellia. What do we use for ingredients?"

"Well, apples, pears, cinnamon . . . Uh, so that's plant things. Salt, chalk . . . that's minerals, I guess. Lizard scales. Unicorn hairs . . ."

"All living things have a tiny bit of magic," she said. "Including . . ."

"Animals."

She nodded. "Most creatures just have a little, like frogs and rabbits. Some have a whole lot more, like pixies and unicorns. A shifter is in the latter category. He has as much magic as a unicorn simply because of who he is. If he shifts into frog shape, suddenly that frog is many times as potent. If he shifts into unicorn shape . . ."

"It's even more powerful than a regular unicorn. And so are his hairs." I took a deep breath, trying not to worry about Leo when I couldn't help him at this exact second. "But if he's so valuable, surely they'd keep him alive," I said.

"Certainly," said the witch. "Threaten him or his family till he shifts into a snake, gather his snakeskin when he sheds it. Force him to shift into a unicorn, shave him for his hairs." She stopped, pivoting to hold my gaze. "But now use your imagination and think what the most unscrupulous witches might do if they needed, say, a particularly potent eye of newt. . . ." The normally stoic Sarmine looked extremely upset, which means that there was the faintest trembling of her fingers.

I swallowed hard. My knees were wobbly and I actually thought I might faint. "Surely that's illegal," I said in a croak. "Doesn't anyone try to stop it?"

"Your father, for one," said Sarmine. Anger flashed over her face, as it generally did on the rare occasions she was willing to talk about losing him. "You see where it got him."

"But I *have* to help Leo . . ." I whispered.

She threw up her hands. "Leave him alone! Get out now. This is dangerous, Camellia."

My voice grew stronger. "Dad wouldn't have run away and neither will I."

"You want me to lose both of you?"

Small, quiet voice. "I want to fight for what I believe in. Just like you do."

She stopped cold. Silence as she wrestled with her own thoughts and fears. Finally she said, "I can't stop you."

"You have *always* told me the witch world is dangerous," I

pointed out. "Yet you always send me into it—to deal with the creep who raises unicorns, to courier ingredients home from Brazil. To try to find elf toenails, which I am still positive are mythical."

"You're correct," Sarmine said. "Not about elves, but about my usual parenting strategy." It was just like Sarmine to talk bluntly about her parenting strategy. "You are correct." She thumped one fist into the other. "I should stay the course."

"The course?"

"Why, to let you handle your part of the bet in your own way," she said. "With minimal assistance from me."

"Ah."

"I simply have an overreaction to this one issue. After all, you could have died during any number of the tasks I have assigned you in the past."

"Good to know," I said dryly. "Now. Please tell me how to protect Leo from the witches."

Sarmine considered. "I don't believe Esmerelda and Valda would torture him," she said. "They might force him to turn into a unicorn and shave him. But the temptation would always be there to go . . . one step more."

"And Malkin?"

Sarmine shook her head. "There are wicked witches and then there are *wicked witches,*" she said.

I knew what she meant.

I hugged the horrible book to my chest. I had to get to Leo. I had to save him. But from what? Surely his best chance was obscurity. I couldn't tell him to leave town. Where would he go?

He needed protection, night and day, until Sarmine's friends left town. They were too close to the high school with their little game. There was too great a chance they would pick up on it somehow. Sense his presence. And that was even if he didn't accidentally turn into a rabbit.

"I need to tell him how to not shift," I said. "Can you help me with that? He's been doing it accidentally."

But Sarmine shook her head. "That's not in witch lore, as you can imagine. Our manuals discuss how to *make* them shift. The best person to tell him would be another shifter. I'm presuming he doesn't know his birth parents?"

"His mother left him with his dads under mysterious circumstances," I said.

"Mm," said Sarmine. "I hate to tell you this, but your best bet is WitchNet."

Of course. I could google it, just like I'd said to Leo yesterday. But . . . "Why do you hate to tell me that?"

"Because you don't know who anyone is on the Internet," Sarmine said. "You might go to a page that appears to have helpful information, but it was instead put up expressly to monitor who might be searching for that knowledge. And then, that person would track your computer's location and know that someone from this town is looking for it. And who else would be looking for it but a shifter?"

My stomach flip-flopped further. "I hate to say it then, but people may already know. He's been researching this ever since it started happening a few weeks ago."

"On the human Internet?"

"Yeah."

She nodded. "He might be safe, then. There's so many fantasy books written about shapeshifters out in non-witch world that real queries may be lost in the shuffle. But I wouldn't count on it."

I straightened up. "What do I need to do?"

"Get him to stop shifting. And get these witches out of your high school before they discover him."

☾

I was so glad to have a bike again. The transit system wasn't bad—but you were at the mercy of its schedule. I wanted to get to school *now,* where I could do something about my worries.

The morning was frosty. I tucked my scarf into my jacket, dug my lock out of the RV garage, and wheeled the bike down the driveway. Devon had done a nice job fixing the tires and handlebars for me. I couldn't wait to find him and thank him. I might not be able to fly it yet, but I could *ride*.

Bike to school.

There was a funny clicking to the gears. I didn't mind it. The rhythm took my brain to another place.

click CLICK click click CLICK click click

save LEo save LEo save LEo save LEo . . .

The houses whisked by like they were on wheels, rolling away from me. It's true, you know. You don't forget how to ride a bike. You might forget the hand signals—and I reminded myself firmly to google them at school—but you don't forget how to go through the streets, on your own, around the hills and up. And up . . . Boy, I was out of shape.

I ended up walking my bike up the last hill to school. There . . . there really were a lot more bikes than normal. I wondered how many cars Sarmine had been exploding. I saw three more bike racks that I was sure hadn't been there last week, and they were completely full. Kids were laughing and chatting as they rolled up on their bicycles and locked them.

There was a pang as I suddenly thought that I could be like all those carefree kids, if my mother weren't a wicked witch. Goof off . . . Heck, I could *still* be like those kids. All I would have to do was decide I didn't care about the chaos caused by my mother's friends. I shook my head as I locked up my bike. No. When you live that close to evil, you see the world differently. Evil was not an abstract to me. I had tried to get off the wicked witch roller coaster before but it wasn't going to happen. I had a duty to help fix things.

Once inside, I cornered a sportsbally sort of guy and got directions to Leo's locker. I walked down to that wing—and saw the guy I really wanted to see at the end of the hall, stowing his guitar inside his locker.

This was where I wanted to be. *This* was what I wanted to be doing.

He looked up at me as I approached. "Devon," I said. "Thank you so much for fixing my bike."

A slow smile lit his face. "Happy to. I owe you one anyway."

I shrugged this aside. "You don't owe me anything."

He was smiling at me as if he couldn't look away. "Well, then. I wanted to."

That answer I liked a lot. It was a metaphorical step toward me. A step in the right direction. "I rode it all the way here," I said. "Except the last hill."

"Easier going home."

"Maybe we can race each other," I said, taking my own step forward. "Loser buys the winner ice cream."

"You are awfully fixated on ice cream for November," he said, teasing.

"Come back in summer and I'll race you for hot chocolate."

"Run through the sprinklers like we're kids again."

"Waiter!" I said in my best snooty voice. "Bring me another and don't skimp on the marshmallows."

"Mademoiselle is busy working on her tan. Requires cocoa."

"A bikini, a jug of cocoa, and thou," I mused, and I got that slow smile back from him.

"Hot chocolate and bikinis is the name of my next song," he said. "Not too racy to get past the censors . . ."

". . . but ever so slightly cheeky," I said. "So yes? The race is on?"

"Today's the tryout," he said. "We're first on the schedule if you want to come watch?"

"Of course!" I said. "If that won't throw you off?"

"I've been practicing," he said. "I've got this." He picked up his backpack. "Off to algebra?"

"Yes," I said. And then, of course, who was finally coming down the hall but a slightly-running-late Leo. "I can't," I amended. "I have to talk to Leo real quick."

He glanced at Leo in a way that I could only interpret as *assessing the competition,* then back at me. There were lingering traces of that smile I liked so much. "See you soon," he said.

Leo reached me right as Devon left. Perhaps there was a lingering smile on my face, too, because he also turned to look at Devon as if assessing the competition. "New guy?" he said.

I nodded. "Devon. Sophomore."

He shrugged dismissively and opened his locker. "What's up? Find anything out?"

"I don't have any good way to tell you this," I said in a low voice. "But I asked about the . . . thing you told me about yesterday?"

His face grew serious, matching mine. "And?"

"And you're in a lot of danger."

"Do you think you'll be able to help?"

"I don't know," I admitted. "But right now I'm your best bet." I patted my backpack. "I've got a book with me that might help us. But we'll need to go somewhere private. Do you have time after school?" Oh no, wait, I had agreed to meet Devon at three.

"After football practice, yeah," he said, shutting his locker. "They're short at this point in the season. So say, four?"

"Perfect." I turned to go and found he was falling into step beside me. Ugh, was this going to be one of those awkward, have-to-walk-down-the-hall-at-the-same-time things? And why were people smiling at us as we passed? Oh, they were smiling at him. He was popular. This was getting odd. "So, uh, where's your class?" I said. It was terrible small talk.

"East hall," he said as he waved back at a cheerleader.

Near mine. Crap.

I mean, not that he wasn't cute and all. And he seemed nice, I guess? But it was weird, weird, weird.

"So that guy you were talking to," Leo said. "I saw him with a guitar yesterday."

"Yep," I said. "He does that."

Silence between us.

A blonde in a pink suit with a green handbag fluttered her fingers at him as she sashayed past. She didn't even notice me. Leo whistled a low, appreciative whistle.

"Stop it," I hissed. "One of them."

"You're kidding, right?"

"Tell you later."

More silence. More high fives from preps and jocks. "Yo," one said to me.

"Yo," I said back.

It had been easy to talk to Leo yesterday, when I was helping him with his problem. Was that because I was the one in control then? I was the one trying to assess the situation and solve the problems. I was in my element.

Now I watched him work the hallway and felt insignificant.

It was a relief when we arrived at my algebra class. Leo waved at me as we parted, and I ducked into the classroom, feeling weird as hell and awkward as anything. At least Devon hadn't been watching. He was sitting at his desk, writing something on a piece of paper. He passed it underhand to me as I sat down and I unfolded it.

Samba for a Contrarian

I know a girl, when we're together
she's sunshine in tornado weather
a palm tree in the purple heather
hot chocolate in bikini weather

I looked up to find him with his head half-cocked, waiting to see if I liked it. "How are you this fast?" I said.

"Doggerel," he said. "Dashed it off." He buffed his fingernails on his shirt and blew. "By the way, did you know it's hard to rhyme things with weather?"

"Feather?" I said. "Leather?"

"Pleather?" stuck in the guy sitting behind me.

"Fine, fine," Devon said, holding up his hands and laughing. "You guys write the next verse."

"What's a samba?" I said.

"Oh. Like 'The Girl from Ipanema,'" he said, tapping out the rhythm for me. "I *know* a girl, when *we're* together . . ."

"And a contrarian?" I grinned up at him. "What exactly are you implying?"

"Not that you have unusual taste in drinks," he said. "Never that."

"Unusual taste in friends, more like it."

"Excellent taste in friends," he corrected me. "Charming and witty . . ."

"And not the slightest bit geeky," I teased.

"I *know* a guy, who *sings* the samba . . ."

"If you're quite through drumming," said Mr. Rourke to Devon, "will you please come to the front and work problem one? Only if the jam session is done, of course."

Devon went to the front, and I drummed the samba rhythm while I watched him work.

Halfway through algebra I realized Jenah wasn't in class with us, which was worrisome. Had Valda gotten her overnight, at home? The idea nagged me all the way until lunch, when I found her in the cafeteria, chatting with a happy-looking Henny.

"You look like you're up to something," I said. I plonked my tray of vegetable soup on the table and sat down with them.

"Jenah is the best," said Henny fervently, gesturing with her spoon. "The absolute best."

"Well," said Jenah modestly.

"She's mine," I said, teasing. "You can't have her. Now what happened?"

"Well, Jenah skipped her first hour for me," said Henny. She tore open her cracker packet, scattering crumbs. "And we made a plan of attack to first, talk to Leo, and second, bring down that horrible witch. Jenah said you gave Leo the love potion so he'd be, um . . . receptive. But I had to actually talk to him." She looked at Jenah for confirmation.

"Correct," said Jenah.

"So I did! I cornered him at his locker after first hour, and then I said, oh, I don't know everything I said, it's a blur. But I talked to him!"

"You did?" I said. "That's fantastic."

"And the best part is," Henny said, "that Jenah said that Adri said that Rafe said that Leo's been talking and texting about some new girl all morning. So that seems positive, right?"

"Er," I said. "Yes," I said.

"And then! Then Jenah came to my art class third hour—"

"How many classes have you skipped?" I said to Jenah.

Jenah waved a hand in dismissal. "One does the things that are important," she said.

"So she waltzed right in," said Henny. "And then Jenah started saying all this funny stuff to Esmerelda."

"Making up slang," said Jenah.

"And the class started laughing but you could tell Esmerelda didn't get it."

"I remembered something you told me a couple weeks ago," said Jenah, "about how witches look the age they feel inside."

"And then the boys begged to draw her again, and she 'gave in,' and then Jenah started asking all these drawing questions—"

"Like, do you want me to leave your eye bags in or take them out?" said Jenah. "What about the neck wrinkles? What about the liver spots on your hands?"

Henny was doubled over with laughter. "You had to be there," she said. "Especially when those things just started *appearing*. Finally someone held up a mirror."

"She ran right out of the room," chimed in Jenah with satisfaction. "Serves her right."

"Looked about like this," said Henny, holding up her tablet. The sketch showed a wrinkly old hag posing in a pink bikini, surrounded by dubious art students, including Henny. "Now that, I can post online. Everyone will think it's social commentary."

I high-fived Henny and Jenah. "You two are a great team," I said.

"I haven't even told you the best part," said Jenah. "After we left art, Henny came back with me to my locker. And there was a freaking bucket of bricks inside, ready to fall on me."

"I caught it," said Henny. She rubbed her shoulder. "Ow."

"We looked around for Valda in the kitchens just now but we couldn't find her—"

"Or smell her," said Henny.

"—and they shooed us out," said Jenah.

"Too bad," said Henny. She hefted up a brick and set it on the table. "I wanted to drop this on her toe."

"Second round of high-fives," I said. "I could not do this without you. Either of you."

"Honorary witch sidekicks?" said Henny.

"Honorary champions of the world," I said.

I whistled as I made my way to the auditorium after school. Devon was going to perform. Henny and Jenah had teamed up to fight crime. Sarmine had agreed to stir her own cauldron so I could talk to Leo. Everything was tentatively on track for the moment. Well, except for Leo. I squashed those fears firmly down. I couldn't be near Leo every second. He had, like, twenty football dudes surrounding him right now. I mean, sure, they weren't as powerful as a *witch,* but maybe they could tackle her.

Right now I was going to enjoy seeing the cutest boy-band boy in the world sing his music, and that was it.

I sat down in the auditorium, near the front, far off to one side where I could duck out the door to go meet Leo. There were quite a few other people in the auditorium—the judges, other band members waiting to go on, and supporters like me. Devon and his band were setting up on stage. The curtains were open and I could see well into the wings.

Devon fiddled with his guitar, tuning it, or pretending to. He looked a touch nervous to my trained-in-observing-Devon eye. But he was disguising it well.

"Blue Crush?" said one of the judges. "If you're ready?"

Devon took his place at the front. He placed his hands carefully on the guitar, keeping them grounded to control their shaking. He grinned around at his band as if everything was totally cool. It was all going to be in the bag.

And then, on the other side of the wings, I saw Malkin.

She also had a grin on her face.

Not a grin I liked.

"And one, two, three," shouted Devon. The drumbeat started.

It was too late to stop her, even if I could think of a graceful way to do it. Still, I reached into my backpack for my fanny pack.

Malkin waggled her fingers at me and I saw her hidden wand tucked under her rings.

The opening chords came from the bassist and the other guitar. The riff into "Liontamer."

Malkin swept her palm across some powder in her other palm, and pointed straight at Devon.

9

Who Malkin Had

I jumped up, fanny pack in hand. But I was far too late. Whatever the spell was, it had already been cast.

Devon opened his mouth to sing the first line. "She's a cool stick of butter—"

But on the word *cool* his voice broke, suddenly and horribly. It skidded up in the air and then went silent, leaving him gaping, like a fish.

There was giggling from the audience and his ears flushed red. Then he grinned, trying to make it a joke on himself, trying to be on the inside of the laughter. He tossed his hair back and did a goofy lion roar that drew applause and whoops while the rest of the band looped that section of music back to the beginning.

He opened his mouth again—and this time nothing came out. Zilch. Zip.

The band played a few more measures, and then, when it became clear that no singing was going to occur, petered out, one by one.

Devon croaked into the microphone, "I'm sorry—" It broke off in a cough and he turned away, coughing more.

The drummer stepped over the cords on stage and took the mic from Devon. "Sincerest apologies to all you party animals out there," she said. "Our esteemed singer seems to have something stuck in his throat."

More laughter. Nnenna rolled her eyes and shouted, "Are you ready to rock?" into the mic.

Whoops and cheers.

She eyed Devon. He waved a hand in dismissal at her, still coughing.

"We're gonna take five, girls and boys," said Nnenna. She looked up at the judges for confirmation. They seemed to be amused by her.

They whispered something, and then one of them said, "We had a cancellation at four. You can return in that slot."

"If your voice is feeling better," chirped the choir director. "We don't want strain."

"No strain," said Nnenna. "Got it." She looked at doubled-over Devon for confirmation, and he gave them a thumbs-up. "Peace out," she said, and put the mic back in the stand.

The band began to gather their things. As much as I wanted to go give Devon a hug, I made myself follow up on my Malkin sighting. She had disappeared in the confusion, of course. But maybe she was still nearby. I ran across the front of the auditorium, up and into the wings. Not there. Out the back door of the stage. The parking lot was half full, and I ran down the main lane, searching to see if she was hiding behind any of the cars. It was hopeless. She was a witch. She could be anywhere.

I went back to the auditorium. The next band was moving onto the stage, chattering, adrenalized by the sudden change of plans. Likewise, Devon was too wound up to sit down. He was pacing at the back of the house, drinking water. His band was setting down their gear a few rows away from him. The house lights were down and it was dim back there, lit only by the aisle lighting, and the ambient light from the judges' table.

I touched his shoulder. "Are you okay?" I said.

He looked ruefully at me. "No."

"It wasn't your fault," I said. I debated whether telling him that Malkin had done it would make him more nervous or less. "A coughing fit could happen to anyone."

"Right when it matters most?" He sank into a seat in the back row and my heart went out to him.

"Devon, I—I'm sorry."

Devon straightened. "You're not responsible." He attempted a smile. "Throat's feeling better already. It can't happen twice in a row—right?"

An idea was growing in the back of my head. Malkin might think she could ruin this boy's week, but he was indomitable. She hadn't even seen him with a demon in him. Devon was the most resilient boy I knew. Probably an odd thing to admire about your crush, but there you go. I liked the way he stood back up again, you know? Smash him, bash him, humble him, and up he got.

But even the most resilient guy could do with a bit of help.

"You stay here," I said. "I'm going to get you a hot tea with honey from the food carts. It can't hurt."

"All right," he said, and he took my hand. My hand suddenly felt very cold in his warm one, and I thought, is this the first time he's really touched me since that kiss a couple weeks ago? I mean, I held his waist on the bike, but now he was deliberately holding my hand. What does it mean if someone takes your hand? It is kind of intimate, isn't it? I mean, I might grab Jenah's hand, but I don't normally grab, say, Kelvin's. Devon squeezed my hand and released it, just as I thought that I was overthinking all of this and I should sink down in the chair next to him and never let him go. "Thanks," he said.

I nodded, quick, short, confused, then turned and fled. My breathing only started to calm as I left the building.

Malkin was not going to get away with this. She thought she could make his life miserable? I was here to prove her wrong.

I texted my mother as I walked over to the food carts. This was her chance to help me when I really needed it.

Need to help Devon recover singing confidence.

Malkin destroyed it.

Would the Power spell work for him?

I walked past a red truck that was laying on its side, apparently abandoned. A blue sports car that sagged like Jell-O. I sat down at the table I had cleaned yesterday. There were new scribbles of graffiti on it—a set of initials in a heart, a doodle of a car going up in a mushroom cloud. My phone cackled with the witch's text.

POWER SPELL USES THE PERSON'S OWN HAIR
THEIR OWN *WITCH* HAIR
THINK ABOUT IT

I guessed that meant no.

Do you know a spell that WOULD work? Can you text it to me?

SHOWSTOPPER SPELL
GIVES YOU UNBEATABLE CHARISMA
ONE PINCH PARSLEY
ONE PINCH POWDERED RUTABAGA

Wait a minute . . . These things AREN'T LABELED

HOW DO I KNOW WHAT POWDERED RUTABAGA LOOKS LIKE????!!

AUDIBLE SIGH
ONE PINCH GREEN CURLY STUFF IN FAR RIGHT POCKET
ONE PINCH TAN POWDER IN FIFTH POCKET FROM LEFT, MIDDLE ROW
ONE PINCH WHITE POWDER IN BLUE GLASS VIAL
ONE DROP WITCH SPIT

I waited to see if any further directions were forthcoming. When nothing more appeared, I figured that dosing Devon with my spit was as bad as it got. I texted a thank you to the witch, then ordered a hot tea from the coffee cart, finally breaking my ten. I took the paper cup back to my table to add the ingredients.

If it weren't obvious by now, the fanny pack the witch had given me didn't have just four or five pockets like regular people's packs probably did. It had been modified to have a ton of tiny pockets, some Velcroed, some snapped, some open. The pocket closest to the stomach had a row of tiny stoppered vials. There were a couple pockets empty, including a nice medium-sized one on the end that would be just right for that bottle of unicorn sanitizer I was always losing in my backpack. . . . No, no, no, I was *not* going to carry around a fanny pack. Just—no.

I measured the ingredients into the tea, and then—with a sigh—spat in it as well. Frankly, this was not the way I had wanted to exchange spit with Devon. I looked up to see the coffee cart guy looking at me with a frown. I looked away.

It was a quarter to four, so I hurried back to the auditorium. Devon was sitting in the back row, listening to the band play. Nnenna was sitting right next to him, which made me take an enormous dislike to her.

I had seen her a couple times now—the minivan yesterday, a brief glimpse at the Halloween Dance. She was the sort of person—like Jenah—who seems so completely, self-sufficiently cool that you have no idea how to measure up to them, and you feel way awkward by comparison. I mean, I don't feel that way with Jenah herself, because she's my best friend, but this was like a Jenah I didn't know.

Nnenna cocked her fingers at me as I approached but she didn't get up or otherwise acknowledge me. I guess she was focused on the music or something. I sat down across the aisle and waited patiently for the music to be finished. I don't really know music, I guess. They were loud. Nnenna seemed fascinated. Devon seemed fascinated. I seemed like a moron, sitting there with my doctored-up tea to help Devon.

After ages and ages the current band finally stopped. Nnenna leaned over and whispered something in Devon's ear and he laughed. Finally, finally, she got up. She had no idea that at that point, I loathed her.

She smiled pleasantly at me and said, "Staying to watch us?"

"Gee, I really wish I could," I said, "but I have to be somewhere else in about, oh, three minutes. I just wanted to bring over this 'tea' for you, Devon," I said. I had sworn that being an ethical witch meant I was going to ask everyone's consent to do things. But I couldn't exactly say it openly with miss super-cool drummer standing right here and not going away. "It's uh, my mom's secret recipe for singers," I told Devon, raising my eyebrows at him. He of all people should understand that code. "You know, to help soothe your throat and stuff. Get your, uh, *confidence* back." Malkin had tried to shake his confidence with the coughing. But she was gone now, and "unbeatable charisma" should solve any of Devon's problems. Heck, even if she did come back, maybe the judges would find his coughing *compelling*. Exciting. Musical.

Devon nodded at me, looking at the cup like he was trying to decide how much he trusted me . . . and how much he trusted my mom. Then he shrugged and took a big swallow. "Pretty good," he said.

The drummer grabbed his sleeve. "Come *on,*" she said. Over her shoulder she said, "Bring me one next time, too, willya?" She towed him up to the stage.

"Swing by tonight and tell me how you did," I said to his back, but I didn't know if he heard.

I really wanted to see him play. But I knew there was at least ten minutes of the judges scoring the last band and Blue Crush setting up and tuning again and everything else. And I had a shifter to save.

I turned and hightailed it back to the parking lot.

Leo was just trudging up the hill in the company of a lot of other football players. They sounded pretty cheerful, talking about the game on Saturday, the practice today, how many of their cars had suddenly died, et cet, et cet. A bunch of them peeled off to the bike rack as Leo came up to me.

"My savior," he said.

"Hush," I said. In a whisper I outlined what Sarmine had told me and watched his face fall. "So we really, really need to stop you from shifting," I said. "We need to figure out how you accidentally became a bunny. Where can we go to experiment?"

He wrinkled his nose. "My house is probably safe," he said. "Just, uh. Don't judge me by my house or anything."

"Don't worry," I said. "When your mom is someone who hangs snakeskins from the rafters, then you become the literal queen of not judging people by their parents."

Still, I wondered what his dads' house was like as we made our way out to Leo's car.

When I saw his car I started to get an inkling. I mean, I don't know cars or anything, but even I could tell that this was a very . . . shiny one. With a convertible top and a little pouncing jaguar figure on the hood. He looked at me looking at the car. "Don't say anything," he warned.

"Lips. Zipped."

We left the school property and drove higher into the hills, winding around until we turned off onto a side road that immediately ended in a gate. So maybe not so much a side road as a personal road. Leo pushed a button on the control panel of the car and the gate opened. We drove along a long winding drive dotted with tall black lampposts, until we arrived at a very lovely old house. He parked the car on the curve in the driveway and we got out.

"The rustic look," he said.

"It's nice," I countered. It really was; a century-old brick house with a long green lawn that disappeared into forest. "What do your dads do?"

"Software," he said. "I didn't get the gene."

"Ha ha."

We walked around to the back, where there were bushes and hedges and little nooks for patios and more long green lawn. Several more lampposts lit the way. The late afternoon was already shading into dusk; they would soon click on. There was a gazebo thing way at the back, only half visible in the forest. "This is pretty private," Leo said. We hiked around the hedges, up the slope of the lawn to the gazebo. It had been cold and windy all day, but the gazebo had some shelter for us.

I plopped my backpack down on an iron table and rubbed my hands. The gazebo had a porch swing and several cushioned chairs with old blankets on them and even a brazier in the middle that we could light if it got too cold. A box of long matches was tucked underneath it.

"Okay," I said to Leo. "Rabbit. Go."

He got a kind of funny look on his face, like he was trying to remember where he'd put a box of cereal. Finally he came back to reality. "Anything?"

I shook my head. "No little cotton tail. No long floppy ears. Nothing."

He sighed. "The times it's happened I've been . . . afraid." He looked down. "Tough to say that, but you know. I was definitely afraid."

"You think fear might be a trigger?"

"Something like that. Makes instinct take over."

"Hmm," I said. Then I lunged at him. "Boo!"

He took a step back, looking at me like I was crazy. But he didn't look afraid, and he didn't turn into a rabbit.

"You need to get into a state where you're not thinking about it," I said. "So your regular brain shuts down and your primal instincts kick in."

He raised his eyebrows. "Primal instincts, huh?"

I held my ground. "That is just the possibilities potion talking," I admonished him. "You don't mean that."

"If you say so."

"Now look," I said. "I'm going to try a spell on you."

He squared his shoulders. "It's weird," he said. "I feel an instinctive response to that. Like deep down inside I know you're my enemy."

"Well, I'm definitely not your enemy," I said. "But good. Maybe that will kick in." I pulled out the fanny pack from my backpack. He smirked at it. "Look," I said, and lied: "I need two red maple leaves and a pinecone with no pieces missing for this spell. Can you find me those things?" That would get him out of my hair.

He nodded and headed off, leaving me alone.

I pulled out a glass measuring cup from my backpack and measured the thyme and ginger for Ye Olde Mystikal Spelle of Great Power and Stuff into it. Now that I wasn't being attacked by a tornado or a Valda, I was going to try the improvements Sarmine had suggested.

I added the hair, the dragon's tear, and a couple tablespoons of unicorn sanitizer. The way that was disappearing, I would need more soon. I pulled out my disguised wand and stirred the mixture several times counterclockwise in the measuring cup. Maybe someday I could trade up to something more dramatic. Like . . . a copper bowl, shimmering with fire! A basin of hammered silver, said to have been used by the witches of Salem! The holy grail! But for now it was measuring cups.

I lit a match and dropped it in.

The unicorn hair vodka flamed off and died away. Scents of ginger and match fire wafted up to me. This time the combination smelled good.

The first time I had tried breathing in the powder, as the book had said. The second time I had tried ingesting it, as Sarmine had said. This time something else was suggesting itself to me.

I held the measuring cup to my face and breathed in the smoke and steam. The wind whipped around my face, fanning my hair back. I was seized with a sense of power, hard and fast this time.

I could do anything, beat anyone. I could bring them to their knees. I could crush them like a bug.

My conscience flickered deep inside, appalled at my violent thoughts. I squashed it down. I was doing this for Leo right now. I was *trying* to frighten him. Let the spell do its job.

I bent my head and breathed again. The smells of the spices filled my nose, my lungs, my hair. I was invincible.

I looked down at my ordinary outfit of T-shirt and jeans, my ordinary beat-up jacket. Even those had changed. They shimmered in the twilight, turning to black, to leather, to silver studs that ran up and down the sides of my legs. Perhaps the spell was pulling from my personal mental images of powerful people, people who didn't care what others thought. From Zolak the demon hunter. From Malkin.

Was this how Malkin always felt? That she could crush the world?

I am on the tall side anyway, but I felt even taller. As if I was both centered in my body and yet could see myself from above. As I moved, a shadow of myself flickered out behind me, moving in tandem with my arms and legs. I was darker, more substantial.

There was someone moving nearby.

Something weak.

Leo strode back into the clearing. "I got your leaves, Cam," he said. "You can do your spell—oh god." His eyes went wide and then he was gone.

In his place was a rabbit, standing in a pile of jeans and a letterman jacket.

Prey.

10

Shifts

The little brown rabbit bounded this way and that, trying to escape. I grinned as I chased it. It would tire soon and then I would catch it. A rabbit was no match for a human in the long run. Humans had stamina.

The rabbit dashed across the yard, zigzagging toward the house. I followed. Around the bushes, across the yard, up to the brick patio.

The rabbit was so little, so tiny. I could scoop it up in my bare hands and . . .

I ran smack into a man in a button-down shirt wearing strong cologne.

The scent filled my nostrils, replacing the smell of wood fire and ginger. I was jolted back into reality. My shadows and leather jackets faded slowly into my normal self.

"Oh my goodness," I said. "I'm so sorry, I didn't see you there."

"Who are you?" he asked, very politely for someone who has just been assaulted by a strange teeth-baring girl in his own backyard.

"Cam," I said, holding out a hand to shake. I hoped he hadn't seen anything funny. But it was dusk, and no one really expects to see someone's clothes mutate, so probably he hadn't noticed. "I'm here with Leo."

Leo, who was momentarily a rabbit. A very naked rabbit. He had bolted back toward the gazebo. I hoped he was in a fit state to come out soon.

The man relaxed. "Oh, lovely," he said. He had a salt-and-pepper mustache and a kind smile. "I'm delighted to see him bringing his friends around again. He's been . . . out of sorts the last few weeks." He adjusted his wire-rimmed glasses and smoothed out his shirt where I had bumped him. "And where *is* Leo?" he asked mildly.

Mm. "Leo?" I said to the backyard.

There was a tense waiting pause and then Leo came strolling out of the gazebo, tucking his shirt in. "Hi, Dad," he called from the back of the yard. "Hi, Pops."

"Pops" turned out to be a slight man with an equally warm smile, except Dad looked Caucasian, and Pops looked as though he might be Thai. He had just now come out onto the patio and was crossing to us. "Hi, kids," Pops said with a hint of an accent.

Leo made the introductions. "This is Richard, also known as Dad; Tanapol, also known as Pops; Cam, also known as a friend from school; and Leo, also known as Leo."

"Would your 'friend from school' care to stay for dinner?" said Richard.

I checked the time on my phone. The witch hadn't texted me yet, but there was a limit to how much I could push her. I was way behind on after-school chores, including her stupid cauldron-stirring.

"We're, uh, working on a science project thing," said Leo. "Outside. Gathering leaves."

"Lots of leaves this time of year," I said helpfully.

"But *after* you gather the leaves," Richard said patiently.

Leo looked at me. "Cam?" he said.

"I'd love to," I said. "But . . . my mom is kind of strict, and I still have a bunch of chores to do . . . can I take a rain check?"

"Anytime," assured Tanapol. He squeezed his partner's shoulders.

"Run along, kids," said Richard. "Go do your . . . 'science project.'"

"Have fun," said Tanapol. They both beamed at us.

Leo and I trudged across the lawn. The evening was dark and the mood was awkward.

"Parents," he said.

"Yeah," I said.

We left it at that for a little bit.

We sat down on the porch swing in the gazebo and I finally broke the silence. "Well," I said heartily. "We know you can turn into a rabbit. Now we need to figure out how to have you *not* turn into a rabbit."

"Brilliant deduction, Holmes."

I tugged a book out of my backpack. "So we might have to approach this backward."

"What is that?" He flicked on a flashlight just as I tried to cover up the title. "*Thirteen Ways to Force a Shifter* . . . What is that thing?"

"Don't judge me by my parents," I warned. "And I'm not going to let you see some of the stuff in this book. But I did find one interesting thing." I flipped toward a page near the end that I had bookmarked. It said:

"The ability to shift lies completely in the mental control of the shifter. However, it is true that at times of high stress (such as if you are coercing a shifter to shift) the necessary control may be hard for the shifter to summon. It is recommended at that time to try an herbal remedy. The scent of cardamom is known to be an aid to shifting."

"Coercing?" he said.

"Cardamom," I said firmly. "Think about cardamom. Do you have some?"

"My dads cook a lot," he said. "I don't think it's something they use frequently, but we might have an old jar sitting around. Let me run in and check." He loped off, leaving me sitting in the dark and cold November evening. The gazebo would be really nice with a fire going in the brazier, I thought. A couple forlorn jack-o'-lanterns sat off to the side, their faces falling in. I could imagine the smell of roasting pumpkin. It would be lovely to sit here with no worries to speak of. No witches to stop from ruining the high school. No witches to stop from destroying my new friend's life.

No worries that *I* would destroy Leo.

I fiddled with one of the maple leaves, breaking it into bits. Okay to scare him a little bit, I admonished myself. Not okay to eat him. Go easy on that Power spell.

Leo returned with the cardamom and sat down on the porch swing next to me, sending it rocking. He stilled the swing with his feet as he held out the jar.

"So we don't know how to make you *stop* turning," I said, "because witches aren't exactly concerned with that."

"You'd think they might be," said Leo. "I mean, what if they caught a shifter and he turned into a bear and ate them?"

"You have a totally valid point," I said. "It does say you can use a pentagram to contain the shifter, so perhaps that's what they use. But that won't help you. At any rate, what you need to know is how, if you're about to turn into a bunny, you can stop it and come all the way back. And it doesn't tell us that. So we'll try the cardamom and see if that sparks a change. It's as good a place as any to start."

I held out the spice jar to him and he took it. He looked over the jar at me. "Cam," he said seriously, and his usual smirk was gone. "I don't know how to thank you for this."

I shrugged uncomfortably. "It's nothing."

"It's not nothing. You're dropping everything to help me, and you barely know me. It makes me feel so . . . safe, I guess, even though I'm in danger. To know that someone with as much power as you is willing to try to help me."

I snorted. "I am not powerful," I said. "I am the beginningest of beginning witches. I barely know any spells."

He touched my hand. "Don't sell yourself short. I saw what you looked like when you did that spell just now. That wasn't a different person, Cam. That person is also you."

I swallowed. I didn't know what to say to that so I just motioned to the cardamom. "Let's do it."

Slowly he uncapped the spice jar. He leaned over and breathed it in.

The first thing I noticed was the spice jar falling. Reflexes made me reach out and grab it.

The next thing my reflexes made me do was run.

Standing before me was a giant wolf.

☾

I raced across the lawn with all my might. The wolf tore after me. I doubled back and forth. "Leo!" I shouted behind me. "Leo, snap out of it!"

The wolf doubled back around and chased me into the deep forest that backed onto his property. I dodged in and out of the trees. I could hear my breathing, hard and fast. The wolf bayed and followed behind me, breaking off twigs and branches. My foot caught a tree root and down I went, hard. I rolled over onto my back—

—and suddenly the wolf was on top of me, licking my face all over.

I scrabbled backward even as my heart slowed. "You're not a wolf," I said, laughing hysterically. "You're a big dog."

He gave my face one final lick and sat back on his haunches. His tongue lolled out in a doggy laugh. With shaky fingers I held out the jar of cardamom—and then yanked it back. "Wait a minute. Clothes." I led him back to the gazebo and threw one of the old blankets at him before setting the cardamom in front of him. He snorted in a giant doggy whiff as I turned around. There was the flappy noise of a dog shaking his head, ears and tongue snapping out, and then—

Boy laughter rumbled behind me. "You should have seen the look on your face."

"About like you, just before you became a bunny?"

"So we're even." There was rustling behind me as he dressed.

My face was slimy where he had dog-kissed me all over, and I rubbed it off with my sleeve, trying not to read anything into it other than that dogs have no manners. "Good thing your dads weren't out here," I said.

"They've seen worse," he said, and I could hear the laughter in his voice. "Okay, you're in the clear."

I turned around to find him with his jeans on, busy pulling on his shirt and jacket. "Better get the leaves out of your hair."

He brushed them off, sobering. "But why did I become a dog?"

"I don't know," I said. "What were you thinking about?"

"The last animal I had in mind was a bear," he said, "because we were talking about becoming a bear and eating a witch."

"Hate to break it to you," I said, dusting mud and leaves off my jeans. "But that was no bear."

"No," he mused. "I remember thinking that I would have to really envision the animal to turn into it, and I couldn't remember the last time I'd seen a bear, not in real life or anything. So then I was remembering the wolves at the zoo, and then how my neighbor had a dog I always thought was a wolf growing up."

"Huh. Did this dog look like your neighbor's dog?" I said.

"I didn't stop to look in a mirror."

"If you try again I could take a picture . . ."

He looked around. "Too dark," he said. "We might have to table this for another day." The grin flickered back into place. "Unless you want to go up to my bedroom and try shapeshifting there while my dads smile significantly and tiptoe around the hallway."

"I'll pass, thanks."

He nodded. "I'll take you home."

We gathered our stuff and headed out to his car. He took us down the long driveway and out onto the twisty roads that ran down the hills from his house.

It was quiet for a few minutes. Dark. The inside of his excessively nice car was excessively nice. Sort of like being cradled in a cocoon of handcrafted artisanal hummingbird feathers and butterfly wings. You could feel the old money wrapping you in a nest of comfort. And Leo, too, was as comfortable as his car. Ease and comfort rolled off him. This was not one of those football players who was going to end up flipping burgers in a few years. This was one who was going to go to an expensive college and play with his equally moneyed friends for fun. And some of those boys were nice and some of them weren't. But I thought this one was.

The realization that I had been looking at a pair of very close lights in the side mirror for about a minute jolted me out of my reverie. "Is that car really close to us?" I said. I turned to see the outlines of a giant SUV right on our tail. The lights blinded me and I couldn't tell who was driving it.

"I'll speed up," Leo said. "This car is faster than theirs." He put his foot down and we accelerated. The roads were pretty darn curvy and he whipped around the next curve so fast that I grabbed the handle above the door.

"You could pull off in a cul-de-sac," I suggested.

"And let him win?" said Leo. "It's probably one of the guys. They think it's funny. But you can't let them win." He whipped around the next curve. The SUV tilted a little as it kept pace with us. "Whoever it is, their car doesn't take corners the way mine does."

I held onto the handle tightly, my life flashing before my eyes. "Soooo maybe it doesn't matter if he wins," I suggested.

"Sure, sure," said Leo. But he didn't slow down.

"Is that—are those blades on his car?" I said.

Leo's eyes widened. "I haven't seen that before."

"Maybe we could turn off now? I mean there are limits to these chicken games, right?"

"I can't turn off here," he said. "He's actually going after us. If I go into a cul-de-sac this jerk will catch up with us."

The SUV bumped the back of our fender, jolting us. Leo growled as he pushed down on the pedal.

"I don't think this is some crazy football player," I said. "Occam's razor and all that."

"You think . . ."

"A witch. Yeah." The car bumped us again. "Oh god."

"All those destroyed cars," said Leo. "And we're next." We skidded past a poor kid walking his bike up the hill and he yelled at us as we squeaked past him.

I didn't want to tell him that the other cars were probably the handiwork of my mother. "Those cars were destroyed in the lot," I pointed out.

"Then what makes this car so special?" His mouth was set tight and his knuckles were gripping the wheel and it was suddenly clear what they hoped to obtain.

"It's *you,* Leo." The words burst out in realization. "The fear trigger. Trying to get you to turn into something. Whoever it is suspects you're a shapeshifter."

He glanced at me. "If I turn into something right now we wreck in a fiery crash."

I swallowed. "Don't think of any animals. Think of uh, majestic ice floes."

"Polar bears," he shot back.

"Ocean beaches."

"Sharks."

"Daffodils!"

"Bees!"

I refrained from yelling at him, as that seemed likely to stress him out. "You are going to drive around this curve like a calm, collected *person*"—the car bumped into us again, rattling our teeth—"until we reach civilization, which can't be much farther."

"Three more curves," he said. "There's a well-lit grocery store. We can pull off there till the witch drives on."

"This is a nice relaxing drive in the country," I said through gritted teeth. I tried to prepare for what might happen if he turned into a rabbit at seventy miles an hour. Would it be better for me to pull the parking brake, which I could reach? To unbuckle my seat belt and clamber across, grabbing the wheel? That seemed like a Really Bad Idea for a lot of reasons, not least of which was that the witch hadn't let me take driver's ed yet.

Three curves. Two curves.

The SUV swung wide, trying to pass us. Leo swung his car into the middle of the road, blocking her way. "Look out," I shrieked, and he swung back into his own lane as another car passed us going the other way.

Last curve.

The streetlights and grocery store were visible up ahead.

Also visible was a police car.

The traffic light was yellow.

At the very last second, Leo took a sharp right into the parking lot, slamming on the brakes. The SUV zoomed on past and through the intersection.

Across the way, the police car put on their lights . . . and swung out after the SUV. We were smaller fish to fry, apparently. I breathed a huge sigh of relief.

Leo's knuckles released their death grip on the steering wheel. He shook his fingers out. And then he slammed his hand on the dashboard several times, cursing whoever it was who had ruined his car.

I waited patiently until his anger wore itself out.

"No rabbit?" I said. "No wolf?"

"None of the above." He shook his head. "My poor car. I don't even know what the dads are going to say." He opened the door and leaned out to take a picture of the scraped and slashed metal. His fingers flashed on the phone as he texted the picture—possibly to the dads, but more likely to friends, I thought. Then he tossed the phone on the dash and sighed. "C'mon, let's get you home before either the witch or the cop comes back. Where's your house from here?"

I gave him directions, and sedately he drove me the rest of the way home.

"Do you really have chases like that down the streets?" I said. It wasn't behavior I'd associated with him so far.

"Yeah," he admitted. "I mean, usually not with a date in the car."

I ignored that particular word choice. "So you have some experience with controlling yourself in high-stress situations, I guess. Between that and football." It seemed like that should help him with his shifter problem, even if sometimes he was the person to get himself into the high-stress situation. What was it that made a bunch of dudes start acting like dudebros? Even Leo, the least dudebro football player I had ever met, apparently still had that dudebro thing that came out once in a while. I drummed my fingers on my leg. "I wonder why this shifting only started now. Did you just have a birthday or something?"

"Like on my seventeenth birthday, woo-woo stuff starts happening? Yeah, no. My birthday was in September. I mean, I guess it could have started then, for all I know. If I need the right circumstances for it to happen automatically."

It was a puzzle. I wished that witches had helpful information about shifters instead of just ways to destroy them. But then, maybe there were more tidbits buried in the book. I should read the whole thing, as much as I hated to spend time reading about the sort of horribly vicious things that were in that book.

Leo pulled his poor battered car into my driveway and I grabbed my backpack. I leaned over and squeezed his hand. "Don't worry," I said. "We'll beat this."

He didn't let go of my hand. "Thanks, Cam," he said. His eyes were dark and his gaze intense. "Your help means a lot to me." Slowly he leaned toward me—

"Uh, yeah, you're welcome," I said, slipping out of his grasp and opening my door. "Anytime."

He nodded at me, seemingly unaffected by my awkward rebuff. Grinned, even. "Another time, maybe."

I let out a long whoosh of air as he drove off. Then turned to go to my front door.

Sitting on my stoop was Devon.

11

Things Suck

"Uh. Hi!" I said brightly. I looked after Leo's retreating car, looked back at Devon. Devon had obviously very definitely seen me get out of Leo's fancy, if a bit smashed up, car. I wondered how much else he had seen. "How are you, uh, doing?"

Devon shrugged. He stood as if to go collect his bike from the driveway, but I was standing closer to his bike than he was, so he stopped as if there was an invisible force field around me. He looked distinctly uncomfortable. "I was going to ask you for some help."

"Join the club," I muttered.

"And you don't have a regular phone, so—" He broke off and tried a smile at me. "Join the club, huh?"

It was clearly an invitation to tell him what I was doing with the guy in the fancy car. But I couldn't tell anyone Leo's secret, because the more people that knew, the less safe he was. It was a tailor-made situation for telling Devon something like, "I'm helping Leo with his biology homework." But I wasn't going to lie to Devon. "I am helping Leo with something," I said, "but it is secret witch business and I honestly can't tell you because the fewer people that know, the better. I would if I could."

"Leo?" he said. "I think I saw him this morning, but . . ."

Sometimes it was hard to remember that Devon had just transferred to our school a couple weeks ago. So much had happened since then. "He is a junior who is on the football team," I said. And then, awkwardly, I said, "And he is just a friend." It seemed important to get that out there, but I will admit, I maybe blushed a little as I said it because it was becoming increasingly clear that Leo might not mind if it was something more. But it was dark, so maybe my awkwardness wasn't as visible as I thought it was.

"Oh," said Devon.

Maybe it was. I wrinkled my nose. How had I ended up with a football player, who—let's be honest here—only liked me for the fact that I could save him from some wicked witches, and maybe also because I had given him a sort of love potion, and that was the guy who wasn't afraid to flirt? And then there was Devon, my Devon, my sweet boy-band-boy Devon, who I thought liked me, but who maybe simply didn't have the self-confidence of a Leo? Of course, that meant that Devon also didn't engage in high-speed car race games of chicken. "You wouldn't ever go seventy down a mountain just because some other guy was also doing it, would you?" I said.

Devon looked at me like I was nuts. "I don't even have a car," he said.

"Yeah." I touched his arm, hoping that would defuse the tension. "So, what did you want help with?"

"Well, first to *offer* to help," he said. "We could spray paint your bike this weekend. If you want. We've got a bunch of spray paint in the garage from one of my dad's projects. You said you liked purple, I think . . ."

"I do like purple," I said. "Particularly as contrasted with avocado green and burnt orange. That would be wonderful."

"Not gonna lie, the retro look is amazing," he said. "But maybe you need a fresh start. . . ." He trailed off, looking at me.

"Oh god, my bike," I said. "My actual bike. I left it at the school when I got a ride with Leo. I guess I'm not used to having it."

Hurt flashed across his face and was gone in an instant. Look, if you were chased by a bunch of witches down a mountain you might forget your bike, too. But the fact that he had just helped me fix it, late at night, and I had stranded it to go off in some boy's fancy car . . . I didn't even know how to fix all the mistakes I was making. You know? When you say something stupid, and you try to dig yourself out but you just keep going in further? That's what this whole week was.

"So, uh. Why did you come by?" I said. "Right, bike. I mean. Well, I'll get it back."

"Also you said to come by later," he said. "To tell you how we did."

We were standing three feet apart but it felt like three miles. "I *did* want you to come by," I said. "I mean, I do. I am currently wanting that. I want to know how you did."

"We squeaked in. We got third. We get to play at the football game on Friday."

"That's wonderful," I said.

"I know you helped me. Something with that hot tea, right? It was pretty cool. I just sang. Everyone was riveted. Standing ovation. We only got third because the rules said they had to dock points for the first disaster."

"I will help you for the game," I promised.

"You will?" There was relief on his face. "I didn't want to impose, but . . ."

"Anytime," I assured him. "Look, I mean, I want to tell you about Leo—"

He hurried on as if he didn't want to hear what I had to say. "The band was great, too. They rallied around. Nnenna said she'd roar if I got stuck again."

Was that code, bringing up Nnenna? Was he trying to tell me not to tell him I didn't like Leo? Because he was going back to his old friend Nnenna? This was ridiculous. However painful a frank discussion was about to be—and it might be very painful—we should be able to cut through this whole mess by talking to each other. I wasn't going to let Devon go without a fight.

I took a breath—

And that's when a bicycle zoomed out of nowhere onto the driveway and came to a dead halt right between us.

A curvy, black-clad figure got off the bike. She looked mad.

"Henny," I said. "What on earth are you doing here?"

"I think I'd better go," said Devon.

"No," I said. "Wait."

"I can't believe you," said Henny to me. "You cheat, you liar, you, you . . . temptress!"

"Hey now," said Devon.

"I trusted you," said Henny, her voice rising. "I trusted you—"

But I knew where that statement ended and it was in words that rhymed with "dove notion." I didn't think it was going to help my case with Devon at all if he heard that I was busy giving Leo love potions.

"It's okay, Devon," I said to him. "I'll be fine." I waved him off.

He picked up his bike and started to wheel it down the driveway. But he didn't move quite fast enough.

"I *trusted* you to give him that love potion," Henny was shouting. "And as far as I can tell, nothing's happened except *you* going off with him to his *house*. If anything, I think he likes *you*."

At the bottom of the driveway I saw Devon freeze. His shoulders tightened.

"He doesn't like me," I assured her quickly and loudly. "He doesn't."

Devon swung one leg over his cargo bike and rode off. I guess he didn't want to hear any more. My heart was cracking in a million pieces.

"Really, Henny," I said on autopilot. My words were here but my heart was going down the street on a cargo bike. "He doesn't like me. He just likes that I can help him." I didn't know for sure that that was all it was but it seemed like a good thing to say. True, things are never black or white, but frankly, I have a realistic assessment of my good looks and charm, which are perfectly adequate, but not necessarily "football star of the high school" level, you know? "Anyway, it's not even a real love potion, Henny. I, uh. I decided that was unethical."

Henny's eyebrows shot up. "You didn't think it was so unethical when you were begging me not to put you in my comic."

This was totally unfair. I blinked back my tears and folded my arms. "Henny Santiago-Smith, it would be just as unethical for you to rat me out to the world and compromise my safety, and you know it. Now look, the kind of potion it is, is a sort of 'opening you up to new possibilities' potion. And it's fine. Leo made me try it, too . . ." Hmm, maybe I shouldn't have said that.

"He did *what*?"

"And I can swear to you that it doesn't cause any harm. It also doesn't make anybody fall in love with people they can't fall in love with. I can see that now. Maybe if you saved his life or something it would be different. But as it stands, I'm really truly sorry, Henny. He's just not in love with you."

Henny rocked back on her heels. Her black-clad shoulders slumped. "I know," she said almost inaudibly. Oh good, *now* she knew how to be quiet. "It was too much to hope for, anyway. How could he be in love with me? I've never done anything awesome. Even my comic has hardly any readers."

"Frankly, even if your comic had a million readers, I don't know if that would be the sort of thing to impress him, Henny," I said. "He's not that sort of guy." And then I had a really random, inspired brainstorm, the sort that comes around only once in a long while. "Henny," I said. "You keep saying the problem with your comic is that you've been fixated on Leo for a year now. You need to move on. Your *readers* want you to move on. You know what you need?"

"A sudden plot twist involving witches?"

"*You* need to take the love potion," I said.

She looked dubious. "But I already have someone I'm in love with."

"And it's not going to work. I'm sorry, but it isn't. Sometimes you have to accept that and move on." Big words coming from me, really. Was I supposed to accept that Devon didn't like me and move on? But no, Devon did, really. Deep down, under all his worries and all my stupid missteps. Didn't he?

I focused on Henny, because I might be able to solve her problems if I couldn't solve mine. "This will open your eyes to who else might be around the high school. The high school is literally full of guys."

"Half-full," corrected Henny.

"At any rate, don't you *want* to move on?" I said. "Don't you want to see who else might be out there?"

"I . . . I . . . don't know," Henny said, a stumble in her voice. "I've been so focused on this one thing, I mean, this one person."

"Henny," I said. "You can't do that anyway. You've got to live your life for you." I had an eerie flashback to Halloween week, telling that to the zombie girls who were magically crazy for Devon. "Don't think of it as letting something go. Think of it as an exciting new direction for your comic. Imagine what it would be like to have so much new material to write about. If you open yourself up to possibility, maybe you can go on a bunch of dates! You can write about them. Think how much fun that would be to read."

"Well . . ." said Henny. And then she straightened up. "All right. I'll try the love potion."

"Good choice." I pulled the honey bear with its last dose from my bag. There was a pang as I handed it over. It would have been nice to use it to smooth over my problems with Devon.

She tipped it into her mouth, squeezing to get the last drops.

"How do you feel?" I said.

She blinked at me. "Actually . . . better. Like anything could happen." She looked at me with new eyes. "Anything at all."

"Nothing needs to happen exactly right now," I reminded the second person this week. Giving out love potions was getting tiresome.

"This could really open up new potentials," she mused.

"You can't mention the honey in your comic, though," I said.

"What if I pretended it was a fantasy comic? Like magical realism?"

"Slippery slope," I said.

"Okay," she said. "I'm just trying to figure out how to throw this curveball at my loyal readers, all five of them. Like do I say one day I woke up and decided to date more people?

"Sure," I said. "Like a New Year's resolution, but in November. Or a bet. Or some final straw that happened." I waved my arms, spitballing ideas. Anything to make her get the idea and go home and write her comic and stop destroying my life. "Like you pretend you saw your crush—I mean, you don't use his real name, do you?"

Henny shook her head.

"Well, pretend you saw him with another girl."

"Like you?"

I reddened. "*Not* like me," I insisted. "The point is, you despaired, you moaned, you whined, you carried on." A lot. "And then you went home and broke all your colored pencils in half and decided it was time to move on."

"Do I really have to break my pencils in half?"

"No," I reassured her.

She sighed. "I'm sorry I yelled at you."

"Yeah," I said, trying not to think about Devon. "Just go home and get some sleep."

She cycled off and I trudged up the steps to go inside. Everything that had just happened hit me like a ton of bricks: a cascade of little adrenaline crashes from the aftermath of the car chase, of seeing Devon, of the argument with Henny.

The witch was inside, reclining on the couch with a martini, watching the glass tubes as if they were the most epic soap opera that ever soaped. Wulfie was curled against her leg, conked out for once. "Goodness, that was exciting," Sarmine said. "First Esmerelda's plummeted—"

"That would be Henny, when she found out that I was off somewhere with Leo," I said.

The witch raised her eyebrows at me. "Leo?"

"The shifter."

"My word, how cliché."

"Whatever, go on."

"Then a few minutes ago, Malkin's sunk like a stone—"

"Devon, also finding out that I was off somewhere with Leo," I said.

"And then Esmerelda's bobbed up and down in the glass and finally went to a middling level."

Well, that was good, I guess. "I gave Henny a plan of action," I said. "But I didn't have a chance to explain to Devon. He was probably pretty high earlier, after placing in the Battle of the Bands finals."

"Oh yes," said Sarmine. "He's been bobbing up and down all afternoon. Better than TV."

She sipped her martini and I laid down flat on the floor. Worst. Day. Ever. And Devon would probably never forgive me. I groaned, staring up at the ceiling.

"Do you want a martini?" said Sarmine.

"No," I said. "God, what is wrong with you?"

"It is far more important for witches to learn how to hold their alcohol than to learn . . . oh, what are those boring things you do at school?"

"Biology? English?"

Sarmine swept this aside. "I can't tell you one good thing I learned in high school."

"Except how to make money selling love potions," I said. I covered my eyes. "Oh god. This is the worst week ever. Why did I even get involved?"

"Ready to give up being a good witch?"

"No," I said to the ceiling. "It's just a few roadblocks." I tried to find my inner optimism. "Look, if I got Henny pointed in the right direction, then all that's left to win the bet is to fix Devon and everyone will be above the midpoint. And if I make Devon a new packet of Showstopper for Friday and that unbeatable charisma helps him win the band battle, I bet he'll forgive me. Do you have the actual spell for me? I need to start labeling my pouches."

Sarmine nodded. "It's in one of my books upstairs. I'll leave it out for you."

"Good," I said. I propped up my head and watched the soap opera of thermometers. Malkin's was pretty low, Esmerelda's was middling, and Valda's was reasonably high. But Sarmine's was the highest. It made me glad to know that she was telling the truth, that we were repairing our relationship. Amid all the disaster, there was one thing I could count on. My own mother did not have it in for me.

Whee.

There was a white rectangle on the table next to the thermometers. Out of the corner of my eye I thought it was somebody's playing card for a moment, until I realized it was the envelope that Malkin had tossed on the table. I stared at it. Why hadn't she told us what she was putting in the pot?

"Sarmine," I said slowly. "What is in that envelope?"

Sarmine was instantly alert. She picked up the envelope, carried it over to the kitchen light, and peered through it. I followed her. "I can't make it out," she said finally.

"I feel like it's a clue." I took it from Sarmine.

"It's sealed against magical tampering," she pointed out.

"But not against mundane tampering," I said, as I put the kettle on to boil.

A few minutes later I was holding the envelope over the steam coming up from the teakettle. "They always say this works in books," I said. "Ouch." Funny thing about steam. It's hot. I nudged the flap back and forth until finally the glue loosened enough for me to slide it open. "We have a glue stick somewhere, right?" I said. "So I can reseal it?" Sarmine nodded.

Carefully I reached in and found a piece of thick, glossy paper. My heart was beating more quickly than it should be. I mean, it probably just said, "Congrats! You win a kraken tentacle," or something. I slid it out.

It wasn't a piece of paper. It was the back of one of the playing cards.

I flipped it over. Instead of a picture of a student there was a big question mark.

Underneath it read: *Shapeshifter.*

"Malkin knows," I said. "She knows he's been here all along."

Sarmine paced. "Why would she set this all up?"

"Maybe to get close to him. Maybe she doesn't know who he is yet."

Sarmine looked at me. "Do you think she does now? How careful have you been?"

"Very," I said. I tried not to think about all the times I'd said "were-rabbit."

"You know it's not just him in danger," Sarmine said. "It's his fathers, and everyone he cares for."

I breathed. I thought maybe pacing would be good for me, too. "She set this whole *game* up to distract us," I said. "You haven't seen her for years, have you?"

"No," said Sarmine. "She's been trying to track down the last known lindworm for ages. A fool's errand."

"Are you *sure* they are extinct?" I said. "What does she want it for?"

Sarmine shrugged. "Supposedly a witch once used the fangs of the lindworm to cause the Black Plague," she said. "Or something along those lines. Lindworms really are extinct, and I don't pay any attention to ingredients that you can't access." Sarmine was practical like that.

"Well, whatever she was doing in the past, now she's here," I said, trying to dismiss thoughts of a giant plague. "And she's trying to get *him*. Random Do-Badders Club/nostalgia/old times' sake: my foot."

"It does look that way," Sarmine admitted.

I rounded on her. "She was *your* friend once, wasn't she? In college?"

"More of a colleague," hedged Sarmine. "Witches tend to clump together whether you want them to or not. We're all from around here originally."

"I thought you moved us to this town when I was little because you were looking for a phoenix hidden somewhere nearby."

"Certainly," said Sarmine. "And I wanted a fresh start, after we lost your father. But, you understand, we're only talking a move of twenty miles. I enjoy this area. There's a number of nice small and medium towns, and we can go to the city if you wish to meet more witches." She sniffed. "Not that anyone would want to do that; I see quite enough of them as it is."

"That's for sure," I said. "Well, clearly it's more important than ever that I keep Leo safe. Especially because at least one witch already knows about him, or has a good guess. So, ditch worrying about the rest of the nonsense and focus on Leo, at least until everyone leaves."

"I wouldn't give up on keeping the other students happy," Sarmine pointed out. "Considering what the prize for winning is."

"What if I just reject that?" I said. "You can't win a person."

"Reject a handshake sealed with witch spit?" Sarmine looked shocked.

"Sometimes it's more ethical to renege on your agreement," I said.

"Fine," said Sarmine, "but don't blame me when you get seven years of bad luck."

"I thought that was breaking a mirror," I said.

"No, it's breaking a witch spit bond," she said.

"Ugh, please stop talking about witch spit," I said. "And, regardless, Leo's life is more important than my bad luck. You can't win a person."

Sarmine nodded. "That's fine and ethical and all. But try telling that to Malkin. I'd say your best bet is still to win this game."

I groaned. "Fine, fine. I'll continue saving the world. Happy? Just be sure to text me the Showstopper spell tonight so I have a chance at fixing Devon. I'm going to bed." I plodded up the stairs and collapsed in a heap on the bed. Reached over to turn off the light, and as I flipped the switch, remembered that I hadn't done any homework.

My howls of frustration sounded about like Wulfie's that night.

I woke Thursday morning with the uncomfortable feeling that things had gone really wrong. It didn't take long for the events of yesterday to wash over me. "Ugh," I said, and pulled the pillow over my head. Maybe I could just sleep until Saturday morning. Wake when the contest was over.

Wulfie jumped into bed with me and nuzzled his nose under my elbow. I squeezed him tight. "Oh, Wulfie," I said. "It must be so much easier to be three years old and not even be human most of the time. Being a human stinks." He licked my face and it reminded me of Leo. I sighed. In the middle of everything else, I had to make the Leo thing stop. I was being put in an increasingly awkward spot. I had to be close to him to help him, but it was leading me into a place that I didn't like.

I got out of bed and trudged downstairs to let Wulfie out. Sarmine was still in bed asleep. I didn't bother waking her. I didn't have the energy to learn any new spells. Especially not if they were just going to backfire on me. The book with the Showstopper potion was open on the counter and I put a bookmark in and took that with me to work through later.

I went outside to get my bike and remembered I didn't have it. Excellent. Anything else the universe would like to throw at me?

I decided to walk to school for a change. I mean, I didn't have morning chores, didn't have a witch to help me with spells . . . no point sitting around moaning, waiting for the bus. I had felt pretty good after the bike ride yesterday. More fully awake. Maybe walking to school would jog something loose in my brain.

It was cold today, but not too cold. The kind of gray fall morning where you see your breath and you smell wood smoke and you remember that winter is on its way. Leaves rattled loose around me, yellow and orange and red, drifting down the gutters. I began walking up the hill. Surprisingly, I started seeing other students here and there as I got closer. I hadn't realized so many people walked to school. There were bicyclists on the road as well, and I saw one of the seniors go past on a cute little motor scooter.

And then I saw the broom.

The *translucent* broom.

I wouldn't have noticed it if I hadn't been walking. It was leaning against some tall bushes at the very edge of the school property, and between the wood color of the broom and the translucence, it blended in pretty well. I moved closer, cautiously, studying it. This must be what invisible eel paste looked like, after it had mostly worn off.

But mostly, if there was a broom, there must be . . . yes. There was a translucent hand holding on to the top of the broomstick. Valda was conferring with someone in the bushes.

Now would be a good time to have my own eel paste. Instead I moved as close as I dared, my ears pricking forward to catch the conversation.

". . . if you're double-crossing me with Malkin again, I swear I'll pull your hair out," said the low, grumpy voice of Valda.

"Daaahhling, when would I have time to do that?" purred the other voice. Esmerelda. "All my free time has been spent reading through those boring archived newsgroups on WitchNet, trying to find what ViciousMalk99 might have said once about a lindworm in the eighties."

"All your free time spent with the football team, more like."

Esmerelda's voice changed to sharp. "I think it's far more likely that *you're* trying to get in with Malkin. What were you invisible for all night?"

"Nothing that concerns you," said Valda. "Now look, we agreed to trade what we've found out so far. In the archives you found . . ."

"Not much," admitted Esmerelda. "The bit of lore about the plague is repeated. ViciousMalk99 doesn't seem to care about that. But then at some point she gets real excited about a rumor that lindworm scales were used in amplification of certain spells."

Silence, and then Valda mused, "Sarmine said something about that spellwork Malkin was doing in college."

"Trust Sarmine to remember a bunch of academic nonsense that never worked."

"Do you think Malkin finally tracked down that scale she was calling me about so long ago?" said Valda. "Or—more than one?"

"I'll tell you what she wants us to think," said Esmerelda. "Is that—Who's that?"

Oh, crap. They must have spotted me. There was nowhere to go—

"Whoa, dude," said some dude from the far side of the bushes. "The art sub is kissing the lunch lady in the shrubbery."

There were indignant splutters from both witches as they emerged into a small crowd of teen boys grinning at them. Me, I hightailed it out of there, thanking my stars for nosy boys.

My brain went around and around as I walked the rest of the way up to the school building, tackling the problem of the witches. The facts tumbled over one another with the locomotion of my legs. Wheels turned, gears clicked. Malkin had set this whole thing up. Malkin knew there was a shifter. Malkin was on the trail of something called the lindworm, which Witchipedia was now informing me was a disgustingly enormous white worm that used to live in caves somewhere.

And then I stopped cold. If I had been on a bike I would have fallen over. Malkin was trying to track down a lindworm for some kind of spell. Malkin was now here looking for a shifter. The connection was obvious.

Malkin was going to force Leo to turn into a lindworm.

12

Thirteen Ways . . .

That had to be the key. Not just that shifters were generally valuable. No, Malkin had some specific spell in mind, or she wouldn't have spent a decade looking for an extinct animal.

But if you had a shifter . . .

"You could get any animal you want," said Jenah when I told her this before school. Her eyes were wide.

"I've got to tell Leo," I said. "I mean, he already knows he's in danger, but . . ."

"Whee, extra more danger," said Jenah.

"The problem is, I can't be with him night and day." I looked down at my fingers, which were really super interesting. "Or at least I shouldn't," I mumbled.

"Hmm," said Jenah. "I'm not sure how you keep getting yourself into these . . . interesting situations."

"Gee, thanks," I said. "My best friend is supposed to build up my faith in my good looks and charm."

"Which you have in abundance," she assured me. "But you have to admit it's a little odd to have like three guys asking you out in the space of a month."

"Coincidence," I said. "That statistics thing Kelvin was trying to explain to me where something looks like a pattern but it's not."

She shook her head. "No, it *is* a pattern," she said. "People are suddenly realizing how awesome you are because *you* are realizing how awesome you are."

"This sounds awfully woo-woo," I said.

"Look, Cam," she said. "There is only one witch in this school and you are it. Don't you think people would notice? I mean, even if they can't read auras like me. They can notice that you look like someone they shouldn't piss off."

This was all very nice and flattering, but something Jenah said made me sit up and listen. "Wait a minute," I said. "I'm not the only witch in school."

"Oh right," Jenah said, wrinkling her nose. "Sparkle. You really want to ask *her* for help?"

"It might come to that," I said soberly. "If we want to save Leo's life." I closed the locker, which ordinarily was the cue to head down to math. Instead I thumped my head into the crook of my elbow and stayed there. I could stay there all day.

"Are you okay?" said Jenah.

"No," I said flatly. There was too much. Jenah had built Henny up yesterday, but then she had found out about Leo. She needed some new boy options to cheer her up. Valda was still trying to throw Jenah off a bridge, and I couldn't be with her every moment to protect her. Malkin suspected Leo was the shifter she was looking for and was trying to frighten him into changing. I couldn't be with *him* every moment, either. To top it off, Devon probably thought I was playing him, which couldn't be good for his happiness level. And if I didn't fix all those things, then one of the witches would win Leo and turn him into a lindworm and pull out his teeth. And I'd be their servant, so I'd probably have to watch. "Even my lists aren't helping me fix all this," was what finally came out of my mouth.

Jenah gently turned me around. "You've done a good job so far this week," she said, like you would to a three-year-old. "Now it's time for you to get some help."

"What, from Sparkle? I don't know any other witches."

"No," said Jenah. "Well, maybe. But first we're going to see what some humans can do. I'll text Henny to meet us at lunch. You"—she eyed me firmly—"are going to go clear the air with Devon and make him come to lunch, too."

"How do you know there's air to be cleared?" I said.

She stared me down. "Did you tell him about Malkin being after him?"

"No," I said in a small voice.

"You see?" Jenah said. "You're evading again. When you get into a tight spot, you start—well, not lying, exactly—"

"I haven't been lying to you!" I burst out. "I've been trying to tell you the truth, even when it's hard." Jenah might understand lots of things, but she did not understand how thoroughly I loathed talking about my personal life.

"I can tell," Jenah said. "Thank you. But you do evade, you know. So you don't look weak."

"That's not fair," I protested.

More gently she said, "I didn't mean it the way it sounded. But you want to take care of everything, and have it look smooth and easy. Which means that you start dancing around the truth if you think we won't like it. You shut us out, and you overstep. Tell me that doesn't relate to your current problems with Devon."

It did. Still . . . "I'm trying to help him."

"I know," said Jenah. "You are very good at being kind and helpful and caring and not at all good at letting other people take care of you. Or even see that you have weak spots."

"I have *loads* of weak spots," I said.

"Yes, and one of them is communicating," said Jenah. "So please. Go communicate to Devon that Malkin is after him so he knows exactly what he's up against. He's not a damsel in distress, Cam. He can *help* us."

She nudged me into algebra. Devon was already there, pretending to be really interested in his textbook. Or maybe he was.

I stared hard at my own textbook. Jenah was right. I was a pretty straightforward person in general. But when it came to my personal life—i.e., witches and crushes—I didn't like showing my soft underbelly. If I told Devon that Malkin was trying to crush him like a bug, then guess what? I was responsible for him getting involved in a horrible witch mess for the second time.

So what if I hadn't technically lied? I had avoided telling him things he needed to know. It was the same thing. And as for telling him . . . it shouldn't be that hard, right? And yet it was. I poked at that a bit. Was it because I was afraid, deep down, that he'd be angry? And then he'd threaten to turn me into a solar panel?

Urg. This was a can full of worms if I ever saw one.

I pulled out my list.

Good Witch Ethics

1. Don't use animal parts in spells.
2. ~~Don't cast bad spells on good people for no reason.~~ Ask people before you work a spell on them (unless in self-defense).
3. Don't lie to people.

"Working out the problem, Miss Hendrix?" said Rourke.

"Yes, sir," I lied. Then made one more change to my paper before putting it away.

3. Don't lie to ~~people.~~ friends.

When class was over, I walked straight up to Devon. Jenah shot me a sympathetic look of encouragement as she hightailed it out of there. Traitor. Your BFF should at least stick around to see your potential humiliation. What if I needed a shoulder to cry on afterward? Where would she be?

Devon was looking at me.

"C'mon," I said. "I'll walk you to your next class." I picked up his textbook so he couldn't get away.

He ran a hand through his hair and fell into step beside me. I didn't have any bubble tea to put off the inevitable this time, so . . .

we were just going to get it over with. The crowd noise should cover our discussion if I kept a low voice. "I've messed up this week," I said. "And I'm sorry."

"You don't have to explain anything," he assured me. "We're not—it's not—"

"Now hang on," I said. "If I lose my focus I can't get through this. Now look. First off, I know I say stupid things sometimes, like that crack about the demon on Monday night. So first, I'm apologizing. It comes from having an upbringing that consists entirely of dusting salamanders and talking to unicorn breeder creeps and being dragged to witch parties where everyone says rude things to each other for the fun of it. But"—and I looked him in the eye, at least for a second—"if I say stupid things I want you to straight out tell me. And then I can try to fix it. So, that's uh, a thing I needed to say." I wound down.

He looked at me without saying anything, so I took a breath and jumped back in. "Okay, and a second thing I needed to say is that you remember the bet thing I told you about? Well, I discovered one of my mother's 'friends' picked you." His eyes widened. "And that's why you choked on Wednesday; it wasn't anything to do with you. And that's why I got you that drink, and I'll get you another for Friday night, because that's not fair. But, uh, you need to know, too. So you can help look out for her. And, uh, help us with the rest of the problems. If you're not too mad at me for destroying your life, take two."

There was another pause and finally he said, "Can I say something now?"

"Please. Anything."

"Of course I'll help you."

"You will?"

"Of course I'm not mad at you."

"Oh thank god."

"I probably say as many stupid things as you do."

"I highly doubt it."

"I think we have a lot more on this topic to discuss," he said, and he was looking at me with a peculiar mixture of seriousness and hope. "But not in the hallway."

"Fair enough."

"Maybe this Saturday?" he said. "After this is all over?"

I was beaming, I'm sure of it. "Saturday." We stopped outside his classroom door. "Oh, but will you come to lunch with us today to make battle plans? You are in 'A' lunch, aren't you?"

"I am, but I can't come," Devon said. "Miss Crane, the choir director, said she'd give me some coaching on dealing with, er . . . vocal anxiety, is I think how she put it. I'm sorry."

"Don't be," I said. "Sing well." The bell was about to ring. There were a couple freshman girls across the hall; no one else. I squeezed his arm—and then, daringly, brushed his cheek with my lips. Then dashed down the hall to a chorus of "oohs" from the girls.

☾

"You are the best," I told Jenah as I sat down at lunch. "I went from feeling like everything was broken to feeling like there's only one problem. And that's Leo, who's a big problem, but still. Way better."

"I take it that means you talked to Devon?" said Jenah.

"Cleared everything up," I said, grinning. I pulled out the book Sarmine had given me and opened it up to the Showstopper spell.

Jenah ate a bite of her curry. "How did he take knowing that he was one of the victims?"

"He did not threaten to turn me into a solar panel," I said.

Jenah raised her eyebrows. "That's good."

"Or actually turn my hands into noodles. Or actually roll me up in a pumpkin patch. Or actually drop me off the roof of the house, shouting at me to 'work the wing spell' on the way down."

"You have made some good strides today," said Jenah. "See you back on my couch next Tuesday."

A tray plopped down next to us, and a girl with it. Henny. She was in her same uniform of all black, but her face was wreathed in smiles.

"You look happy," I said. I got out a piece of scratch paper and a pen to work through the Showstopper spell.

"Today has been epic," said Henny. "Epic!"

"Spill," said Jenah.

"So I posted my Esmerelda drawing on all my social media last night," Henny said. "And this morning I have so many likes and hearts and shares, you don't even know. All the girls that wanted her brought down loved it—and even the guys thought it was funny, too. It's the highest ranked of any of my 'Pathetic Love Life' strips, by far."

"That's amazing," said Jenah. "Are you going to do more?"

"I spent all morning on them," said Henny. "Doodling and thinking up ideas my first couple classes. So look, I'm going to change Henny's name, so it's clear it isn't me. Get a new name for the strip, in case it goes big. I promise, there will be no identifying details linking back to you, okay?"

"But writing about witches?" I said dubiously. It seemed awfully close.

"Oh, no," Henny promised. "Superheroes. Totally different sub-genre. The Esmerelda witch character will die with the Henny strips."

"Too bad it's not that easy to vanquish her," I said. "Write her out of your life."

"Oh, but it is that easy," said Henny. "During art I ignored Esmerelda and sat there sketching the whole period. Occasionally someone else would share the picture around on social media and then laughter would burst out but it was never me! I was innocent. She was so mad, guys. But I mean, what was she going to do, turn me into a toad in front of everybody? And then, I just smiled at her whenever she said anything mean—thank you for that tip, Jenah."

"You're welcome," said Jenah. "And thank *you* for sending that bodyguard second hour to protect me."

Henny lit up. "She works for my grandmother," she said. "She's used to going undercover."

"Well, she stopped Valda from dropping the free weights on me in gym," said Jenah.

"Wait, hold up," I said. "Why does your grandmother have bodyguards?"

They looked at me in the same way as when I admitted I didn't know who Leo was. I was beginning to feel pretty out of it.

"Uh, she's our governor?" said Jenah.

I shook the cobwebs out of my head. "You're related to *Maria* Santiago?"

Henny ticked off on her fingers. "Some people don't like that she's a woman. Some people don't like that she's Hispanic. Some people don't like that she's Catholic or that she likes watching basketball or the way she does her hair and sometimes, every so often, some people disagree with her on actual matters of policy. So yeah, bodyguards."

"And the bodyguard rocks," said Jenah. She pointed to someone who looked like an ordinary—but very fit—teenage girl, in black jeans and shirt, prowling the perimeter of the cafeteria. "I told her this was one of Valda's favorite places to strike, and she should keep her nose peeled for a cigarette smell."

As we watched, a short, dumpy woman in a lunch lady's uniform emerged from the door to the kitchen. She was carrying a large pot in gloved hands.

I stood up. "Jenah, she's coming this way. I bet that's like, boiling tomato sauce or something."

Jenah tugged me back down. "Just watch," she said.

Valda had barely made it past the first table when the bodyguard was suddenly there, blocking her path. A short, heated exchange—

And then somehow Valda was on the floor with a pot of water

turned upside down on her head. A great howling emerged from under the pot. A student lifted it off to reveal three lobsters clinging to Valda's face. One of them had firmly crunched her glasses. Another was crunching her nose. The bodyguard had melted away, back into the crowds.

"What did I say?" crowed Jenah.

"She's good," I admitted.

"If only the cafeteria served lobster," Henny said wistfully.

"But can she be trusted?" I said.

Henny raised her hands. "I swear I did not once say the word *witches.* I asked my grandmother if I could borrow her to do a routine inspection of my space. So she's here for one school day only, but I figured one day was better than nothing."

"It is," Jenah assured her.

"Teamwork is amazing," I said. "Who knew?"

"Everyone but you," said Jenah with a grin.

"So look," I said. I was working out the Showstopper spell with one hand and eating a sandwich with the other. "I need your guys' help at the game tomorrow night. I'm sure Malkin is going to try something there."

"Like what do you think?" said Jenah.

"For starters, attacking Devon again," I said, pointing to the spell I was deciphering. "But Showstopper gives him unbeatable charisma. It should counteract anything Malkin tries to do to his performance, short of dropping a piano on his head. He'll be armed and ready."

"You know, if we all know that people are deliberately trying to make us miserable, it seems like it should be pretty hard for any of the witches to win," Jenah said.

"True," I said.

"Like you can't be gaslighted if you know someone's doing it," Jenah said.

"Gaslighted?" I said. I crossed out the part of the spell about the cup of dirt. Good to know I hadn't given dirt to Devon.

"If someone tries to tell you your own experiences aren't true," Jenah explained.

"Ah, like the witch thought I should tell Henny, 'No, you didn't see us clean Jenah's jeans.'"

"She said what?" said Henny.

"You should put that on your ethics list," said Jenah. "No gaslighting."

"We need a Good Witches Oath," I said.

"'On my honor I will try . . .'" quoted Henny.

"To be brave, ethical and true to my friends," said Jenah.

"And have lots of gumption," I finished. I glanced up at Henny. "Speaking of gumption . . . have you made progress on asking anyone out?"

She flushed, and toyed with her sandwich. "I don't know," she said. "I mean, no, not really. I mean, I was busy doing my comics all morning and it hasn't come up."

"Which is perfectly fine," assured Jenah.

But I was still excited by how my convo with Devon had gone and I wanted to share the happiness. I set my pen down on my spell. "Let's find someone for you to ask out right now."

"I don't . . ." Henny demurred. "I mean, I'm still getting over Leo, and I—"

"Look, there's my friend Kelvin," I said. He was sitting with a rather weedy-looking kid down at the far end of our table. "He also likes geeky things. I could introduce you two."

"No, I . . ."

But I was already standing, gesturing to Henny. I knew how to keep her on track. "Show your readers some gumption," I said cheerfully. "Or I'll turn you into a newt."

Reluctantly she followed me down to the end of the table.

"Hi, guys," I said. "We were just on our way to get some, uh, napkins. And I wondered if you two knew each other." Terrible but enthusiastic, that's me.

Kelvin looked at the boy sitting opposite him, carrot stick half in, half out of his mouth. "Rajesh and I have known each other since fourth grade," he said.

"I meant, I wanted to introduce you to my friend Henny," I said, gesturing to the girl standing stiffly at my side. "I thought you guys should meet because you're both, like, geeks, and stuff."

They eyed each other.

"Who's your favorite Clue character?" shot off Kelvin.

Henny rolled her eyes. "I haven't played that since I was seven. What's your favorite Ghibli movie?"

"Boring," said Kelvin. "If you could be a *Star Wars* character from the original trilogy, who would you be?"

"All the best characters in those movies are dudes," returned Henny, "except Leia, and I refuse to be objectified in a metal bikini."

Maybe this wasn't going to be as easy as I thought. "Okay, so you might not have the same, whatchamacallits—"

"Fandoms," they said in unison.

"—but I still thought you might get along."

Henny shifted from foot to foot. "I have to get to the computer lab before lunch is over," she said. "It, uh, was nice to meet you guys." She turned and fled.

I guess I hadn't done that very well at all. "Well, uh. Sorry to bother you," I said to the boys. "Nice to meet you, Rajesh."

"I like Studio Ghibli," offered Rajesh.

I trudged back to my spot at the table. Henny had taken her things and vanished.

Jenah was in tears of laughter.

"Not funny," I muttered.

"No, you're right," said Jenah, wiping her eyes. "I'm sorry, you're just so—so on the wrong track."

"What, does Henny like girls now?" The laughter overtook Jenah again and I waited patiently. "If you're quite done laughing at how hopeless I am when it comes to understanding people," I said.

"I'm sorry, I really am," said Jenah. She forced her face into a serious expression. "Let me explain it to you in biology terms. She's like a little caterpillar coming out of her shell."

"You mean a butterfly coming out of its chrysalis?" I said dryly.

"Look at her, with her comics," Jenah said. "Let her find her own way. She's going to be all right."

I shook my head. "If you say so."

"I promise you," said Jenah. "I've got her back and she's got mine. Now how's that spell coming?"

"Almost done," I said at last. I picked up my pencil and finished writing down the last couple steps. Oh no. Oh no nononono. I double-checked my work and triple-checked my work, but the answer was always the same.

One pinch parsley, one pinch powdered rutabaga, one drop witch spit . . .

And one pinch powdered pixie bone.

That was what had been in the vial. *That* was what I had used to make Devon's spell.

"What is it?" said Jenah.

I was livid. I pushed the paper over to her as I picked up my phone to call Sarmine.

She answered on the fourth ring and said, "Can't you text me like a civilized person?"

"Sarmine, you tricked me," I shouted. "I said I wasn't going to use animals as ingredients and you told me to use the powder from that vial."

"Don't you dare raise your voice at me," said the cold voice at the other end of the line. "You asked for the spell and I gave it to you. Perhaps you should have bothered to ask what was in it—or, dare I say—learn your own damn spells."

I was so angry I hung up. I was probably going to hear about it later, but at the moment I didn't care. "She has no empathy. None! She can't even think of me as my own person. She . . . aaagggh." I trailed off in frustration, unable to fully express my current loathing for Sarmine Scarabouche. "And now how am I supposed to help Devon when I can't use this spell?" I banged the table in frustration. "She's trying to back me into a corner with her whole 'the spells are the spells' nonsense. And I'm not going to do it, I'm just not."

Jenah reached across the table and squeezed my arm in sympathy. "Now look," she said. "Remember when we were trying to find a substitute for goat's blood? And there were a bunch of suggestions in one of your mother's books? What if we find a substitution for this?"

I calmed down at that. Thank goodness one of us could keep a clear head when dealing with my mother. I supposed it was easier if you didn't have to live with her and her snakeskins and her newt eyeballs. "You're right," I said, and I picked my phone back up. "We are going to get on WitchNet and google something else that will work."

Ten minutes later we had finished our lunch and I had a list of three potential substitutes for pixie bones. I read them out to Jenah.

"The first suggestion is a vanilla bean pod infused in balsamic vinegar, with a pinch of baking soda," I said. "The plus side to that is I can dash across to Celestial Foods to get that, and be only a little late to fourth hour."

"The drawback?"

"If you don't get all the vanilla seeds out you will invoke a 'small but terrifying natural disaster.'"

"On to number two," said Jenah.

"Basilisk urine," I said.

"Next," said Jenah.

"Okay, so the last one has potential," I said. "Supposedly you can use an infusion of three unicorn hairs to one-quarter cup of green tea in place of any powdered or liquefied pixie bone. So this has real possibilities, except Sarmine has cut me off from any more supplies because I refused to use her invisible eels." Jenah raised her eyebrows and I explained about the pitcher of water that wasn't really a pitcher of water.

"Charming," she said.

"So now, if I could just get out to the Unicorn Ranch." I drummed my fingers. "I could bike after school . . . no, I need to find Leo and get him handed off . . . I could ask Leo for a ride, but . . . hmm."

Jenah got that manic gleam in her eye that she gets whenever I mention certain magical creatures. "I'll go," she said.

"The guy who owns the ranch is kinda creepy," I said. "Are you sure?"

She nodded. "Oh, definitely. Oh, except I have scene study with one of my acting partners this afternoon, and then my grandparents are here for dinner . . ." Now it was her turn to weigh the calendar. "Heck, I'll dash out during fifth hour."

"You can't cut American history," I said.

"I loathe American history," she said. "All those amendments."

"All right," I said dubiously. "I could use the help."

"I'll make it work," she assured me.

"That would be amazing," I said. "You can even take my bike. Just don't use the set of shifters on the left-hand side."

"Because?"

"Long story," I said. I told her how much three unicorn hairs should cost, and gave her directions, my bike lock key, and most of my cash. "Don't let him cheat you."

"Please," said Jenah.

☾

There are benefits to having a class you really love and are making A-plus-plusses in. I got to fifth period early, cornered Ms. Pool, and pitched her a special self-directed project that would let me use one of the unoccupied lab benches in the back of the room while everyone else was up front doing the next two days of genetics. "It's technically a chemistry experiment for something that might become a science fair project," I explained. This was skirting around the edge of lying, but on the other hand, I had in fact once done a science fair project on the theoretical genetics of werewolves, so why not develop a science fair project based on vegetarianizing spells? Kill two birds with one stone—two tofu birds anyway. "I'm testing the reaction between several different compounds." That was an understatement. "But I don't have chemistry this semester, so I was hoping you'd let me use the equipment here."

"You'll be ready for the test next week?" she said.

"Absolutely," I assured her. "Plus I'll listen while I'm working." Genetics had been going all right so far, and I would have the whole weekend to catch up, after the Friday night bet was all finished and Leo had been officially saved.

"All right," she said. "Just don't blow up the lab."

I took my vanilla bean pod to the back corner and laid it out with the other ingredients. Despite the "natural disaster" possibilities, it was a good strategy to try a backup. After all, Jenah might not be able to procure the unicorn hairs—or I might not get that spell to compound correctly.

I had measured the vinegar and witch spit together outside the classroom, so no one would see. Next order of business was to carefully separate the seeds from the vanilla bean pod. I got out the scalpel . . . and the safety goggles.

Out of the corner of my eye I saw Leo come in the door. He made a beeline to me. "Did you tell me that the new art sub was one of those witches?" he said in a low voice.

"Yes," I said. "And you need to be careful. I have confirmation that a different one actually came to town looking for you."

His eyebrows rose.

"I don't think she knew who you were at first."

"But after last night . . ."

"It does seem likely," I admitted. "Has the art sub been stalking you in particular?" No matter what Esmerelda had claimed in the bushes, I wouldn't be shocked if she were busy double-crossing Valda with Malkin. And vice versa.

Leo shook his head. "No. But she's been hanging around the football team."

"That's slightly creepy," I said.

He shrugged. "The other football players don't think so."

"Yeah, but you don't know how old witches are on the inside. She could be, like, fifty or something. Or eighty."

He snorted. "Tell that to the team. I think she's angling to get hired on as the new cheerleading coach. The boys are for it and the girls are ticked."

I put the safety goggles on and tugged the strap over my hair. "Would you date her?" I said.

He looked sideways at me. "Honestly, yeah. Does that weird you out?"

"No," I said. Which was half true. "Anyway, maybe it's just because you're open to possibility and all. You are still feeling open to possibility, aren't you? It hasn't worn off?" Despite the disaster with Kelvin, I thought I should make one more plug for Henny's sake. Or, actually, one plug at all. She was right that I had never really tried to set them up. One more thing to put on my ethics list. Number 4: Don't be a weasel.

"I *am* open to possibility, Cam," Leo said. "I've been waiting to see if something revealed itself this week." He looked at me in my lab coat and hideous goggles and there was an awkward pause.

I jumped into it with both feet. "Gosh, yes, ha ha, I'm sorry nothing's worked out for you yet. I mean, you wouldn't believe the troubles I've had this week with . . ."

"Yes?"

"Well, you know," I said feebly. "I already told you, I mean. I have an almost sort of—" What did you call it? Boyfriend? Tentative baby steps thing? "Well, I have someone, you know. I told you that."

"Right," he said, but not like he understood and we were now done with the subject. Much more of a dismissive "right," like maybe he'd never believed me to begin with and had always thought—or wanted to believe—that the potion was straight from me.

I couldn't do this. This no-man's-land of whatever this thing was with Leo. It wasn't for me. I blurted out, "So, hey, how do you like that Henny who's always in the computer lab. She's nice, huh?"

He did a bit of a double take as he realized who might have asked me to make the love potion. "I am an idiot," he murmured.

"Of course not."

He looked a little angry, just the fraction of a tinge. "You know, we've never even met before this week?"

"Ah," I said. I held the scalpel like a shield.

"Do you really think that's fair? Does that seem right?" He squeezed the side of the table. "Does she even *know* me?"

There was a negative feeling in the pit of my stomach. I mean, he was right. Henny really did only like him for his superficial qualities . . . and that probably didn't feel good to hear. "But you've gotten to know her a little bit now?" I said feebly. "She said she came up and talked to you yesterday."

He sighed and let go of the table. "Oh, I suppose."

"So you think she's nice? Now that you know her?"

He smiled absently at me. "Sure, sure."

"Well, good," I said, fake-heartily. "That's done and dusted." Up front, the class was settling down at the lab benches and Ms. Pool was writing the first set of problems on the whiteboard. The bell rang. Leo should be taking his seat.

Instead he pulled a chair over to the second spot at my lab bench and sat down, opening his laptop to take notes like he belonged back here.

"What are you doing?" I whispered.

"Hush," he said. "Go on with your work."

I looked at his profile as he settled in. I have to say I could sympathize with Henny a little bit. He was in fact a very attractive sportsball person, with more intellect than I would have expected a sportsball person to have. Which is probably shortsighted on my part. But all the football players I knew were straight-up jocks. I wondered how well Leo got along with his team members. It probably helped that it looked like he could hold his own in a fight. I mean, not that I was looking at his arm muscles or anything. Man, this honey stuff was intense.

Leo looked sideways at me while sketching out the diagram for the first genetics problem on a piece of paper. "Cam," he said. "I want you to come with me to the football game."

"You do? Oh, right. For the witch business." Concentrate, Cam. I slid the glass under the microscope and adjusted the focus. Delicately I teased at the seeds on the vanilla bean pod. Every last seed had to be removed, the Web site had said in blinky purple letters. I wasn't sure my dexterity was good enough, frankly. They clung to my hands.

"I've been practicing with the cardamom," Leo said. "I'm just not sure what's going to happen on the field. If I suddenly turn into—"

"A bunny—" I said to the microscope.

"A majestic lion, proud and untamed—"

"Mm."

"And then a squadron of witches—"

"A *coven* of witches—"

"Descends on me like I'm next up on the witch menu, then . . . I honestly don't know what I'm going to do."

"Turn into a velociraptor and rend them end to end?"

"Don't tempt me."

I stopped then, and rested my scalpel on the table, thinking. Gently he touched one of my fingers with his own, then stopped and put his hands back on his work. I didn't know what any of it meant but I did know that Devon had the Battle of the Bands at halftime during the game, and I couldn't be in two places at once, even if I wanted to. "You need help," I said. I began measuring out the parsley, rutabaga, and baking soda.

"Cam, I'm no weakling."

"No."

"I can hold my own in a fight."

"Definitely." I dropped the vanilla bean pod into the vinegar and studied it. What sort of a minor natural disaster were we talking about, really? "Maybe you should put some goggles on, too."

He ignored this. "You know who I need in my life right now? Not just someone who cheers me up, or is fun to talk to. Definitely not someone who just likes me for my triceps presses, or the number of touchdowns I made last year." He looked right at me. "I need someone who can protect me."

"First step in that is safety goggles," I said.

"Fine," he said, and reached for a pair.

This love business was in fact tricky. We had just determined that it wasn't the best that Henny only liked him for his good looks and superstar prowess. But why did I like Devon? He was also good looking. That was okay, right? I thought about his kindness to people and animals, his sweetness. The way he had fought against the demon inside him. Leo was like that, too—stubborn, a fighter. But Devon thought more about others. About his own ethics and morality. Sure, Devon and I had been thrown together when I had to save him. But I liked him for who he was inside . . . and I hoped he felt the same about me.

Now here Leo and I were in a similar position. But my instincts about Leo told me that this was a boy who—as much as he was complaining about Henny crushing on him—he was a boy who was used to being liked. Used to having girls fall at his feet. That made you a different person, in the long run. You couldn't help it. He gave his heart lightly and easily, certain it was not going to get broken. He didn't fall hard for people. And if he did think he liked me, it was only because he liked the new possibility—and because he liked having a protector.

I felt certain that he didn't really, truly like me, any more than Henny really and truly liked him. It might be one step up to like me for my witch skills instead of my looks. But it amounted to the same thing in the end. He didn't really know me.

I held my breath as I dropped the powder mixture from my glass bowl into the glass beaker of vanilla-vinegar. The mixture was smooth and still. Would it work? I had been as careful as I possibly could with the equipment that the school had.

A tiny whirlpool opened up in the beaker. This did not look promising. The liquid began bubbling up out of the center as if pushed by an invisible volcano. It rose to the top of the beaker, and then bubbled over in an endless cascading head of foam. I couldn't give this to Devon. It would be like turning him into a washing machine with too much detergent.

"Are you making a baking soda volcano?" said Leo.

Ah. I had been punk'd by a witch. "Yes. Yes, I am."

I pulled out my list and crossed off *vanilla beans*.

Leo had gone back to his genetics problem, but it was clear in the set of his shoulders that he was still waiting for a response to his earlier question.

Very slowly I said, "I do see what you mean. About needing a protector."

"You do?"

"Yeah." It was clear that Henny's hopes were going to be dashed. But as interesting and charming as Leo was, I knew this was the moment for me to bow out. He needed someone powerful to watch over him. And he didn't care how old she really was. "Meet me after school at the food carts," I said. "I know just the girl for you."

13

Sparkle to the Rescue

"*Sparkle?*" said Leo. "I've known Sparkle for years. What makes you think we should go on a date? She's kind of, um . . . intense."

"Ah," I said. "You only *think* you know Sparkle."

Sparkle was the most popular girl in the junior class, and she was my ex–best friend from grade school. Our falling out had been replaced by increasingly vicious bickering over the years. And then a couple weeks ago I had discovered that she was actually another witch. An older witch, forty or so—which, for a witch, is practically a teenager—who had put an amnesia spell on herself and come to live with her Japanese grandfather here in town, waiting for a magical plot to come to fruition. Since witches look the age they feel inside, as long as Sparkle thought she was six, seven, eight . . . she appeared to be a normal kid growing up.

She knew who she was now, of course, but she—like me—had decided that she was less than thrilled with the idea of being a wicked witch. She had grown up as normal Sparkle for so long that she had decided to try to continue being a regular teenager for a while, and maybe take a different path in life this time through.

She still ruled the school, though. She hadn't changed her personality one bit.

But she did remember all the spells from her former life as Hikari. You can't keep your witchy side suppressed completely. So far she had—from what I could tell—used her newly refound magic to a) make her magical nose job permanent, and b) magic herself up an impressive new wardrobe.

We found her at the football field. Sparkle is, among her other ruling-class traits, head cheerleader, and when we got there she was busily and happily ordering the other girls around. What grown-up office job could compete with that?

I was about to go up to her, but Leo stopped me. "I need to wrap my head around this," he said. "You say she's a witch, too? How many witches are there at this school?"

"Oh, that's it," I said. Although I guess I couldn't be sure. Still, no need to make him more worried. "Sparkle and I are the only two I know of."

"And of course that substitute teacher."

"Don't forget the lunch lady."

"But then . . . how old is Sparkle really?"

"That's your first question?"

He shrugged.

"Maybe forty? I dunno. I get the feeling it's rude to ask. Like they aren't maintaining their mask well or something."

"She definitely doesn't look it," said Leo.

I could tell he was more interested in her than he had been when he thought she was just an ordinary cheerleader. Of course, she had probably always thought he was an ordinary football player.

Which meant . . .

"How do I know she won't try to cut me apart for her spells?" said Leo. "I mean, I trust you. But her?"

I paused. This was, in fact, a good point. Sparkle had been a classic mean girl for so many years that it seemed like you couldn't trust her anymore for anything. On the other hand, her mean-girl ways were focused on running the school, and you could be someone who wanted to run the school and not someone who wanted to torture the local football champ.

Plus, I knew Sparkle from when I was five and she was six. One of the main things that had started us drifting apart was when we saw the witch work a horrible spell. She had helped me believe that I must be adopted, frankly, because we were both so appalled by what a wicked witch would do.

Slowly I shook my head. She had changed over the years.

But she wouldn't condone *torture*.

"She's safe," I said finally. "We might have to talk her into it. But she won't go after you."

Sparkle had been glancing over at us. I waved at her the next time she looked our way. She rolled her eyes, but she called a halt to practice. The girls went for their water bottles, and she came over. "Hi, Leo," she said. "What are you doing with her?"

Ugh. "Sparkle, I know we haven't been friends for a long time," I began frankly.

Sparkle waved a hand to cut me off. "Nuh-uh, Cam," she said. "I have no interest in talking about what happened on Halloween. Brushed under the rug. Never happened." She stared me down. "Things are going on as normal."

I sighed. I wondered if we could ever go back to being friends. "Okay," I said. The wind whipped around my ears. "But things can't go on precisely as normal, not right now. I need your help."

Her eyes flicked to Leo and back. "You have ten seconds to make your case," she said.

"He's a shifter."

Her eyes went wide. She grabbed our arms and dragged us off the track and into the stone cave of the bleachers. "You shouldn't say that out loud, Cam," she scolded. "Especially not if it's true." She looked at Leo with new eyes. "Is it true?"

He nodded.

She looked him up and down. "But I've known you for years," she said.

"I've known you for years and I didn't know *your* secret," I said.

"Hush," Sparkle said absently. She was studying Leo like he had suddenly turned into a cheese plate. She brushed back her black ponytail and moved a little closer to him. "How is it," she said, "that we've never dated? The head cheerleader, the star quarterback?"

Leo shrugged. But his eyes were interested.

She was practically purring. "I mean, I would have had your

secret out in a red hot second," she said. "And then you would have been under my thumb."

"*Sparkle,*" I said. "I do not want him to be under your thumb. I want you to *protect* him. From the other witches."

Her head went up sharply. "Other witches? Who else knows about him? Your mother?"

"Yes, but she isn't going to harm him," I said. "There are these other three witches in town, and they're here till tomorrow night for sure. Esmerelda, Valda, and Malkin. Do you know any of them?"

She got a faraway look like she was accessing her old witch memories. Slowly she nodded. "Malkin in particular is bad news."

"I was definitely getting that idea," I said. "Look, I think I know part of Malkin's evil plan. She's been trying to find a lindworm for years." I rounded on Sparkle. "Do *you* know anything about lindworms? So far the suggestions are maybe she wants its fangs for a plague and maybe she wants a scale for unspecified witchy mayhem."

Sparkle shook her head. "I never studied mythology."

"Well, at any rate," I said, "obviously it occurred to Malkin that if she could find a shifter, she didn't have to find a lindworm. She could make him turn into one and pluck off a few lindworm scales or something."

Sparkle looked at me funny, and Leo said, "What is a lindworm?"

I shrugged. "Big white worm. I guess she'll show you a picture?"

"But that's exactly it," Sparkle said. "He can't turn into a lindworm."

"Why not?"

"He can only turn into animals he's touched before."

Leo and I looked at each other. "Of course," I said. "The rabbit. Your neighbor's dog. A giraffe—?"

"At the zoo once," he said. "Pops knows a zookeeper who let me pet it when I was little."

"That's why you couldn't turn into a bear," I said.

"No velociraptors, either," he said. "What a shame."

I shook my head. I had been so certain the lindworm was part of Malkin's plan. That explained why Sarmine had been so dismissive of the idea. There must be something I was missing. "So how does this usually work?" I asked Sparkle. "A shifter would need to go around and build up a collection of animals, so to speak, that he's touched?"

"Yeah," said Sparkle. "That's why every so often a shifter will die under mysterious circumstances that have nothing to do with evil witches and everything to do with the fact that they tried to get into the polar bear cage."

Leo swallowed. "But if a polar bear started to bite me, that'd be touching, right? And then I could become one, too."

"True, but the other polar bear might be better at being a polar bear," said Sparkle. "You do get some instincts—" She broke off. "I mean, from what I've heard."

I refrained from asking. I mean, Sparkle was my only hope. I had to trust that she wasn't going to turn him into a frog and go poking around for his magical spleen. "You'll protect him?" I said. "Teach him everything you know?"

Sparkle patted his arm, practically purring. "Study partners."

"You can help me stop it?" Leo said.

"Oh, yes."

"Good. I didn't like the idea of being witch mincemeat."

She slipped her arm through Leo's. "You'll be safe with me," she cooed. "I will attach myself to you. By your side night and day. We'll get through this."

I grimaced and looked over at Leo. Surely he wouldn't be crazy about that part of the plan. Sparkle was so . . . obvious.

But he was grinning like anything. That honey potion must have opened him up to all kinds of possibilities. It was a good thing he wasn't forlorn and forsaken over me. I mean, it really was. Really.

"Save me, Sparkle," he said, grinning. "Save me from myself."

This is what I did Thursday night while other kids practiced their trombone and drew comics about superheroes and kissed each other and prepared for the Battle of the Bands. I stirred banana-smelling cauldrons, rotated the jars of pickled herring, and then combed through all of Sarmine's bookcases looking for any other solution to my Showstopper problem. A different potion I could do, or another substitute I could use for the pixie bone.

I also texted Sparkle several times to make sure she was still shadowing Leo. She had a WitchNet phone, and I had made her trade numbers with me. I got the feeling that she was simultaneously annoyed that I was checking up on her and delighted to rub in the details of everything she was doing with Leo. Things like, "playing pool w/ Leo, probly hot tub next," and "omg u didnt tell me his dads were such amazing cooks + the caviar lol." All accompanied by selfies, of course. I wanted to tell her that if she was trying to make me jealous she was barking up the wrong tree, only she wasn't, not exactly. I hadn't completely fixed things with Devon, and until then, I was going to continue being jealous of the way Sparkle could take her romance from zero to sixty in one afternoon.

Meanwhile, the only thing I found in Sarmine's books was confirmation that unicorn hairs in green tea might work—that it *had* worked for the writer, once, but that very many other times it had exploded. So it was good that I had actually found some valid information on WitchNet, but bad that the substitution was not going to be as easy as I had hoped. In the margin of the book Sarmine had written notes like: *Does the concentration of the tea make a difference?* and: *What about decaf vs caf?* So basically, this would be a perfect spell to do a long experiment with—running through every permutation and making notes—except I didn't have that kind of time or ingredients.

Sarmine came into her study on a waft of rotten-banana stink that meant she had been working on her spell in the RV garage.

She retrieved a book from her shelf, stopped to give me encouragement ("Give up, Camellia. You'll never find a substitute in time"), and I brought her up-to-date on my encounter with the shrubbery witches. Sarmine lit up at the idea that ViciousMalk99 had once heard that lindworm scales might be used for amplification.

"That must be the missing piece to the sympathetic resonance spell," Sarmine said.

"You keep saying that pair of words," I said. "Would you care to explain what they mean?"

Of course Sarmine did, because Sarmine loves to lecture. "Malkin was trying to create a spell whereby if you do something to one part of a set, you can do it to all the items in that set. For example, you kill one mosquito and all the mosquitoes in the area drop dead."

"That could be useful."

"She couldn't ever get it to work for more than a few inches in any direction, though," Sarmine said. "If a lindworm scale really is the catalyst to make it work on a large scale, it would explain why she's spent her whole life hunting for one."

The thought was a little frightening. Whatever Malkin had in mind, it probably wasn't killing off mosquitoes for the good of all mankind. And I still didn't know how Leo was involved. Maybe she just wanted to turn him into an extramagical unicorn and shave him for his hairs. That would probably juice up her Power spell nicely.

I sighed and closed the book of substitutes. "Right now I'm mostly concerned about Devon. Is this unicorn-hair tea solution really going to explode?"

Sarmine considered. "I'd say your odds are eighty-twenty."

"Whee."

"Give up now while you can still get some sleep," Sarmine said as she left the study. "Big day tomorrow."

"You're telling me," I muttered as I lugged the books up to my room. It might be a long shot, but still. If Jenah managed to get me some unicorn hairs, I would try it at least once in AP biology. It was my only chance to help Devon.

☾

Friday morning dawned cold and clear. Yet again, Sarmine was nowhere to be seen. I guess she had given up on setting her alarm clock after I refused to use the eels and the pixie bone. No point wasting precious sleep on a daughter with an inconvenient ethical code.

The eels themselves were still swimming around in the pitcher in the kitchen. I mean, I presumed. I poked at the pitcher. I wondered how long the eels would survive on our countertop. I should really return them to the creek before Wulfie decided to drink from that pitcher and make himself disappear. Yet another thing to do, I thought as I grabbed a Mason jar. Maybe Jenah was right that I needed to let everyone take care of themselves. I mean, I'd set Leo up with Sparkle, and Henny with Jenah . . . maybe nobody needed me anymore anyway.

Somehow that made me even more depressed.

Jenah still had my bike, so I walked to school, surrounded by loads of other kids. It was getting to be a more familiar sight. The parking lot was only half-full of cars, and several rows of parking spaces had been taken over by bike racks. A school cop patrolled the cars that were there, no doubt trying to see if there was something more than mere coincidence involved in their destruction. Although Sarmine had been overly dramatic with some of the cars, most of them she had simply encouraged to succumb to entropy. They wouldn't start, the brakes went out, the wheels rotted away . . . some random reason they had to be towed. I doubted the cop would find anything, unless it was a trace of cinnamon or nutmeg.

I didn't see Jenah around the bike racks, so I went to our locker, hoping to find that she had managed to get the unicorn hairs. But it was a woebegone Jenah who met me there. Her thermometer bubble must be below the midline now. "My parents found out about me cutting class," she said.

I didn't say I told you so, because a) she had been helping me, and b) nobody likes that.

She looked at me, a little bit grumpy. "Yeah, yeah, I know," she said. "But I was doing it for a powerfully good reason, and that's more important than rules."

"But now?" I said. I hung my jacket in the locker and draped the scarf over it.

"Now my parents said I can't try out for the spring play if I have any more absences."

"I thought your parents were pretty loosey-goosey about that stuff?" I said.

"They are, but all four grandparents are very strict, and two of them were in town last night visiting and after they descended on my father with, 'We would never have let you do that' he finally broke down and said that I have to shape up." She massaged the bandage on her wrist while she talked.

"Parental peer pressure, man," I said. "It's the worst."

Jenah frowned at me. "Have you ever met *any* of your extended family?"

"A cousin, once, I think?" I said. "Sarmine hates her family, and my dad's family hates Sarmine." They still blamed her for not doing enough to find him, and for once I was on Sarmine's side about that. She worked some pretty dark magic to try to track him down, and still failed. I shook my head, coming back to the hallway. "Look, I hate to ask, but were you able to get the hairs?"

Jenah brightened. From her skirt pocket she produced six hairs and all the money I had given her. I boggled at her.

"Well, you said he likes to haggle and cheat," she said.

"Like all witches."

"And also that he's kind of a pervert," she said.

"Jenah," I said sternly. "You did not barter him anything inappropriate, did you?"

She looked offended and rightly so. "What I did," she said, "is ask him to show me around the unicorn stables. And while I giggled at his dumb jokes, he totally did not notice me taking the hairs off of one of the brushes they use to groom them. And then I waved and left."

"Ah. You stole them."

"I helped maintain his brushes in perfect working order," corrected Jenah. "And, I got one up on him for all the times he's tried to cheat you." She grinned. "It was fun. Next time he said he'd let me ride one. I'm sure I could get you a whole handful of hairs that way."

"Hmm," I said. It was clear that Jenah and I were not going to share the exact same ethics in this matter. On the other hand, I now had twice as many unicorn hairs as I needed, which meant that if today's test on them in biology worked, then I could use the other three to make into a potion for Devon tonight. I tugged the Mason jar out of its swaddle in my backpack and stowed it in the locker.

"Forgive me for asking dumb questions," said Jenah. "But why is there a jar of water in our locker?"

"Remember the story about the invisible eels?"

Jenah blinked at it.

"They need to go back to the creek. So, you know, if anyone felt like taking them there after school . . ."

"On it," said Jenah. She poked at the jar, marveling at it. "By the way, how did the testing on the vanilla bean go?"

"It was a prank," I said. "Devon would bubble over."

"You never told me what the drawback to the unicorn hair substitution was," she said.

"He might go boom," I said.

"That would be a dramatic halftime show."

I squeezed her shoulder. "Thank you so, so much."

"See you at lunch?"

"I have to check on Leo," I said. "See you after school?"

"I have to take your eels to the creek," she countered. "See you at the game?"

"Done."

So, at lunchtime I swung down to the football field and checked in on Leo and Sparkle. After I texted Sparkle like five times to see where they were, she finally responded that they were down in the boys' locker room. She knew I was coming, and I presume they could hear my footsteps echoing long before I could see them, and yet somehow they still had to jump apart when I entered.

I rolled my eyes and ignored whatever I had interrupted. "How's it going?" I said. "Still using the cardamom?"

Sparkle fixed her lipstick. Ostentatiously. "Please, Cam. He catches on quicker than any shifter I've ever seen. He doesn't need cardamom anymore, do you, my little lion?"

Leo grinned at me. "I don't, actually," he said. "It's amazing how quickly you can learn this stuff when you have such a good teacher."

"Gee, thanks," I said.

"Oh, no offense," he hastened to add. "But you and me, we were kind of stumbling around in the dark. And now—look at this." He started bouncing on his toes, like he was raising his energy level. Getting his heart rate going. Up and up—and suddenly there was a potbellied pig in his place. It wriggled out of his jeans with a snort.

"We drove out to the petting zoo to get some more samples," explained Sparkle. "We need to find a way to get him acquainted with some more . . . dangerous creatures. Then he'll have a better ability to protect himself. Why, I remember this one time . . ." She closed her mouth again.

"*Sparkle,*" I said. Leo was running around grunting and looking for leftover food. "How do you know so much about being a shifter? Do you have a secret history of making shifters change for you? Using them to get extramagical unicorn hairs?"

Sparkle sighed. "Well, yes and no. Promise you won't tell?"

I held up my little finger. "Pinky swear." We locked fingers like we used to when we were kids.

"I used to know a shifter girl, long ago. Back when I was Hikari. When I was a teenager the first time."

"And what did you do to her?"

Sparkle held up her hands. "Nothing, I swear. We were really close. And she told me everything she knew about shifter lore, and I helped protect her. She would also donate hairs and scales to me for the spells I was working on." That sounded awfully nice of Sparkle. I narrowed my eyes at her and she added, "Well, and I *wouldn't* have done anything to her, I swear, but you have to admit, that was a pretty good incentive to keep her secret."

That sounded more like the Sparkle I knew. I supposed Leo would be donating hairs to her before too long. She already had him eating out of her hand, and I don't mean while he was a bird or cat. "Then why didn't you say that before? Why is it such a big secret?"

Her eyes flicked over at the pig rooting around. "Because she disappeared on me. When she was pregnant. She went into hiding and I never saw her again. And I think—"

I couldn't help it. I laughed. "You think it was maybe Leo's mother?"

"Hush," she said crossly. "That would weird him out. I'm determined to be a normal teenager."

I sobered up. "I suppose you practically are anyway, if you witches all live at least a couple hundred years."

Now she was the one to laugh. "You know that means you, too, don't you?"

My mouth fell open. I had only started admitting I was a witch a couple weeks ago. I hadn't spent a lot of time thinking about the implications.

"It comes with the package. You're going to be around a couple centuries as well. You'll see humans come and go. So I wouldn't make too much fun."

I could hardly take it in. What would it be like to live—not eighty years, but two hundred? I counted the decades on my fingers, looking forward into the future. What kinds of changes would I see? Changes in technology, in the world, in the environment . . . And how many people would I lose along the way? Put that way, it made sense that witches paired off with other witches. I mean, I didn't know many male witches but there must be some. My dad had been one. "Are there more female witches than males?"

"Starting to think about breeding, are you?" said Sparkle, leering.

"I thought you were trying to sound like a teenager and not like a two-hundred-year-old witch," I sniped back.

"Ugh," she said, and waved her hands like she was shaking me off. "Yes, there are more women *practicing* witchcraft. But that's just because having witch blood isn't enough; you still have to actually study the spells. Male witches tend to breed unicorns and whatnot instead."

"Ah."

"Point is," said Sparkle, "have fun with your human boyfriend now. He won't be around forever."

"At least mine isn't busy rooting in the trash can," I said. It fell over with a clang and Leo squealed and dove for a crumpled-up fast-food sack.

Sparkle went around the trash can to Leo and ran her hands over his snout. "Come on, sweetie, do you remember how to snap out of it? Let's lay down calmly, let instinct turn you back . . ." Under her touch the pig gentled. He lay down on the ground. And then, with very little transition, there was a boy curled up behind the trash can.

I sighed and tossed him his jeans, turning away so he could get dressed. Honestly, it seemed like somebody else could worry about general decency beside me. Leo seemed to think it was hilarious. Were all boys secretly ten years old inside?

"I really am getting better at it, Cam," Leo said from the locker room floor. "Problem is, once you're a pig, you kind of enjoy being a pig. Or a dog, or a bunny, or whatever."

I stared at a poster taped to the tiled wall. NO HORSEPLAY, it read, and showed a bunch of wild horses wearing football jerseys. They didn't know the half of it. "Just don't turn into an elephant at halftime," I said.

All too soon it was fifth-period AP biology, and one last chance to try the unicorn hair recipe before the game tonight. Sarmine had said that basilisk urine had to be flown in from a witch who was breeding them in Peru, so that was definitely out. Unicorn hairs it was.

Leo had returned to his old seat, which was good. No distractions.

I laid out the ingredients and boiled some water over a Bunsen burner to steep the packet of green tea. Apparently the mixture was volatile enough that Sarmine's book had also given directions for neutralizing the mixture, should you produce an explodey one. Simply use your wand to inscribe a pentagram around your sink drain before pouring it out. I patted my disguised wand, making sure it was close at hand.

I measured out the rutabaga and parsley, and stirred them in. Carefully turned my back to the classroom to spit in the mixture. Lastly I slid the unicorn hairs in.

The potion was quiet. It looked good so far. But the explosion was supposed to happen on contact with the actual victim, er, human.

I was going to have to test it.

This is where a regular wicked witch would test on humans, and a regular human scientist would test on animals. But I didn't want to harm anybody. I had started this whole crazy scenario to make *sure* that I wasn't harming anybody. So animal testing was not in the cards. Not to mention the fact that all the animals that lived in the biology lab had names, and if I blew up Fluffy the Frog I was going to hear about it for the rest of my school career and beyond. Anyway, I liked Fluffy.

I liked me, too, but there didn't seem to be another alternative.

I lifted the beaker to my lips, then stopped. I didn't have to test this with my face, right? Or test the entire mixture? Or use a glass beaker? C'mon, Cam, I admonished. Use your brain.

I carried the beaker over to one of the fume hoods against the wall. It had a glass shield, so I could keep my hands and the mixture away from the rest of me. First, though, I tested a drop with a pH strip. It was right in the middle. Too bad there wasn't a way to test magic as scientifically as you could other things. If the spell said it might explode on contact with a human then that's what it might do.

One drop, in a small metal bowl. Place the bowl deep inside the fume hood, behind the tempered glass.

I pulled out a pair of yellow rubber gloves to sacrifice to the cause. I cut the fingertip off the left index finger. Maybe if it exploded I would only get a tiny burn. (But what if it was like napalm, I asked myself. What if it stuck to my skin? Or what if it ran up my glove and ate me alive?) I almost dumped the mixture out in the hazardous-waste bin right then, except the spell had specifically said to dispose of it with a pentagram and the sink, and anyway, darn it, I was going to try it first. I was.

Nerves of steel, Cam.

I reached out with the tip of my finger and touched the drop of potion in the bowl.

It exploded in a yellow burst of flame.

I jumped back.

Everyone turned to look. Ms. Pool swiftly crossed the room,

ready to douse the lab or me with the fire extinguisher. Thankfully, since I had only used one drop, the fire had already burned up. There was nothing in the sink, nothing to see. "I, er. Got the results I was looking for," I said. My finger smarted like anything.

"Any injuries?" she said.

"No," I said. "I know how to dispose of it correctly," I said. "And then I'll come sit in my regular seat," I said.

"Good," Ms. Pool said.

She returned to the front of the classroom and I inscribed a careful pentagram around the drain with the hand soap before using my gloves to pour down every last drop. I rinsed the beaker with water and poured that down too, several times, and finally I dared to touch the beaker with one of my nonburned fingers.

Nothing happened.

At least I wouldn't explode the school.

But I was no closer to figuring out a way to help Devon.

After school, I looked around for Jenah. She wasn't at our locker. Then I saw a flash of curly graying hair down at the end of the hall. Valda. What was she trying to pull now? We were so close to the end. I didn't trust her not to throw Jenah out a window if she thought it would help her win. The team of Jenah and Henny had been proving too resilient—that was going to be Jenah's downfall.

I raced down the hallway after Valda, and skidded around the corner in time to see her disappearing into a classroom. Mr. Saganey's room. I crept closer. Saganey taught American history. Jenah was in American history. I didn't like the answers I was coming up with.

I dashed across the hallway and hid just inside one of the other classrooms, where I could peek out to see when Valda left. Before too long she came out in her usual fast, stompy sort of way.

Saganey must not be in there, or I would have heard them

talking. As soon as Valda was out of sight, I hurried into Saganey's classroom. There was a pile of tests loosely scattered over his desk.

I could see Jenah's name on top as I neared it. Valda *must* have been tampering. Messing with a test seemed out of character for her—except that Jenah and Henny and the bodyguard had forestalled all Valda's usual blunt-force tactics. She must be grasping at straws. And there—with her usual lack of subtlety, she hadn't even bothered to put the test back in the right place.

The damage was clear at the top of the page.

Valda had changed Jenah's grade to a 64 percent.

I ran through the list of spells I knew and was willing to use. Love potion, Power, and a weak self-defense spell. Nothing useful there. Spells I knew but wasn't willing to use. Showstopper. Invisible eels. I didn't have any spells to undo what another witch had done.

I looked hard at the paper. I could change that six to an eight. It would look a teensy bit tampered with, but not too bad. Still, Saganey might notice, and that's the last thing I wanted. If only I could rub out that fractional bit of red, right there. . . .

Of course. I pulled the unicorn sanitizer from my backpack and barely wet my finger with it. Took a breath. I had never done anything like this before. But Jenah was going to get grounded if she messed up one more time.

What was the right thing to do?

Slowly, delicately, I wiped away the top of the six.

Then I picked up Saganey's red pen and changed the six to an eight.

14

The Big (football) Game

The evening of the big football game was cold and clear. Okay, maybe it wasn't a big football game to the football players, just a regular one. But to Devon, who was about to have his big competition in front of several thousand people, and to Leo, who was really hoping not to turn into a were-elephant in front of several thousand people, it was a big deal.

And all I had to do was keep everyone happy till the end of it.

Oh, and keep Leo from getting torn to bits. That, too.

I ended up not going home, but prowling the school for witches. Then I headed over to the football stadium so I could check it out before everybody got there. Football was a reasonably big deal at our school, and there was a nice new stadium, with plenty of bleachers on both sides of the field, along with a covered-over area for the players' locker rooms, concessions that different school fund-raising teams staffed, and everything else. Including security. Good thing Jenah had brought back my cash. I paid for a ticket, showed my ID to the guard, and slipped inside the stadium. I made a complete circuit of the grounds, but saw no wicked witches.

It was getting closer to game time. People were filling the stands now, laughing and chattering, their gloved hands wrapped around hot chocolate from the concession stand. The chaos meant it would only get harder to find the villains. I trudged toward the front entrance, keeping my eyes peeled.

"Good place for ro-bot uprising," said a voice behind me. I turned to find Kelvin.

"Kelvin!" I said. "What are you doing here?"

"Euphonium," he said, tapping the massive music case he was carrying. Kelvin himself is tall, white, and built rather along the lines of his case. "Our halftime show's been canceled for some rock musicians?"

"Battle of the Bands," I said. "Yeah."

"But we're still playing the pregame and pep rally in the stands. You know."

"I don't, actually," I said. "I was just thinking about how I've never made it to a game before."

"You've been missing out," he said seriously.

"So look," I said. "Speaking of that 'ro-bot uprising'"—and I used my best robot voice for him—"if you were a robot, or no, not a robot . . . Okay, let's pretend for a moment that you were a wicked witch, or something."

"Or a supervillain?"

"Sure. You're a supervillain and you're about to wreak havoc on the football game. What would you do and where would you come in from?"

The best thing about Kelvin is that this is the sort of question he gives serious thought to. He put his red mittened hands out in front of him like a picture frame, surveying the field. "Is there something in particular I'm trying to achieve? Or just to cause chaos?"

"You specifically want to disrupt the Battle of the Bands somehow," I said. "And you might also be trying to snatch a certain football player."

"Hmm," said Kelvin. At that point his friend from lunch came up behind him, wearing an oversized sweater and holding a rather smaller case. "Ah, Rajesh," said Kelvin. "We are going over a rather interesting point. Imagine you were so angry about the disruption of our halftime that you became a cackling supervillain called—"

"Clarinet Man," said Rajesh.

"And you wanted to disrupt the band battle. What would you do?"

Rajesh pivoted slowly, considering. "You know, if you filled in those outlets, it would be pretty easy to make this stadium a lethal trap."

"Exactly what I was observing," said Kelvin.

"Oh god, I don't want there to be anything lethal," I said.

"Imagine this bowl filling up with water," said Rajesh.

"Or Jell-O," said Kelvin.

"Or sharks."

"Or lunchmeat." We both looked at Kelvin. "What? I'm hungry."

We both shook our heads at Kelvin. "Okay, thanks, boys," I said. "Look, keep an eye out, will you? Let me know if you see anything . . . weird."

"A stadium of lunchmeat would definitely be weird," said Kelvin.

I did another loop around the stadium while the crowd took its seats, looking for places the witches could hide. Esmerelda would be looking for Henny, Malkin for Devon and Leo, and Valda for Jenah. I wasn't too worried about Jenah at the moment. Valda thought she had Jenah's history grade screwed up, and I knew I had it fixed. So Valda would be relaxing, confident of her victory. The others, though. . . .

The band started playing the pregame. Leo must be down in the locker rooms. Sparkle was on the field with the cheerleaders, doing her own circuits. I exited the security gate and headed up the slope from the stadium to the school. Maybe I could find Devon.

I walked around to the front of the school, and saw the turquoise flash of Jenah's brightly colored peacoat, trudging up the other side of the hill from the houses below, walking my bike. "Is Leo safe?" she called.

"As far as I know," I said. "Sparkle's supposed to be glued at the hip to him. I think they're enjoying that." I did a double take as she neared me. Her wrist and ankle bandages had been joined by a strapped-up finger, a selection of Hello Kitty Band-Aids on her neck and jaw, and an eye patch. "Are you okay?"

She sighed. "Even with Henny's help and the bodyguard's help, your witch has now tripped me in the lunchroom with a bike, on the stairs with the water puddle, on the back porch with a cat, on the sidewalk with a skateboard, and in the hallway with the candlestick. I didn't even make it to the creek yet—thought I should check on you before I head over there. It's a good thing there aren't any auditions coming up or she probably *would've* got me depressed. No one would cast me for anything when I look like the bride of Frankenstein. Not to mention that being on guard all the time wears on you."

"I really am sorry," I said.

"Not your fault," she said with a shrug. But I could tell she was, in fact, on edge. Even cheerful, positive people have their limits, and Valda, as blunt and unsubtle as she was, was managing to find them. "She almost got my grandmother with that skateboard stunt, though. We would have had some real words about that."

"Look, Jenah . . ." I said, my words trailing off. I had promised her I would share everything with her and I needed to tell her about changing her grade. "Do you have a minute?" From down the hill came the roar of the crowd and the echoing sounds of the announcer as the game began.

Jenah looked up into my face and her eyebrows looked suspicious. I couldn't blame her. Lately everything I was telling her was bad news, and it involved me.

"So I was outside your American history teacher's classroom earlier today," I said. I walked through the story for her. About halfway through I could tell she was getting more and more mad. This was frustrating, because she had said I had to tell her everything, and I was telling her everything, but I was getting a worse feeling inside instead of a better one, like it should be. "So, uh," I finished. "After I saw Valda sneak back out I knew what she had done. So I put it back the way it was. I had to make a guess but since she made it sixty-four percent and I knew you're usually a B student in

American history, I put it back to eighty-four percent. I hope that was right."

Jenah groaned. "What am I going to do with you?"

I took a step back. "Me? I mean, I'm sorry the witches drew you in the bet. That is totally my fault. But I'm trying to fix it." A peppy tune from the marching band underscored my words.

Jenah's shoulders slumped. "But I've been going around trying to help *you,*" she said. "Between all the demonic excitement before the Halloween Dance, and Valda trying to break my ribs this week, I haven't cracked the history book in like three weeks. A D is better than I deserve."

"You mean . . ." But I couldn't fathom this.

"Valda probably didn't change my grade at all."

"She just made me think she had changed it." I said. "Ugh, I hate cheating, lying, double-crossing witches." My voice rose on every word.

"This is the overstepping I was talking about," said Jenah. "You can't 'fix' people's lives without asking. You just *can't.*"

"But I didn't think I was," I protested. "I thought I was undoing what Valda did."

Jenah looked at me. "That is a slippery slope and you know it."

The thing is, I did know it. My intentions had been good. I even thought the setup had been good. Just undo something that had been done. Set things back to normal. And now I had blundered in and wrecked things again.

"How did you change it?" said Jenah.

"With the red Sharpie," I admitted.

Jenah buried her eye-patched face in her hands. "What if he thinks I did it? You get suspended for that kind of thing."

"Well, uh." Crap. I had really messed up. "Your parents might be pleased that you finally did some real rebellion?" I said hopefully.

Jenah glared at me. "The real rebel doesn't do things just to rebel," she said. "I have standards. And anyway, you know how much auditions mean to me. I just finished telling you I couldn't mess up again."

"Jenah, I—"

She was busy gathering up her things. "Whatever you have to say, don't bother," she said. She slung her leg back over my bike. Then turned. "You know, Cam, one of these days you're going to go too far," she said. "Friendships can break, you know. They can break for good." She turned and pedaled down the hill, away from me.

Tears pricked the corners of my eyes. Jenah had good reason to be mad at me. Sure, this was a little mistake in the context of things. But the bigger picture was there. If I had power I had to use it responsibly. Heck, I'd barely used power in this case—mostly just a red Sharpie. But I had to use red Sharpies responsibly, too.

I pulled out my ethics list and stared at it, or maybe through it.

Good Witch Ethics

1. Don't use animal parts in spells.
2. ~~Don't cast bad spells on good people for no reason.~~ Ask people before you work a spell on them* (unless in self-defense). *OR FOR THEM.
3. Don't lie to ~~people.~~ friends.
4. Don't be a weasel.

Despair took me, hard. I had failed at every single one of these. If I couldn't be a good witch, maybe it was time to give Devon the Showstopper potion made with pixie bones and be done with it. At least someone would be happy.

As I retraced my steps to the back of the school, I slowly became aware of more noise coming from the parking lot. The lot had filled up more as parents arrived at the game. No doubt they were all excited about finally being able to park in the school lot. But it sounded more like . . . shouting?

I hurried around to the side of the school. Was Malkin finally striking? After managing to distract me with witches and grades and ethics? I turned the corner onto the parking lot.

My eyes couldn't make sense of it for a few moments. There seemed to be a large metal cylinder—no, a small tanker truck—in the middle of the parking lot. But around it was . . . a swamp? I picked my way closer, to where a number of parents were standing on the edge of the swamp and gesturing angrily at the truck driver, who sat on top of his overturned tanker, gesturing angrily back at them.

The air smelled sweet. Cloyingly sweet. Like sugar? Syrup? This swamp was a clearish, goldish color.

Corn syrup.

Clinging to all the remaining cars in the lot.

How had a corn syrup tanker gotten stuck here and why? Everyone was yelling so much there didn't seem to be anyone to ask, even if they knew. I stepped around the corn syrup and recognized the peculiarly anise smell of pixie sweat.

An entire tanker of love potion.

But why? Distraction?

I called Sarmine. "Tell me you don't know anything about the parking lot full of destroyed cars."

"Oh, good, did that work?" she said. "I wanted to come up and see it in person, but you know how I loathe crowds."

"I'm trying to stop several witches from killing my friend," I said. "Do you think you could hold off on your regular taking-over-the-world shenanigans for, I don't know, a day?"

"I'm simply making Caden as happy as possible," protested Sarmine. It was belatedly occurring to me that, even though she had promised to help me, at the same time this was awfully unlike Sarmine to try to make the son of an auto dealer happy.

"You have some other plan, don't you?" I said.

"Naturally," Sarmine said. "I merely want to destroy all the cars in the world."

15

Who Wins the Game

Sarmine's words echoed in my ears as I looked harder at the stranded people in the parking lot.

"Of course," I said. "It's not a love potion, no matter how often I call it that. They're being opened to new possibilities. Of *transportation*."

"The local bike store owners I've called should be arriving right about now," Sarmine said. "Also the skateboard store, a scooter salesman, and a Segway dealer. I think this will be exactly the push some people need, don't you?"

I could not even deal with Sarmine Scarabouche right now.

She was still talking in my ear. "And then, tomorrow, you can help me activate the spell that destroys all the cars in the world," she said, and for Sarmine she sounded rather happy and upbeat. "Obviously we have to wait till tomorrow, because I think it would be a bit of a downer for Caden if every car his family owned suddenly became inoperable, don't you? So we'll wait till tomorrow morning. And then maybe some celebratory waffles."

"I am not going to help you with that," I said.

"What a shame," said Sarmine. "You've been so helpful in stirring the cauldron all week. And the other ingredients are waiting in the RV garage, ready to be combined. All that's left to procure is whatever Malkin's got up her sleeve. The final piece of the sympathetic resonance spell. I bet it's a lindworm scale, don't you think?"

I *really* could not even deal with her. "You can't *do* this!" I said. "I don't care how good you think your motives are. You can't waltz in and mess with people's lives!"

"Hogwash," said Sarmine.

"You can't make decisions for them!"

"People," said Sarmine, "are too stupid to live, let alone make good decisions."

"You have to give them the *chance* to change."

"Nonsense," said Sarmine. "Make the decisions for them. Never look back."

Across the parking lot I could see the minivan belonging to one of Devon's band members. They had the door open and were trying to negotiate getting out without stepping in the goo. I kicked one of the corn-syrupy car tires near me in frustration. "I have to go save some boys," I said. "We'll talk later."

I slammed the phone into my backpack and hurried over to the minivan, skirting the biggest puddles of syrup. I mean, maybe if I ate some it would give me better ideas on how to save the day, but also maybe Sarmine was triple-crossing me and it wasn't even the Possibilities potion. I mean, who knows, right? That's what witches were. They lied, all the time, and they were quadruple-crossing weasels. I had wasted so much time listening to her. So much time letting them, all of them, get under my skin.

I buttonholed Devon and pulled him away from the minivan, out to the edge of the lot. "If you fall, you get back up and try again," I said.

"What?"

"That is going to be number five on my Good Witch Ethics list," I said, "and also, the only advice I have for you tonight."

"No drink?"

I shook my head. "I can't give you the charisma drink because it uses powdered pixie bone." My voice rose in frustration. "I can't find a substitution that won't explode you, and I can't"—I waved my list of paper in front of him—"go against my ethics, even though it would be super convenient and save the day for you. I can't work this spell."

Devon stared at me. "The first drink used what?"

I could see him remembering the demon making him kill a hundred pixies for one of the witch's spells. "I didn't know," I said firmly. "I didn't know when I gave it to you, and I'm sorry, and you know me, you know I wouldn't have done that. I didn't know!" I was practically shaking him, willing him to believe me. "So I can't give you the drink, and you just have to go on, in front of . . ."

"Everybody."

"Yes, everybody. I'll keep looking for Malkin. I'll try to stop her from destroying you again. But I don't know if I can."

Devon nodded. "I trust you to try." He tried for a smile. "Hey, at least it's not like she's going to try to kill me in front of a thousand people, you know? Just humiliate me."

"That's it, though," I said. "She *is* going after Leo. She is trying to catch him."

"Leo? The Leo you—?"

"Yes, that Leo," I said. "Who'll be a rabbit. She's trying to catch the rabbit so she can pull out its fangs and start the apocalypse—"

"Cam," he said. "You're raving."

"Look," I said. "I may not survive tonight."

"It's that serious?"

"I may get arrested for the murder of my mother. And if I do, if I don't survive this, I just want to tell you one thing. One thing I've been trying to tell you all week."

"What?"

"I like you, you idiot."

I grabbed his collar and kissed him. Then I turned and ran.

I hurried down the hill to the stadium. The second quarter of the game was just starting, and I did the only thing I could do, which was keep my adrenaline-fueled self on the go, up and down the stadium, in and out, looking for witches. There was one point when I spotted Esmerelda's pink suit on the bleachers opposite me, but by the time I got over there she was long gone. The musicians for the Battle of the Bands were slowly gathering on the sidelines, Devon among them. Leo was on the field, and Sparkle was watching him closer than any cheerleader had ever watched a football player. Which was pretty close.

We were only a few seconds from halftime when Malkin finally struck.

It began the same way her other attacks had. The flags whipped and snapped. The ends of scarves lifted, flapping. A paper plate flew out of a woman's hands.

I whirled, looking around for Malkin. Leo was in the middle of the field, running with the ball, all eyes on him. Popcorn bags and napkins blew past the cheerleaders, and I saw Sparkle, lowering her pom-poms, her gaze sweeping the field for the threat.

Leo threw the ball, the buzzer for halftime sounded—and then, while all eyes were on the football's spiraling arc—the lights in the stadium cut out. Everything was plunged into darkness as a hurricane wind swept through the stadium.

I cast my own Power spell, making just enough of a calm place for me to run down the stairs to the field. I reached it right as the lights came back on and the wind died to ordinary November-strength winds. There was still chaos everywhere, but I clearly saw Malkin cut across the field, chasing a bunny.

Sparkle saw it, too. She pulled out her wand. The bunny dodged, this way and that. I hurried down—maybe I could catch it . . .

And then there were bunnies everywhere.

Malkin turned, her face livid. Sparkle's face was pure satisfaction.

Which one was Leo, though? Did he know where to go? I wasn't sure how much he knew when he was in bunny form. Malkin headed toward the east end of the field, chasing what she thought was the right bunny.

So I was the only one to see Devon sidle onto the field and scoop up a little brown rabbit.

I ran to him. There were so many people and rabbits now that we might be able to sneak away.

The rabbit trembled against Devon's chest, and he stroked its fur, soothing it. On the field, thirty other rabbits darted around the confused football players and cheerleaders, and Malkin plowed through them, searching for the right one.

"Get out of sight," I said. "Quick." I put a hand on Devon's back and steered him to the exit, trying to get us away from the witch on the field.

"I take it this is someone you know," he said, when we were outside of the stadium.

"Leo," I said. "Yes. If we find some cardamom we can help him change back."

"Or maybe we should get him out of here first," said Devon. "Take him somewhere safe. I've got my cargo bike." The little rabbit nestled in his arms.

"We can text Sparkle once we get to safety," I said. We hurried up to the parking lot—and stopped. There was Esmerelda, coming around the school toward us, her pink suit clearly visible in the dim evening light.

"This way," said Devon, and we turned—but there was Valda. She had her wand raised.

"Put the rabbit down," said Valda.

"Back away from the bunny," said Esmerelda.

The two of them glared at each other. "I'm bringing the shifter to Malkin," said Valda.

"No, I am," said Esmerelda.

"I knew you were a double-crossing—"

"Lying, cheating—"

"You can't have him, either of you," said Devon firmly. He held the shivering rabbit closer.

"You'll change your mind when I turn you into a toad," said Valda to Devon.

"No, a weasel," said Esmerelda.

"Are you nuts?" said Valda. "Weasels bite."

"Behind me, Devon," I said. He obeyed. I could work the Power spell on the witches, if I could only get the ingredients out of my backpack. I wasn't as strong as them, but maybe I could hold them off a little bit.

The witches straightened up, focusing on us again. It must be hard to keep your squabbles suppressed enough to get anything done. Valda reached for her fanny pack. Esmerelda stuck her hand into her green purse.

"They're dangerous," I said to the boy and bunny behind me. "I don't want to see either of you get hurt. You'd better put the bunny down."

"No," said Devon.

And then I felt a wind snap toward us. Malkin was coming.

There wasn't anything left to do. I had to call in the reinforcements.

I began to text Sarmine.

HELP

"Put down that phone," said Valda, "or I'll make you."

"Okay, okay," I said, but apparently I wasn't moving fast enough for Valda. A small sandbag dropped out of nowhere, banging my arms and knocking the phone to the ground. "Ow!"

"And you," said Esmerelda to Devon. "Put the bunny down or I'll cast Going Up on you."

"What, like floating?" I said.

"Makes you forget every one of your lyrics," Esmerelda said. "Sounds perfect, doesn't it?"

"Go for it," said Devon. "I'm not giving you Leo."

"Don't!" I lunged for Esmerelda. Valda dropped another sandbag on me. I tumbled and rolled, narrowly avoiding a third sandbag to the head, when I sat up and saw Esmerelda flick her spell out at Devon and the bunny.

Devon coughed as the mixture hit his face, but he held on to Leo. "Are you trying to sneeze the lyrics out of me?" he said. "I'm not going to forget the songs that easily."

Esmerelda smirked.

"She's a cool stick of . . . Oh god," said Devon.

"Devon, you wrote those songs," I said. "They're in there somewhere."

"Cool stick of . . . cool stick of . . ." He looked sick. "I know a girl . . . They're gone, Cam. Gone."

Then Malkin was there, and I knew I couldn't hold them off anymore. I moved to be with Devon and the bunny.

"I'll take that," said Malkin. She plucked the bunny from Devon's hands. "Who's got the ingredients for Moving Sidewalk?"

"I do," said Valda. She mixed something in her hand and tossed it at Devon's feet, chanting words.

He left. His feet took him and he headed away from us, back down the hill, back toward where he was supposed to play in the Battle of the Bands. "I'm sorry," he shouted to me. And then, from farther away I could hear the words drifting back: "Cool stick of . . . cool stick of . . ."

"Excellent," said Malkin. "Now to go somewhere where we can inscribe a pentagram for this shifter. Inside, please." She glared at me. "March."

I marched. We went in the side door, into a hallway. "I'll need a marker," said Malkin.

"I think I have one in here," I suggested, reaching into my backpack. If I could get my fanny pack . . .

"Drop it," said Malkin. She turned the wand on me and I obeyed. "Kick it into the corner," she said. I kicked, annoyed with myself. I should just have worn the stupid fanny pack. Ugh.

The backpack slid to the wall just as the side door opened and Sarmine strode in, carrying a large bubble-wrapped package.

"Sarmine," said Malkin unenthusiastically. "So nice of you to join us."

"So kind of you to invite me," said Sarmine. "I was relaxing on my sofa, looking at the thermometers and counting down the minutes, when I realized no one had come to my house for the usual celebratory unveiling, discussion of techniques, and martinis."

"I'll take a martini," said Valda. "Did you bring them?"

"And then I began to get worried," said Sarmine in a not-at-all-worried tone of voice, "that one of my dear friends might be jumping the gun, so to speak, and declaring themselves the winner before the final minute. I would hate to see a witch-spit bond be broken in so cavalier a fashion. Why, think of the bad luck!"

"All right, you've made your little speech," said Malkin. "You're correct that I had presumed that I would win in, what—fifteen minutes from now? But of course I want to do this the right way." She smiled nastily at me as she set her phone with a countdown timer in the middle of the floor. "It's only fun if you do it the right way."

"Exactly what I thought," said Sarmine. She unwrapped the thermometers and set them on the hallway floor.

I went closer, looking at the bubbles floating in the thermometers. Two were still above the line, but the one I sought out first was Valda's.

I had destroyed Jenah's faith in me. Her bubble hung just below the line. I had failed.

Then I looked at Malkin's bubble, the one that was Devon. His hung even lower than Jenah's. Like rock bottom. So not only had I failed both of my friends, and failed to win the bet, *Malkin* was the winner. She didn't have a shred of conscience in her entire body, and the other witches would help her tear out Leo's teeth and pluck out his toenails and god knows what else.

I slumped down.

Malkin laughed at me. "Time for the unveiling of the cards," she said. "We might as well do this up right. Happiest to unhappiest, kids, let's go."

That meant Sarmine was first. She, at least, had played me fair, and her bubble was well above the line. She pulled out the card from her fanny pack and tossed it on the floor. Caden. He and his family had raked in so much money from the families who'd been able to buy new cars that he was doing just fine. It made me feel a little better to know that Sarmine really was on my side, no matter how funny of a way she had of showing it.

Esmerelda was next. She pulled the card from her purse and tossed it to the floor. Then flipped it off. Henny. Esmerelda had done her worst, but Jenah and I had encouraged Henny to take control of her own life, and that had worked out. There was one thing I had done right.

Valda sighed. "This one is resilient," she said. "No matter what I did she maintained a positive, can-do attitude. Wouldn't have thought it from such a little punk." She smirked at me as she tossed down the Jenah card. "But finally it occurred to me to enlist the help of someone who really knew her."

"Go to hell," I said.

Eleven minutes left. Malkin grinned at me as she held up the very last card, the Devon card, the card of the poor boy who must be bombing on stage right this second, mad at himself for not being able to rise above the spells the witches had worked on him. "Well, this might be interfering with the results a little," Malkin said, "but I'm counting on your complete and utter despair at losing to see us through." She tossed the card on the floor to reveal . . . me.

I looked at her, uncomprehending. "But you wrecked Devon's life. I saw you. And the agreement was that you would only try to make your own student's life miserable."

"And it worked," she said, leering at me.

"But then . . . But then it wasn't Devon at all," I said. "He's safe." The bubble bumped up, just a little, at the thought.

Malkin glared at the bubble.

"Wait wait wait. That means . . . that means *I'm* in charge of my own thermometer," I said. "I control that bubble. What if I refuse to give up? What if I insist on being happy?" I stared at that bubble. If it really was me, then I could force it to rise. All I had to do was decide that Malkin wasn't going to win after all. The bubble buoyed up a notch. I had control. I could do this. Another notch.

Malkin waved a dismissive hand. "Go for it," she said. "But you still can't get us all above the midline." She nodded at Valda. "We have a deal, you see."

"Fifty-fifty investment in the shifter," said Valda.

"Eighty-twenty," said Malkin. "The brains of the operation gets more."

"Now wait," said Esmerelda. "I helped distract Camellia, too. I should at least get ten percent."

Malkin considered this while I despaired. Ten minutes left. Even if I could change my own thermometer, I could not change Jenah's. I could not win.

Knowing that I could not win sent my bubble plummeting back to the bottom.

I looked at the three bickering witches, each loudly announcing how they would divvy up Leo, and I thought hard. No matter which of them won, I was screwed. Leo was screwed. That meant . . .

Slowly I looked from Sarmine's quite happy thermometer up to Sarmine. She wore the self-satisfied expression of the patient teacher who has just watched his dullest student arrive at the correct answer.

"If I help you destroy all the cars in the world," I said slowly, "I can make you win. And you're the only one of them who won't destroy Leo."

"I'll go one better," she said. "You make me win and I'll hide your shifter for you forever."

I shook my head. "But you could have won at any time," I said. "You have the spell all ready to go. If you destroy the cars Caden's family owns, then you destroy them. Just find his family in the stadium and, I don't know, explain to them in graphic detail how their lives will be destroyed. You could still win."

"It would not be any fun for me to win all by myself," said Sarmine. "I want your help." She pulled a folded piece of paper from her skirt pocket and held it out to me.

Malkin was getting redder and redder in the face. "Now wait a minute," she said. "You're not supposed to be working together."

"Really?" I said, eying Valda.

"That was different," protested Valda. "That was cheating. Cheating is practically fair play."

"This isn't cheating if you're doing it out in the open," explained Esmerelda.

"Consider it backstabbing," I said. "Except from the front."

My fingers were shaking with the adrenaline. I held out my hand for the paper, and Sarmine put the completed, worked-out spell in my hand.

In Sarmine's familiar spiky handwriting, it read:

Malkin's Sympathetic Resonance Spell—Updated

2 tablespoons monkey brains
8 squished pixies
15 butterfly wings
2 lizard tails
1 pinch powdered eye of newt
1 cauldron of 10 bananas + 3 gal milk, steeped for 5 days
Sympathetic resonance catalyst, which Malkin will give us once we win, 2 CENTS SAYS IT'S A LINDWORM SCALE.

I closed my eyes. Backstabbing, all right. Sarmine's plan was clear. I could save Leo forever. But what did I weigh it against? One monkey, eight pixies, eight butterflies, two lizards, and one newt. How did you measure lives against each other? How could you?

And not only that, of course. Sarmine's plan to destroy every car in the world would certainly achieve her goal of burning less fossil fuels, and making people remember how to bike and walk and everything else.

But it would destroy so many lives in the process. That wasn't any kind of slow change. That would wipe out families with jobs in auto factories and car dealerships and everything else. It would wipe out taxi drivers. It would destroy everyone who couldn't afford to live near their job, or their school.

And it wasn't right to be blackmailed into it, even to save Leo.

I closed my eyes tightly. Sarmine so wanted to toughen me up she was willing to sacrifice her own plans to do it. When would she get a lindworm scale again? Never, unless she won it now.

I shook my head. Maybe it would be different if my back weren't against the wall. But I wasn't going to give in to bullies.

"I can't help you, Sarmine," I said. "I can't."

Sarmine's face set into angry lines. Malkin high-fived Valda.

The clock ticked closer.

"And you." I rounded on Malkin. "You can't win Leo, anyway. He wasn't yours to offer up as a prize and he's not yours to win now. He's a person, not a thing."

"He may not be mine to win," said Malkin. "But he's mine to take."

The clock began to strike and she plopped the bunny into Esmerelda's purse, then held out her left hand to Valda and Esmerelda. They both seized it, and with her right, she cast a powder up in the air and slashed her wand through it. She chanted, "Aljeni, Aljeni, Aljeni . . ."

"Now wait a minute," said Sarmine, rising. "I can't let you do this."

But the other three witches must have had their plan all worked out. Malkin was busy working some sort of transportation spell, but Valda and Esmerelda each had one free hand. Valda held out a green powder and Esmerelda scraped her wand through it and blew it straight at Sarmine.

The green powder turned into vines that wrapped around Sarmine's arms and legs, covering up her wand and her fanny pack. She stumbled backward, the vines tripping her. The mean girls had momentarily bested her.

I didn't know exactly what they were doing but I knew it involved Leo. And I knew I was the only one left.

I scrambled across the hallway, grabbing the witches' hands just as Malkin chanted the very last word. Behind me I heard the glass of the tubes breaking as Sarmine fell across them. Her head went down hard as the glass shattered on the floor. "Mom," I shrieked. But it was in the distance already, because we were zooming through the school, around hallways, through doorways, until Malkin brought us to a sudden stop in the gymnasium.

I rolled and came up again with my wand. My ingredients were still in my backpack in the hallway, but maybe they wouldn't realize that immediately.

But Valda was quicker. She had her wand out and on me.

Esmerelda pulled the bunny out of the purse and set him down on the basketball court, keeping her hand on him. Malkin pulled out a marker and began drawing the pentagram. . . .

And then the back door to the gym opened. I craned my head—was it Sarmine?

Sparkle and Henny rushed into the gym, disheveled and panting. Sparkle's black ponytail was in tangles around her face and Henny's glasses were at an angle. "We've been looking for you everywhere," shouted Henny. "I've got Leo!"

Everyone turned at that. Each of the girls was cradling a bunny.

"No, you don't," shouted Sparkle. "I do!" They came closer, arguing back and forth.

Esmerelda laughed. "Girls fighting over a boy," she said. "How amusing."

But I saw the girls' eyes flick to each other. They were coordinating. As the witches laughed, Sparkle said, "Now!"

They released the bunnies. All three bunnies bounded in different directions.

Esmerelda swore, and all three witches dove for the bunnies. I raised my wand.

Then Malkin had her wand at my throat. "I wouldn't," she said.

"Hunnngh," I said. Esmerelda came up behind Malkin, a

frightened rabbit kicking in her arms. Valda had another one by the ears.

Malkin grabbed the third. "We'll solve this," she said. She pulled out a jar of cardamom from her jacket pocket. "Which witch has the shifter?"

"Maybe none of them," I said as she waved the jar under the nose of her bunny, then Esmerelda's. "Maybe he's still on the field, and . . . and . . . he got away."

Malkin held the jar up to Valda's bunny.

Suddenly Valda was holding a very naked boy by the ears. "Ew," she said, and jumped back.

"Mm," said Esmerelda.

Malkin rolled her eyes and finished inscribing his pentagram. Valda magicked him up a towel, which he wrapped around himself. Esmerelda focused her wand on Sparkle and Henny while dusting rabbit hairs off of her pink suit. Sparkle was still in her cheerleading uniform and her hands were empty—if her wand was with her, it must be in her kneesocks or something.

"I was watching him," said Sparkle, "And then she tricked me." She glared at Malkin, who shrugged.

"*C'est la guerre,*" Malkin said. She advanced on Leo, who was looking like he was only a whisker away from bunnying himself. "And now you, my little lion, are going to become a very special animal for me." She grinned. "The lindworm."

"I want him to be a unicorn first," said Esmerelda. "If I just shave the hairs off of his neck I'll be set for life. You don't need the neck, do you, Malkin?"

"Dibs on the tail," said Valda.

Leo swallowed.

"But you can't make him turn into a lindworm," I pointed out. "Not if there aren't any more."

"It is true I have been searching for the lindworm for a while," Malkin said. "And it is true that they are, sadly, extinct. But halfway through my search it occurred to me that I didn't have to find a lindworm. All I had to find was a shifter . . . and some lindworm DNA."

My eyes widened.

"See, I could've been a velociraptor," Leo said under his breath. Gallows humor.

"I found the last scale known to man in a tiny museum in Italy," continued Malkin. "Mislabeled, of course. They didn't know what they had. And it just sat there gathering dust. But I recognized the tint, the shine, the sparkle! All so clear to anyone with witch blood. It was exactly as it had been described." She pulled out a small vial from her pocket. She was right. To me, the scale emitted a glow. "Once you touch this, you will be able to change," she said to Leo. She uncorked the vial and slid it through the pentagram to him.

"And then what?" I said. "You'll pluck his canines out, start a plague, and call it a day? He can go to the dentist and we can go home?"

She shook her head. "Of course not, Sarmine's daughter." She looked up at Leo, her eyes soft and caressing. "I need his heart."

16

If You fail . . .

"Can't give you my heart, I'm afraid," said Leo. "It's already taken."

"Oh, Leo," cooed Sparkle.

I admired his bravery even as I wanted to tell him to shut up. Malkin wasn't joking around.

"You will turn into a lindworm for me," Malkin said. "Or else."

"Or else I'll turn into a rabbit?" said Leo. "I'm good at that one."

"Or else I'll go strangle your fathers," Malkin said coolly.

Leo shut up.

"The legendary lindworm," rhapsodized Malkin. "With it I can rule the world." I settled back against my heels. This could take a while.

"All the world?" said Henny. "I didn't know wicked witches were usually so vague about their plans."

"You shut up, too," said Malkin. "I plan to use the catalyzing power of the lindworm to gain control of all the remaining oil in the world. It's the sympathetic resonance spell I've been working on my entire career. Without the lindworm, the spell had very limited range—a few feet. Now, scales will definitely give me the range, but not the long-lasting control. But with the heart . . . I work my spell on one drop of oil, and it gives me control of every single drop, everywhere, forever. I'd consider that 'ruling the world,' wouldn't you?"

Oh, Sarmine would love to hear that. I wondered if I had had the choice again, if I would have chosen differently. Picked Sarmine's evil instead of Malkin's.

"Now, where did I set the cardamom?" mused Malkin.

"You'd better be careful," I said. "Leo and Sparkle were practicing at the zoo. Who knows how many vicious creatures he's touched by now? He might rip you from ear to ear."

Malkin glanced over at me. "So you do have some witchy knowledge in that mundane little head. Did your father teach you about shifters?"

"I never knew my father," I said.

Malkin snorted. "That's rich."

"What?"

"Your father is the one who helped his shifter mother get to 'safety,'" she sneered. "The witchness protection program, such as it is."

"But he's not . . . I mean, you're not . . ." I looked at Leo. I didn't want to date him, but that would be a little too weird for comfort if he were my half brother.

Malkin rolled her eyes. Witches do that a lot. "No, your father was just a bleeding-heart softie," she said. "We could never figure out what Sarmine saw in him."

I saw hope forming in Leo's eyes. "Is my mother . . . Is she still alive?" he said.

But we both knew the answer. How else had Malkin finally tracked Leo down?

"She died well," Malkin conceded, and I shuddered.

Leo's chest was rising and falling, huge racking breaths that echoed in the basketball court. He looked like he was only controlling himself from shifting with great effort. Even I wanted to smash Malkin's face in and I am ordinarily the least violent person there is. "She would never have told you where I am," he managed.

"Nah," said Malkin. "I had to ransack her place. Her problem was she was unwilling to cut you off forever. See, her apartment was clean and tiny and had almost nothing in it. But she had two laptops. One that was brand new and one that looked, oh . . . how old did you say you were?"

Leo did not answer this.

"Well, you know how long laptops last. And why would she have two? She wasn't in tech. She wasn't a hoarder. Most importantly, she wasn't a witch. She didn't have any way to check up on you. That is, unless a certain softhearted witch had bespelled her a device that was brand-new seventeen years ago. Her only possible connection to you." Malkin shrugged gracefully, like a cat. "Once I cracked the password, there you were."

You could have heard a pin drop in the gym.

"It was set up to grab little videos of you now and then. Seemed to be keyed in to important events. It got your first bike ride, wobbling around a long driveway. The first book you read all by yourself—*Go, Dog. Go!* wasn't it? First trip to the zoo. There were about a hundred of them, all neatly labeled and dated."

My eyes were filled with tears and Leo's didn't look much better. Sparkle's teeth were clenched. She really *had* cared for her shifter friend.

"The most recent one was labeled *Homecoming Game*. But when I clicked on it, it only showed me a second before the screen went black and an error message popped up. Then the laptop fried itself. It knew what had happened."

Go Dad, I thought.

"But I had seen a flash of the team colors. Orange and forest green. I have to tell you that narrowed it down considerably. And when I realized that one of those schools, Hal Headley High, was in the exact same town where my dear old friend Sarmine lived—well! I knew it couldn't be coincidence."

"Evil villain monologuing," said Henny under her breath.

But Malkin had heard. She snapped her wand over to Esmerelda and ordered, "Bring up the girlfriend."

"Excuse me?" said Sparkle. "I am a wicked witch in my own right, you know."

Malkin shrugged. "You'll bleed like any old human." To Esmerelda she said, "Threaten her."

Esmerelda held her wand on Sparkle. Sparkle, to give credit where credit was due, looked more pissed than terrified. Mean girls of different generations, squaring off. "What threat would you like?" inquired Esmerelda. "Purple boils? Slugs down your neck? Public humiliation?"

Sparkle sneered. "Pathetic."

"Fine," said Esmerelda. "How about good old-fashioned torture?"

"Ugh," said Sparkle as the wand tip poked into her throat. "So . . . very . . . gauche. . . ."

"Stop!" said Leo. "I'll change."

"Don't do it, Leo," I shouted. "You'll save Sparkle but we'll lose everything."

"Gee, thanks, Cam," said Sparkle. The wand dug in. "Huunnngh. I mean, she's actually right. Don't do it."

"I have to do the right thing," Leo said. "No one else should die for me."

He reached down and touched the lindworm scale. His eyes closed and I wondered what he saw. Did he see that exact lindworm from so many years ago? Did he see it slithering around in the wild; see the end of its life? There was an imploding feeling as if he was sucking all the air toward him.

And then rearing overhead was the lindworm.

Violently it strained forward, attempting to swat the witch with its massive white bulk. It slammed into the invisible sides of the pentagram and slid down. Malkin laughed. She held her wand high. . . .

And then there was a terrific noise behind us. Some sort of cavalry, I thought, someone coming to save us. Sarmine, perhaps. Malkin had too much sense to turn, but we all did, just in time to see Jenah zooming up the stairs from the locker room on a flying bicycle.

"I'm coming, I'm coming!" she shouted. She had a baseball bat in her hand and I almost cheered. "How do you stop this thing?"

She crashed right into Valda and bowled them both over. Malkin gracefully hopped over the bat that came sliding across the floor. She did not move her wand from Leo, and Esmerelda did not move her wand from Sparkle's throat. "Over there with the others," she barked at Jenah, and Jenah eeped and ran to us as my last hope fell.

I looked down at her. "You tried," I whispered.

"No talking," barked Valda. "Malkin needs to work the spell."

Malkin started laying things around Leo's pentagram. A mermaid fin. A Bigfoot claw. Uncooked bacon.

Jenah's hand found mine. If I was going to die with someone Jenah was a good person to do it with. Although of course I wasn't very interested in dying at all. I would much rather . . . wait, what was Jenah putting into my hand?

My fanny pack.

It had an unpleasantly greasy feel to it . . . oh. Jenah had rubbed eels all over it. It was invisible.

That was what Jenah was really bringing. The baseball bat was a red herring.

I breathed. Now was the moment when I needed to be Sarmine and have an army of spells in my memory. She would be able to combine what she had and come up with something to save the day. What had I learned this week? I already knew my Power spell couldn't stand up to Malkin's. And I seriously doubted that the Possibilities potion would suddenly open her up to the idea of being a good witch.

And then I knew.

The spell itself was the longest of long shots, and worse, it would involve me changing my Good Witch Ethics list yet again.

Don't use animal parts in spells—*unless it's to save a life.*

I hadn't been willing to work Showstopper to help Devon sing. But I would work it now.

Luckily I was really familiar with the ingredients by this point. I stuck my hand into the invisible fanny pack and combined the parsley, rutabaga . . . and pixie bone. I pretended to cough and spat in my hand.

Esmerelda was busy enjoying the intense gazing going on between Sparkle and Leo the Lindworm. Malkin was preparing her spell. But Valda was watching us, smoking a cigarette.

I nudged Jenah's foot and she knew what I meant. That's the best thing about best friends. They know when a foot nudge means "distract that wicked witch right now."

"Hey, the school's going to be pissed about that," Jenah said to Valda.

Valda laughed. "So?"

"So, uh. They've got sensors all over the school. The sprinklers will kick in any moment."

Malkin looked up from her work. "Put it out, Valda."

"This is not like the good old days," said Valda.

"Now," said Malkin. "I don't need anything messing up my pentagram."

Valda sighed and threw the cigarette on the floor. She pulled her skirts aside to rub it out with her shoe, and as she did, Jenah "accidentally" tripped into her. Valda swore as she went down.

I swiped my wand through the spell on my hand and flung the Showstopper formula all over the lindworm.

Immediately Leo turned into the most charming lindworm I have ever seen in my life. I mean, it was sheer animal magnetism. And Leo was already kind of charming, so trust me when I say that this was the most charming entity in the northern hemisphere at the moment.

Lindworms unfortunately lack the power of speech, but he turned his great, soulful, puppy dog eyes on Malkin and she melted. I mean figuratively, not literally, as nice as that would have been. Her wand lowered. Her lip quivered. She walked up to him in a daze and began to scrub out the chalk outline of the pentagram with her toe.

"Malkin, it's a trap!" shouted Esmerelda.

Leo swung his giant puppy dog eyes over to Esmerelda and her wand lowered, too. Just enough that Sparkle could wiggle out of her grasp, and get a headlock on her, just when Leo needed to turn back to Malkin, who was beginning to suspect something was not quite right.

"Kiyah!" said Henny, and she jumped on Valda, sending her sprawling again. Jenah sat on her head.

Malkin rubbed some more chalk outline free . . .

And then Leo was out.

I thought he was simply going to turn back into Leo, but lindworm instinct is apparently a powerful thing. He seized Malkin's vest in his teeth. He slithered with her, down the hall, heading down the stairs. He humped along rather quickly for a giant worm.

"Whoa, is he going to eat her?" said Henny.

There were chomping and slurping sounds from the stairwell, punctuated by some howls from Malkin. I didn't really want to know, to be perfectly frank.

Sparkle had magicked up a rope and was busy tying up the witches.

"What are we going to do with them?" I said. "We can't let them go, or they'll come back to get Leo. He'll never be safe."

"I'll take them," said Sparkle. "I can do an amnesia spell that will take out just this week." She glanced at me. "It'll take my last vial of dragon tears, though," she said. "Amnesia's tough."

I sighed. "I'll give you one of ours." Even though the dragon had left us, we were still the main source in town for dragon tears.

"Monday morning," Sparkle said. She considered. "You can give it to me at lunch if you wish."

Sparkle was allowing me to come up to the cool kids' table? To be seen with her? It was so unbearably condescending I almost called her on it. Except . . . I wouldn't mind repairing our friendship, at least a little bit. "I will," I said.

She trained her wand on the witches and they left.

I turned to look for Henny and Jenah. "This was totally awesome,"

Henny said. "I have enough emotional material for a million comics."

"I don't have to make Sparkle give you the amnesia spell, too, do I?" I said. "You won't tell anyone about any of this?"

"I swear," said Henny. "By the time I've changed it over to *Captain Awesome and Amazing Punk Girl Save the Day from a Radioactive Inchworm Gone Haywire!* you totally won't recognize it."

"Ahem?"

"With a little help from their good friend, ScienceGrrl?" said Henny.

"That sounds just right," I said.

"I have to go find my tablet before I forget any of my ideas," said Henny. "I'll see you Monday."

She ran the opposite way from the disgusting lindworm trail and then it was just me and Jenah.

"Thank you," I said. "For saving the day."

"You're welcome," she said. "You'll have to thank your mom, too. When I came back to apologize, she was just groggily sitting up. Trying to untangle the magic vines."

"Was she . . . ?"

"Yeah. She's okay. She gave me your backpack and pointed me in the right direction. So she did help."

"But you thought of the invisible eels."

"I also thought about drinking them," she said, "but I didn't think it would help you if I was puking all over the floor."

"You were perfect and brave," I said.

"You know what? I kind of liked this week. Bandages and all."

"Don't get too used to it," I said. "I'd like things to go back to normal right about now. Normal is easy."

"It isn't, really," said Jenah. "Because it was never true. This is true, you know."

"Speaking of true," I said. "First thing Monday morning I will tell your history teacher the truth about the grades. What's the worst he can do to me? Cut out my heart?"

Jenah sighed. "I know you were just trying to help," she said. "I overreacted."

"No, you were right to be mad at me. I was messing around with your life."

"What kind of person complains that their best friend tried to give them a B? Especially when they thought they were just trying to fix the thing the witch did that wasn't the thing they thought it was but was something else . . ." Jenah laughed. "Oh, honestly, the only thing that could make this more confusing is time travel."

"Don't tempt fate," I said. "I don't want to hear that the witches have a time machine next."

"If they did I guess I'd have to go back and try to get a better grade," she said. "Of all the boring uses for a time machine."

"Finals are coming," I said. "I'll make everything up to you by helping you study."

"You're in the video-watching American history class," she said. "You don't know any more about the Civil War than I do, do you?"

I shrugged. "No, but I do know how to make flash cards," I said. "And I know how to sit down with you at your kitchen table and stop you from sewing a new skirt or watching clips from Broadway musicals on your phone. I can make you work."

"Let me get this straight," Jenah said. "You're going to make it up to me for almost ruining my life by making me *study*?"

"I'm going to make up for giving you a passing grade by making you *earn* it," I said.

Jenah squeezed my hand. "I can always count on you," she said. "And you can always count on me. I shouldn't have yelled that thing about friendships breaking because it isn't true, so you have to forgive me for that one. When you and I make mistakes we can fix them."

I dashed tears out of my eyes. "Yes," I agreed.

The Nice Little Epilogue

It was a glorious Saturday afternoon, the last gasp of good weather until spring. Sarmine and I biked up to the park and spread out a picnic blanket. The winning band was playing a concert in the park, and people were out in full force, biking or strolling around the park. From up here I could see loads more bikes all over town. Like it or not, it was clear that Sarmine had made a difference. Families were smiling as they spread out their picnic blankets; bikes and cargo bikes littered the hill. We could see everything.

Including our RV garage down in the valley. It was belching a surprising amount of pink smoke. "So I'm, um, surprised you didn't work the Kill the Cars spell anyway," I said, feeling her out. "After the bet was over and your promise to me was over. I know you were out late last night on the football field retrieving shed lindworm scales."

The witch wrinkled her nose. "I tried," she said. "But something was off with the mixture." She took a sharp glance at me. "You did stir it every day as requested, yes? One hundred turns counterclockwise, no more or less?"

"Scout's honor," I said.

"Hmm," she said. "It almost seemed as if something was added to the spell that negated it." She looked out across the distance. "I would be quite impressed if someone in my own household had figured out how to double-cross me by negating my spell."

Er. What had I done to that potion? I thought back to that first day, when I had gotten all misty-eyed about the dragon. Hmm. I would have to look up in Sarmine's books and see if "tears of a witch" had any known properties. Really, someone should compile all the known substances into one clear, accurate textbook. Not that any witch would ever do that . . . I came back from my reverie to remember what her last statement was. "Er, yes," I said. "That would indeed be very impressive. That person might be well on her way to becoming a True Witch."

Hastily I switched the subject. Might as well leave her thinking I was cleverer and craftier than I actually was.

"So Sparkle wiped this week's memories out of Valda and Esmerelda," I said. "But you know there are loads more witches out there. And a secret's not safe forever."

Sarmine nodded. She seemed to be admiring her pink smoke.

"So you won't help Leo?" I said. "You know a spell to hide him and you flat-out won't do it?"

Sarmine leveled her brows at me. "There *is* a spell to hide someone permanently from witches," she said. "Used as a last resort—because, for example—*you* would never be able to interact with him again. He would simply slide past your notice."

I didn't like that idea. Sparkle wouldn't, either. But for Leo I'd do it. "Well, what are you waiting for? Prove you're not the most horrible person in the whole world," I said.

"The spell uses a substance found only in the stomach lining of dolphin babies," she said.

"Good god, what?"

She shrugged. "So please, Camellia. Go ahead and work this spell anytime you wish."

I rocked back on my heels. I could see that Sparkle and I were going to be protecting Leo for a long time.

"I need to start doing more research," I said. "There have to be vegetarian substitutes out there that can do what these animal parts do." Isolate the compounds that caused something to levitate, for example . . . could spells possibly be reduced to chemistry? Just because the unicorn hair/green tea compound hadn't worked the first time as a substitute for powdered pixie bone, didn't mean there weren't more things to be tried. I mean, look at the way my small variations to the Power spell had caused it to work better and better each time. There was more research to be read in the witch's library, and in other witch libraries around the world.

Really, when you came right down to it, witchcraft and ethics weren't all that dissimilar. There was never just one right answer. And you didn't give up just because one time you made something explode.

I leaned back on my elbows. I guess it was time to forgive the witch . . . for now. After all, she'd kept her promise, and hadn't destroyed her student's life, as much as she wanted to. And if she hadn't stepped in to rescue Leo . . . there was also the point that she hadn't murdered any little dolphin babies to do it. Some days the best thing you can say about your mom is that she hasn't murdered any little dolphin babies recently.

And that's all right.

We lay back on the hill and watched the city full of bikes. I saw Henny and Jenah pedaling side by side—Henny appeared to have a big folding easel strapped to her back. Farther down—Leo, back in human form and without his fancy car, balancing a laughing Sparkle on his handlebars.

A cargo bike separated itself from the pack and began winding back and forth up the zigzagging path toward us.

Devon.

He slung his leg over his bike and came up to me. "Cam," he said, "I owe you an apology."

I glanced over at the witch. She stared at me for a moment. Then she rolled her eyes. "Fine," she said, and stalked off to go wreak havoc elsewhere in the park.

Devon sat down next to me on the blanket. The band playing in the distance sounded like a good group. If not for me, it could have been his band up there.

"No, I owe *you* an apology," I said. "I could have given you Showstopper after Malkin made you forget all your lyrics but I chose not to. And then I know it seems like I flip-flopped immediately to give it to Leo, but . . ."

"You made the right call," he said. "Both times."

"How did it . . . ?" I trailed off. I mean, obviously it had been a disaster.

He snorted. "The band found me babbling 'cool stick of butter' so they stuck me in the back, handed me a triangle, and told me to look pretty. Then Nnenna sang all the songs from a mic at the drum set. She was amazing, frankly. We might end up making it a permanent change." I could hear the tinge of regret at his own failure behind the genuine happiness for Nnenna. "We only didn't win because when *she* went up on the lyrics, she swore a blue streak into the mic. Parents didn't like it but gig requests started rolling in."

I was glad something good had come out of that performance, even if it wasn't quite what he or I wanted.

Devon brushed at the dirt on his knees. "But look, that's not it. I wanted to say I'm sorry for being weird this week. I've still been trying to figure out who I am post-demon. And deal with the fact that I am definitely not as cool as he was."

"I think you're plenty cool," I said firmly.

He laughed. "Well, you might be the only one. And then I kept seeing you with Leo, and it's not that I was jealous exactly—" He broke off. "Okay, maybe I was."

"That's okay," I jumped in. Don't lie, and don't be a weasel. "I mean, I was even jealous of Nnenna for part of the week, so . . ."

"Nnenna? She likes girls."

"Oh. Oh!"

"It's okay," he assured me. "I'm frequently jealous of her myself. At any rate, it wasn't you. It was me feeling . . . not up to standards. I know you were just helping Leo with the shifting, and so what? Even if you weren't, you have the right to live your own life.

It was just me trying to deal with not being as cool as I think I should be. To, uh. To deserve you."

"That is the first time anyone ever said they should be cool to deserve me," I said.

He looked at me like I was bonkers. "Cam, you rescued a football hero from a pack of witches. You have a *flying bike*. You are the coolest girl I know."

I sighed happily. I was going to have to readjust my internal expectations to the idea of being cool. I mean, not that anyone else in my life was going to think I was cool. But Devon thought I was cool. That was enough.

Besides, not only was I cool, I told myself, I had gumption.

"This is weird," I said. "But you remember back when you had that demon in you a couple weeks ago, and you kept trying to kiss me? And I obviously couldn't let you because it was an evil plot?"

"Would you like me to pretend there's another evil plot?"

I wriggled closer. "Demonic plots seem a lot simpler than everything that's happened this week."

He wrapped both arms around me. I felt safe and protected, and I have to admit it was kind of a nice change, because lately I had been the one protecting everybody. That's all right. Everyone should get a chance to pretend that they're the big strong one. I looked up into Devon's sweet, kind face.

"Kiss me," I said.

He obeyed, and I will now direct your attention to the beautiful autumn morning going on behind us, at least for a few minutes. It was leaf-filled and lovely, and after a few minutes he took a breath and said, "Cam?"

"Yes?" I said.

"I just have one question."

"Is it whether you need to stop? Because you don't need to stop."

"Is life at your high school always going to be this exciting?"

"Perhaps," I said. "Perhaps."

Appendix

SPELLS

☾

A Mystikal Spelle of Great Power

- If the day of the week begins with *S*, find some slugs.
- If the day of the week begins with *Y*, find some yak fur.
- If the day of the week begins with *W*, find some walrus tusks.
- If the day of the week begins with *T*, find some thyme.
- If the day of the week begins with *M*, find some monkey brains.

Let the DAY=*X*. For ye olde occasions when *X* doth equal *S*, carefully extract the intestines of one slug and combine with blackest coffee. For all occasions of *X*, use thou a pinch of ginger. For all the many occasions when *X* doth equal *Y*, the clumps of fur needed shall be equal to the number of letters in the day that begins with *M*. Let the YEAR=*Q*. For ye verie interesting occasions when *X* doth equal *W*, extract both tusks by hand, and shave twelve tablespoons of Ivorie under a bright sun. For all occasions of *X* where *X* equals *X*, use one of thine own hairs. If *X* doth perchance equal *T*, combine you then one dragon's tear and one pinch of thyme. If *X* should equal *M*, depart to yon nearest zoo and returneth bearing your prize.

Mix all necessary ingredients and breathe in, imagining yourself a full ten feet tall, clad in the trappings of power. Exult in the superior might that you have shown. Disregard all those who said you couldst not do it! You totally could. You are a Moderne Witch, the Equal of Anything! You got this.

A Lovelie Spell to Open You to Possibilities

Ingredients

dark chocolate	rubies of the cave nymph
candied violets	pomegranate juice
caramel	tears of the lake dryad
pixie dew	syrup
hazelnuts	dew of the bayou orchids
rose petals	spearmint grown by a bogwitch

Preparation

This recipe is so lovely, isn't it? I love all these things. I can hardly tell you which to choose. Perhaps it should be three leaves of a bogwitch's spearmint, grown in the sun-soaked terraces of Sicily, plus a quarter cup of finest caramel, made by a local pastry chef whom you have fallen madly for. Or perhaps start with a bouquet of violets, candied on a misty night by the light of a single beeswax candle . . . [spell continues for three pages] . . . but in the end, I think the classics are usually the best. Combine one tablespoon syrup, one drop pomegranate juice, one finely ground rose petal, and one drop pixie dew. Stir and serve to one who would be entranced by an opening of possibility.

Invisibility Spell

Ingredient: Invisible eels

Usage: Ingested or as ointment

Taste: Disgusting

Showstopper Spell

Ingredients

one bright idea
one pinch parsley
one cup of dirt
one martini
one bag of oats
one lucky star
one folding chair
one pinch powdered rutabaga
one carton eggs
one pinch powdered pixie bone
one stack of playing cards
one drop witch spit
another martini
another martini

Preparation

1. Deal out the playing cards.
2. Combine the dirt and the oats.
3. Play a round of solitaire.
4. Throw out the oats-dirt mixture—what were you thinking?
5. Cook up the carton of eggs.
6. Have a martini.
7. Have another.

8. This is way too many eggs.
9. Have a third martini.
10. Wish on a lucky star.
11. Disregard all previous steps. I mean, they made for an interesting evening, but it won't get you the effect you want. (A dozen eggs? Really?)
12. How to get unstoppable charisma:
13. Combine the parsley, rutabaga, and pixie bone.
14. Spit in it.
15. Give it to the would-be superstar of your choice.
16. Relax in your folding chair and watch in fascination.

Good Witch Ethics—FINAL LIST!!!

1. Don't use animal parts in spells, unless it's to save a life.
2. Ask people before you work a spell on them (or for them), unless in self-defense.
3. Don't lie to friends.
4. Don't be a weasel.
5. If you fall, you get back up and try again.

ACKNOWLEDGMENTS

I like getting a chance to thank people. In this case, we'll start vith Meghan Sinoff, Tinatsu Wallace, and Caroline M. Yoachim, or talking me down from ledges during all the first drafts that I ept trying and throwing away. Next, to Kij Johnson and everyone everyone!) at the KU CSSF Repeat Offenders workshop, where finally got on the right course and wrote the first draft (the real ne this time!) in one burst of lightning. (A particular thanks to Dominick D'Aunno for pacing me—outpacing me—as we raced o complete our drafts.) After much revising, I can then give nore thanks to Caroline again, Brian Allard, Kirsten Lincoln, nd my dad, for reading final-er and final-er drafts.

The production of a novel is a team effort. Thanks go to the ver-sharp Ginger Clark and the team at Curtis Brown, the fabu-ous Melissa Frain and the fantastic Desirae Friesen at Tor, Amy tapp for her able assistance, NaNá V. Stoelzle for copyedits, mma Goulder for yet another amazing cover image, and every-ne else at Tor/Tor Teen for your help and support. Many thanks lso to the Tor.com team, including Chris Buzelli and Irene Gallo, or the gorgeous artwork for my Tor.com prequel story to this eries (It's called "That Seriously Obnoxious Time I Was Stuck at Vitch Rimelda's One Hundredth Birthday Party," it involves Cam attling some inflatable kraken, and you should check it out if you aven't).

An especial thanks to everyone who hosted me on tour or for lks this year—the bookstores (Powell's, Mysterious Galaxy, eattle Mystery Bookshop, the Raven, the Kansas Union, Reader's

Guide, B&N Tanasbourne, B&N Clackamas), the libraries (Ledding, Stayton, Redmond, Hillsdale, and North Plains), the cons (Orycon, WorldCon, World Fantasy), and the et ceteras (Cascade Writers, Willamette Writers). I am also tremendously grateful to everyone who came out to one of those stops, as well as those who helped me bypass the limitations of my ancient phone by doing cool modern stuff like taking pictures and tagging me. (Jenna! Tracy!)

Many thanks to Tinatsu again for the addition of the *Seriously Wicked* bracelet to my event fabulousness (also, Desirae supplied cupcakes to the Powell's event and Danielle brought homemade sandwich cookies—so it was pretty amazing and I'm sorry if you missed it). I also want to particularly thank Kate Ristau and Dale Ivan Smith for their help this year in connecting me with many great events. And now I have to stop listing all the people who helped me at events this year because otherwise I will leave too many people off and then there will be guilt. So much guilt. Let me just say that I appreciate all of you, so much.

The usual big thanks to my family, particularly my parents for watching the darling little irrepressibles last summer while I wrote that first draft. A special thank-you to Uncle RJ (who helped me with the Thai name for Pops), and in memory of Uncle Rick. I am sorry you didn't get to see this one—I always loved reading your stories, and I had hoped you would like this one.

And finally, an apology (for failing to stop Cam from foiling the witch's plan) as well as huge thanks to Eric, without whom none of this could be done. I suppose that last bit's grammatical, and yet it sounds fishy. Alas, we've already passed the copyedits stage. You see? I can't do this without my team! Did I ever tell you how they stopped me from saying "spring solstice" in *Ironskin*? Also, they know the difference between *sank* and *sunk*. Let me tell you, without them, I would be.

January 2016
Portland, Oregon